To Kate

I hope you enjoy it

Colours

About the author

Karen Medlin is a slightly scatty mother of five grown-up children. She lives in Cornwall with her equally scatty son and twin chorkie dogs.

When the colours of the flora and fauna and the ever-changing moods of the sea planted an idea in her head, it grew like a weed and became her first novel. She must be a glutton for punishment, because she's started her second.

Colours

Karen Medlin

NILDEM

British Library Cataloguing in Publication Data
A catalogue record for this book is available from the British Library.

ISBN 978-1-3999-6117-2

Typeset by Amolibros, Milverton, Somerset
www.amolibros.co.uk
This book production has been managed by Amolibros
Printed and bound by Ingram Spark worldwide

Dedication

To my mum, Jill

This book is dedicated to all those that have ever supported and loved me, you know who you are. To Warren and Kelly for listening to endless re-writes, and to Tam and the Moon Hut writers for the five-minute exercise that started this novel. To Hilda Bronstein, Ruth Gunstone, Lynda Morgan and Steve Speed for lighting the fire. To my beautiful granddaughters Cheyenne, Delilah, Mariama, Matilda and Mimi, I love you. Lastly, to my hero, my dad David, who is cheering me on from heaven. I did it, Dad!

Sally

I don't think I set out to kill him. Oh I thought about it a few times, don't we all when we've been wronged in some way? It's the first thing you say to yourself isn't it? But most people don't actually go through with it. If I can plead my case at all, it would be that you can only take so much before you snap. You let your mind mull over the taunts, the punches like picking at a chicken bone, gnawing on the details, till they take over your emotions, your rationale. Anger is a strange thing, isn't it? It starts pink. Niggling, goading, until it becomes an orange ball of rage in your gut, as you realise someone's taken over your soul, and left a person you don't recognise anymore. I've never been much to write home about really, but now I am nothing at all.

So as I said, I really didn't mean for it to end like this, but when Larry came home stinking of a thick, cloying perfume that I wouldn't wear in a million years and ordered me to get him a beer from the fridge, I was on alert. I could tell it wasn't his first, or probably his fourth drink of the day. Straight away the pink feeling began fizzing in my stomach. I couldn't let it out. Unless

I wanted an extended trip to A and E. So as always, I did his bidding. It was then that the humiliation I'd felt earlier that evening, when I found his little surprise, came back hard and fast, Orange turned to red. I was on fire, but I was also scared to death.

It had been about nine o'clock. I know that because *Coronation Street* had just finished. It's the only thing I really watch on television. Larry laughs at me, but, despite all the ups and downs the families on the street have, I would swap my life with any one of theirs in a heartbeat, and before you say it's not real, I know that deep down, but it takes me out of my head for an hour three times a week and it's cheaper than drugs. I turned the TV off and went upstairs to put his clean washing away. I was always careful to sort them in order of type and colour. I knew the consequences of mixing socks and underwear, believe me. All my life I've had to tiptoe around people, been made to conform. So it shouldn't have come as a surprise when Larry turned out to be just like the people that made me what I am. As I tried to shut the drawer something snagged, so I put my hand in to flatten it down and my fingers touched something hard. I yanked the drawer open sending tighty whiteys flying everywhere, and I knew I'd have to clean that lot up before he got home. It turned out the offender was a little black note book about the size of a mobile phone, just lying there in the near empty drawer. My first thought was don't look, just put everything back as it was and he will never know, but curiosity got the better of me. I bet at this point you are shouting, put it back, Sally, put it back. I picked it up anyway and opened up a whole new can of worms.

I know it's a cliché, but why are harbingers of doom

always black? You never find bad news in a pink fluffy journal, or one with little puppies and kittens on the front, do you? If I had just put it back and not peeked, I wouldn't be in the mess I'm in today, but peek I did, and there they were, all of Larry's conquests rated out of ten on a sliding scale, in small tidy writing. All their names and addresses in midnight blue ink swam before my eyes. He had put notes in red in the margin for his special mentions. For instance Nina Swan, he stated, had enormous tits that were so absolutely symmetrical, they could only have come from under the knife. I on the other hand have the equivalent of two fried eggs, so I admit I was a teensy bit jealous for a minute. But for the money they must have cost, I could have bought a one-way ticket to anywhere in the world. Anywhere, as long as it was away from Larry, big boobs I could do without. All the women on his list were far more elegant, more alluring than me according to him. Nina Swan and her tits rated a six. Audrey Brown was top with an eight. She had a beautiful neck and lustrous hair apparently. As my finger travelled down the page, past Mary and Pauline and Sheila, I found my name. I was right at the bottom and rated a two with no outstanding qualities. Reading his opinion of my worth in his neat script confirmed my place. It was the same as it had been all my life. On the shit heap.

When Larry and I were first together I must have rated higher, maybe to the dizzy heights of Audrey Brown; he married me after all. But time and tide and all that, plus the odd bruise and busted eye socket here and there, took its toll on my looks I guess. I'll bet he didn't push Nina Swan down the stairs, or strangle Audrey Brown to the point of unconsciousness. No, that was reserved just for me, how lucky am I? Anyway! I got the beer, took a deep breath and walked back through the sitting room door into a nightmare.

When I handed Larry the bottle, he slapped me so hard I fell, hitting my forehead on the doorjamb on the way down. It took me a few seconds to come to and wipe the blood out of my eyes, but when I could focus again, he was standing over me, laughing in my face. "Stupid bitch," he snarled, "could you have gone any slower?" I scrabbled backwards toward the kitchen, managed to get to my feet and head for the back door. He followed me, tripping over nothing all the way, jabbing his finger hard between my shoulder blades, calling me filthy names. As he got close enough to grab my hair, he pulled a knife out of the block on the countertop and touched it to my neck. A part of me was terrified, but just for a moment, I wondered what it would be like to cease to exist. To feel true peace before the blackness claimed me. He was swaying all over the place, drawing blood. This was it! I was going to die. All of a sudden Larry seemed to tire and let go of the knife. The blade clattered to the tiles, echoing in my ears like a tuning fork. I'd always wanted to play the piano.

The next thing I knew the knife was in my hand, then in his chest. He dropped like a stone, scarlet spurting from his heart. I must admit, I was mesmerised for a second. I was watching the life ebb from his body in short, sharp squirts knowing I could do nothing about it. Wondering if I cared? After a while, he began to look kind of grey round the lips, but, at least the hurtful words, delivered with his stinking breath were silenced now. His eyes were still open, but the once searing blue, was now mostly white as they rolled back in his head. I thought when someone died it would be more like in films. You know? Where the actors make a right meal of it. I didn't actually know what it would be like to watch a person take their last breath, but safe to say, it wasn't like the movies at all.

Kneeling down in the crimson slick that was forming around us, I placed my hands around the knife that had made the hole in his heart. I didn't want to take it out. I wouldn't be able use it again anyway so I left it there. With each beat blood splayed over my fingers, but it had changed from a spurt, to a sort of dribble and I remember thinking, that in that moment, as Larry's heart was fluttering under my hands, that it truly belonged to me, and not to any of his conquests in his little black book. Trouble was, I no longer wanted it. I hadn't for a long while if I'm honest. Oh, I tried long and hard to get him to see me, but whatever I did was wrong. I began to over-compensate and instead of making him happy, it had the opposite effect. That's when I ended up in hospital. Oh, not every time. I was an expert at patching myself up. But the fractured jaw, broken nose etc. required better skills than mine.

As I watched, the blood flow stopped and the beats ceased completely. I must have lain down beside him then, I hadn't done that in a while. Intimacy it seemed, was reserved for the Audrey Browns of this world. As Larry's body began to cool, I closed his eyes and stood up. Blood was beginning to pool outwards from his body, framing it in red. I know it sounds funny, but I was cross with him for messing up the kitchen floor when earlier that day, he'd loomed over me as I mopped it, pointing out the bits I missed. But as my anger ebbed back to pink it seemed silly to blame him, I was the one who had spilled the blood after all.

He now looked harmless lying there next to the swing bin, and the devil in me thought how the tables had turned. Larry had used his size against me for years. He was six-four, built like the proverbial outhouse, and used every inch of it to make me feel small. Now I was the one standing over him. I won, for once, but it didn't feel as good as I dreamed it would. He couldn't even see my little victory, could he? His eyes were closed. His clothes, caked with congealing blood, were making cloud-like patterns on his Chinos and I began to worry. He didn't like to be dirty. Everything had to be pristine. Orderly. His obsession with neatness was absolute. Believe me. I knew to my cost what would happen, should a line of T-shirts be the least bit wonky. I had a swirly feeling in my head like oil on water. It felt like a dream, like I was acting a scene from a scary horror film. Any minute now the director would yell cut! Everything will go back to normal. Any moment now…

When I came to I remember looking at my hands, sticky with his blood. The enormity of what I'd done hit me like one of Larry's punches. I tried to wipe them on my already sodden nightdress, but the soaked cloth felt so cold against my skin I whipped it off over my head, and threw it as far away from me as I could. The sweet coppery smell, like old pennies, made me retch, so I rubbed my hands down the wall to dry them. The magenta, so startling against the woodchip, reminded me of last week's nosebleed running down my dress. Larry had screamed in my face, because I couldn't take a slap without making a mess. Then he'd clamped his hands around my throat and squeezed, all because a tiny drop of my blood from the wound he'd inflicted, had reached the front of his best shirt. I must confess, my anger went straight to red and threatened to boil over. I screamed at him, hurt him like he was hurting me. Only in my mind of course! Beige little Sally would never do such a thing in real life. if I did, I knew that his face, contorted with hate would be the last thing I would ever see.

I shook my head, hard, willing the memory away. It was then that I caught sight of myself in the hall mirror. My face speckled with red freckles, my lips purple, the blood from the gash on my forehead dripping slowly into my left eye. I looked grotesque. It was then I started screaming. My body began to shiver uncontrollably and realised at this point I needed help, so I pressed redial and hoped it wouldn't be Ikea. We wouldn't be needing the new wardrobe now, and the thought annoyed me, because Larry had made me ring them every few hours, for three days straight, chasing the order. It wasn't Ikea. They wouldn't be open at this time of night anyway. It was my friend Miriam, thank God. She was the only person in the whole of my life who had ever truly cared about me. The only one I could count on, no matter what.

The phone rang a long time. I was just beginning to worry that she wasn't there, when she answered. I heard her say hello and my heart immediately slowed. I couldn't find the words to tell her what had happened. A funny sort of squeaking noise was all I could muster, but she knew it was me and that I needed help. She said she would come as quickly as she could and I believed her. As I put the phone back on its cradle, I was fascinated by the large flower pattern made by my grip on the handset. It was quite pretty really. I stood there for some time, transfixed by the petals in every shade of red and pink imaginable, then went to wait on my special stair trying not to look at the thing that was once Larry. Most of his body was in shadow anyway, but his feet were pointing into the hallway straight at me. He was wearing shoes I had never seen before, and I realised I knew nothing about his life outside this house at all. Apart from all the other women I'd just discovered of course. I began to laugh, crazy, I know, but I had the thought that If he could see me now, he would probably rate me a one in his little black book. The lowest mark possible on his shitty sliding scale. He couldn't though, could he? He was dead.

What little grip I had on reality slipped away. The laughing stopped as quickly as it started and I pressed myself into the stairs, making myself as small as possible, hoping I would just disappear. The hallway, once bright and homely, looked stark. The light harsh, cold. I wrapped my arms round my bare skin to try and get warm. I was freezing but I couldn't make myself move. I just sat on the fourth stair from the bottom waiting for Miriam to save me, because God knows I didn't have the strength to save myself. If I had, I would have done it a long time ago. I often sat there to think. It was the stair I'd chosen myself with no input from Larry. He controlled everything else in my life and he would have jeered at me for taking refuge there, but I felt safe in small spaces. I always had. I pressed myself against the wall, seeking comfort from something solid, unmovable, but it was smeared with the blood from my hands and I immediately sat bolt upright. I didn't want any part of him to touch any part of me ever again.

Things were going to change now, weren't they? I knew that. It stood to reason. Part of me welcomed it. No more living in fear of upsetting him, of saying the wrong thing. On the other hand I could go to prison, or the nuthouse? Oh, it scares me, but it's a different kind of scary and is no match for Larry's particular brand of sadism. I realised suddenly that this may be the last time I saw this house. I would miss it, in a way. It hadn't been a happy place for me, but I had tried so hard to make it a home, despite everything. It was also the last time I would see Larry. I wouldn't miss him at all, but the aloneness I felt right then, was so overwhelming that I could have borrowed him back. Just for a few minutes you understand. It was Miriam I really wanted of course and I began to worry that Brian had stopped her coming. Just then, I heard her key turn in the lock and I knew everything was going to be OK.

"What the hell as happened here?" I think she said, her eyes darting sideways and coming to a stop on Larry's feet. I could tell she was swallowing a scream but she came towards me, shrugging her arms out of her coat as she went. She wrapped it around my nakedness and I felt the heaviness of the wool envelop me. It was warm, like a hug after the chill of all the blood.

Miriam called the Emergency Services. I couldn't really grasp what she was saying. My head felt thick, fluffy, like Miriam's coat, but I could hear the urgency in her voice as she tried to tell the operator what had happened. When she came off the phone, she sat down gently next to me on my stair and put her arms around my shoulders. She smelled of face powder and clean washing. It was familiar. Comforting. She wouldn't make me tell her what had gone on. It was kind of obvious really. There was a six-foot-four corpse laying in the kitchen in a pool of blood, a five-inch carving knife sticking out of his chest. The black handle was still pointing at the ceiling. Shiny. Like his shoes.

"They're coming, lovey, they'll be here in a minute," she said softly. I remember thinking that there was no rush. They wouldn't have to come on Blues and Twos. There was nothing they could do for Larry now, was there?

The ambulance and the police came and she let them in. Miriam dealt with the police. She'd stopped shaking and had taken charge as usual, thank God. I just sat there on my stair, watching everyone move around me but I felt disconnected. As if I was seeing things through that thick plastic we had to put on the back door once when Larry shattered the glass with his fist. I saw a paramedic put two fingers on his neck, trying to find a pulse. I knew he was out of luck. Was it bad not to feel sad about it? Miriam, and a policewoman, were standing by the mirror, speaking in hushed tones. It looked a bit like they were conspiring against me, but I knew Miriam better than that. Just then the lady officer started towards me. I must have panicked, because she backed off, then Miriam came forward. She sat with me as before, shushing me, stroking my hair. She said the lady's name was Vicki and she was here to sort everything out. I nodded, and tried to look the woman in the eye but it was hard. Just then the male officer rushed into the hallway and all I could see was Larry coming at me with the knife in his hand. I ran. Past the fifth stair. The sixth. The seventh. I hid in the bathroom. Not very well as it turned out, because Miriam and Vicki found me quickly. They gently put some clothes on my frozen body and guided me back past the fourth stair into the melee. I tried to stay calm as I was ushered past Larry's body. The paramedics had covered him in a black sheet. It reminded me of the bag I had put out for the bin men early that morning and a part of me thought, good riddance to bad rubbish.

Two more police cars pulled up in front of the house. They too came without sirens, but the blue lights shining through the glass in the front door made me relax a little. The rhythmic flashes calmed me. They were predictable, safe. Everything that Larry wasn't. Do I sound crazy? Comparing Larry with a blue flashing light? My life, up to this point, had been so precarious you understand, that I tried to anchor myself to anything solid, like Miriam, or since I was a kid, walls. In the lights of the police car I saw peace. Freedom. Not in the physical sense, oh no! I knew I would probably have to go away for a while, but I no longer had to put up with Larry's purple mood swings, his kicks, his punches. So in that sense I was free. I knew I wouldn't ever be truly alone, because Miriam would not abandon me, even if I did get locked up in the loony bin. At least I knew I had one person who would be there for me. Always. No matter what.

Miriam gently told me it was time to leave. I looked round for the last time, taking snapshots in my mind, filing them away to bring out when I felt the need to torture myself. I had hoped, when we first got married, that this house would be a place where I could finally feel safe from the world. Of course, it hadn't worked out like that, because the danger was inside with me all along. It had gone now. I would be sorry to leave 4 Mulberry Crescent despite what had happened here.

My friend led me out of the front door, flanked by

Vicki, to a big white van with a cage in the back. You know? The ones they put murderers in. I remember bucking my body and pulling back. I started to scream. I didn't want to be locked in there like a killer, staring out, shaking the bars. I'm sure all the neighbours standing around watching thought I was nuts! They wouldn't be far wrong, to be fair. I didn't care about them! We had lived in this street for a long time and not once did they ask if I was all right, or pass the time of day, even though they could plainly see the rainbow of bruises on my face, every time Larry decided I'd done something worth beating me for. Vicki got in the backseat of the van instead of the cage and that confused me, because I didn't know where I was supposed to go. I took a glance at Vicki, then at Miriam who held me tight for a minute. She helped me into the backseat and got in beside me squeezing my fingers gently. Sitting between the two of them, Miriam's hand in mine, knowing they were there to help, made me feel safer somehow. Safer than I'd felt in forever.

Miriam

When I first got the call I was a bit annoyed really. I'd got meself comfy, Brian had just made me a cuppa and put a couple of chocolate digestives on a plate, when the phone began to burp. I think it sounds like a burp but Brian says it sounds like a little bird and...oh Lord what am I saying. I'm a bit all over the place at the minute... . Well! as soon as I answered it I knew it was poor Sally, she's me friend did I say? She couldn't speak. She just sounded like a little kitten mewing. I tried to ask what was wrong but she couldn't answer me. Flaming heck, I thought, Larry's punched her again, so I said, "Hold on, sweetheart, I'm coming." When I put the phone down, I realised the biscuit I had rested on the rim of me cup had fallen in me tea and was floating about in the tar. I have it strong enough to stand the spoon up in, but Brian prefers to wave the tea bag at his cup and call it done. He might as well have hot water.

I put me mug down and ferreted about in the drawer for the spare keys to Larry and Sally's place. I shouted to Brian, "I've just got to pop to Sal's a minute, darlin'. Can you tape the film? Something's not right over there.

Larry's probably beat her up again. I shouldn't be long unless she needs the hospital like last time."

"What if the bastard's still there, Miriam?" Brian called.

"Not bloody likely. When he does this, he scarpers to the 'Dog and Duchess' and their famous 'lock ins'. Don't worry, pet."

"Well I do worry, Miriam, I don't want anything upsetting you, shall I come?"

"No darlin'. It will be easier without a bloke there. Save me a couple of biccies will you, and don't eat all the party rings eh!"

"OK love, phone if you need owt, I can borrow our Garry's truck and be with you in no time."

I heard his voice wobble as I shut the front door behind me. I've got a goodun there, bless him. Blimey, if he only knew what I was going into, he wouldn't have let me go at all.

On the way over to Mulberry Crescent, I tried to think of a way to get Sally to leave Larry. She'd been a doormat and a punchbag for that long, you'd have thought she'd have got the message by now that things weren't going to get any better. He was the same as her ruddy parents. Maybe, in Sal's mind, even if he was a bastard, it was still someone to warm your bed at night. My Brian's the opposite, his feet are ruddy freezing. While I were parking the car I was still sorting in me head what to say to Sal. I took a while. Something was giving me the willies.

When I finally did get up to the front door, the lights were off everywhere except the one in the passage. I thought that was strange. At the very least, the front room light should be on. It was only half ten at night and Sal never went to sleep till Larry got back from the pub. If he came back at all. Sometimes he doesn't. Sometimes I wished he wouldn't. Always does in the end though. He knows where his bread's buttered that one. I took me time fiddling with the keys. I had no ruddy idea what I was going to find? It might be a bloody nose, or a cracked rib or something much worse. I put me key in the door and waited a sec. If he was still there I didn't want to barge in and have him swing for me an' all. I know it sounds awful, thinking about meself when I'm supposed to be there for Sal, but it was all quiet so I went in.

The first thing I saw were feet sticking up towards the ceiling. I nearly wet meself when I saw what had happened. Larry was dead! Brown bread! HIs body lay sort of half in, half out of the kitchen, the light bouncing off his shoes. They were still shiny, which was a ruddy miracle because the rest of him were covered in a river of red. I could just see the shadow of a bloody great knife sticking out of his chest, but I couldn't see his face thank God! The kitchen light were off as I said before.

"Bloody Saints alive," I whispered. "What's happened here, love?" Daft thing to say really when it was bloody obvious. When I looked over to Sally, she were sitting on the stairs naked as the day she were born, head to toe in claret. She looked like something out of that film that Brian rented once. *Carrie*, that's it! Bloody scary as I recall. Something clicked in my brain then and I knew I'd have to take charge of the situation. Sal had lost it completely and was shivering so much that her teeth sounded like my washing machine on fast spin.

"Oh darlin', I'll get you warm," I said to her. I took me coat off and draped it round Sal's shoulders, all the while trying not to look at Larry. I couldn't do anything for him now, my focus had to be on her. She had a deep cut above her left eye that would probably need stitches, not for the first time neither. She was looking right at me, but I don't think she saw me at all. She seemed to be locked up in her own mind, somewhere safe I shouldn't wonder. Well you would do, wouldn't you? If you'd accidentally killed someone. Even if the bloke concerned was a piece of scum.

I took Sally in me arms to try and stop her shaking. I didn't want to think about the blood seeping into me clothes. When me husband saw me later, he thought it was me that had been stabbed. As I cuddled her, I realised I had Brian's mobile phone in me pocket cos it was pressing into my side. I remember taking it with me when I left the house, just in case. I didn't own one of me own. I hate the thought that you can be summoned at all hours of the day and night. I have enough of that, what with me husband, me son, and Sally! I gently moved over so I could get it out of me coat. I showed it to her and said, "I'm going to call the ambulance now, lovey, OK?" She didn't seem to hear me, so I said it again and still got nothing, so I just did it. I gave my name, and the address to come to and just said to hurry up. I didn't know how to describe what'd gone on, so I just said someone's dead and put the phone down. They came bloody quick. About five minutes if I remember rightly. I saw the lights coming closer, turning the street blue as they came. I was bloody glad they weren't using the sirens. That would have sent Sal right over the edge. If she wasn't there already.

As they came in the front door, I felt the tension seep from my body, just like Larry's blood had done, all over the kitchen floor. They took charge, thank the Lord. They knew what they were doing, so I closed me eyes for a second to give me brain a chance to catch up. I was all over the place, thinking all sorts, but I couldn't let Sal see that. I had to be strong for her now. I prayed that this was all a dream. I prayed for Larry not to be dead, and for Sally to come back from round the bend and tell me what happened, even though I didn't really want to hear it. I couldn't make sense of any of it. What had gone on here tonight? How had it ended with a dead body and a naked woman hugging a wall? I didn't want to be here. I just wanted to be at home with Brian and a packet of Hob Nobs. I felt sick.

The muttering of the paramedics and the unearthly noise Sal was making all began to roll into one and I began to shiver the same as her. We were a right pair both of us, sitting on the fourth stair, shaking like a pair of maracas in a mariachi band. The police arrived a couple of minutes later. A man whose name I didn't catch, and a young woman who said we were to call her Vicki. She had striking bleach blonde hair and lovely brown eyes, so I concentrated on her face, trying to listen to what she was telling me. I needed something to focus on to stop me joining Sally in La La Land.

The police were very good under the circumstances. I think they realised Sally wasn't with us, and asked me what I thought had happened. I told Vicki what I knew, which wasn't much, but I gave her a quick rundown of Sal's life with Larry. I told her what she'd had to put up with all these years. The beatings and such like. She wrote everything down, smiled at me, then looked over at the shell of my friend on the stairs. Sally met Vicki's eyes for a split second then pushed herself into a clean bit of the wall. She were jumpy, she looked ready to make a run for it, and that's what happened, when all of a sudden a male police officer rushed in the front door and came full pelt towards us. Sal lost it. She jumped up, nearly knocking me flying, it was then me coat slipped off her shoulders. "Flaming hell" said the policeman as he watched Sally, naked as a jaybird and covered in blood, turn and run up the stairs.

Between Vicki and me we got Sal dressed in a sweatshirt and joggers. I wanted to wash her off first, but Vicki said I couldn't because of collecting evidence or something? When we brought her back downstairs all the male police officers had disappeared, but there were still lots of people in that tiny passage. I'm sure they all had jobs to do, but Sal went stiff as a board in me arms. The paramedics had already covered Larry's body in one of those sheet things you see on the telly. I'm glad I didn't have to see his body again, but I could still make out the shape under the cloth. One of the policemen told Vicki that her partner was waiting in the van. He said to take our time coming out. I couldn't go any faster anyway, because Sal had wrapped her arms around me body and I were dragging the both of us. I kept saying to her that everything was going to be all right, but in me head, I was thinking that this was the first time I'd ever lied to her.

Vicki explained to me that when we got to the police station, Sally would be seen by the ME, which, she said, meant the Medical Examiner. A doctor to you and me. It would be up to a psychiatrist though, as to whether she would be fit for interview tonight. I didn't need to be a ruddy psychiatrist to know the answer to that I can tell you! More cars had arrived outside and Sal stared at the lights flashing through the front door. She seemed to calm a bit, as if she were listening to them. What am I saying! Lights don't talk. I think I'm finally going round the twist, but I won't be alone, I'll meet Sal on the corner. Vicki came over and spoke softly to us. Letting us know what was going on. I suppose she'd been in a lot of situations like this. She seemed to know there was more to what happened tonight than met the eye. She was kind to us. A policeman standing in the garden signalled to me to bring Sal to the van and Vicki came with us. With Sal draped all over me, we must have looked like conjoined twins walking out of that house.

She freaked and started screaming when she saw the van. She was so frightened, poor love, I could feel the tremors going through her like an earthquake. Lights had come on all over the cul de sac. People were streaming from their homes to get a good look at the loony woman from number four, losing it in the street. I wanted to give them a right gob full, but I wanted to get Sal out of there more.

When we got to the van, she saw the cage at the back and tried to climb me. "Don't worry," Vicki said, as she got in the van. "You'll sit in the backseat with me and Miriam." Vicki nodded at me to bring Sal in. She went like a little lamb and I got in beside her.

We sped away from the house. From Larry. Thank God. The flashing blue lights made the wet street shine like his shoes. I thought about him still there, head in the kitchen, toes in the passage. I couldn't get it out of my mind. He was a bastard and I didn't like him one bit, but a tiny part of me was sorry he died like he did. Having said that, me sympathies lay with the poor girl sitting in a police van, her hair matted with blood. With all she'd been through it's not surprising she'd gone a bit gaga.

Megan

Why is it the minute your hands are full the phone decides to ring? Well not decides exactly, as it doesn't have a mind of its own, much like me after a full day's work. But ring it did. It came at a crucial moment too, as I was attempting to steer a large triangle of deep pan margarita with extra cheese into my mouth which, can be difficult at the best of times. On top of that my arthritis was playing up, so my grip on the crust was shaky to say the least. As the end, heavy with mozzarella, dipped past my lips. I corrected its trajectory and took a huge bite. Silly really when the phone still needed answering, but I'd missed lunch and I was starving. I tried waving frantically at Leo and Gina, but they were absorbed in the film *Ghost*. It was the bit where Demi Moore and Patrick Swayze were getting hot and heavy over a potter's wheel. Some people have all the luck, don't they? Chewing furiously to clear my mouth, I picked up the phone and swallowed hard. That, in turn, made me cough making it sound like I had a forty a day habit as I said "Hello?" Just then a big wodge of the remaining pizza slid off and landed on my new work shirt "Oh damn," I grumbled.

"Pardon? said the voice on the other end of the line. "Hello, have I reached Dr Standage?"

"Er yes?" Another cough! "Sorry, yes it is. How can I help you?"

"Sorry to trouble you at home, Doctor. This is Winston Green police station. We have a situation with a woman involved in a domestic death. The Psych on call is in the middle of another case and can't get away. Also, he's a man and we think, that from what we've been told, you would be better for this one being female and everything"

"I understand, Officer?"…

"Kemp Ma'am. The lady in question goes from silence one minute, to absolute hysteria the next. The ME tried to examine her, but he couldn't get anywhere near. She needs a psych opinion on whether she's fit for interview. I realise you're off duty but…"

"I'll be there in about twenty minutes. Is there anyone with her at present?"

"A friend, and one of our female officers, Ma'am. The lady came in with her. She was the one that called us. We couldn't separate them. When we tried to put the woman in an interview room with just Officer Thomas she damn near screamed the place down, so we kept them together.

"You did the right thing, Officer Kemp. Her friend being there will help keep her calm."

"Thank you, Doctor"

"Oh and Officer Kemp?"

"Yes Ma'am?"

"Don't let them discuss what happened tonight. They will both have to give separate statements at some point "

"I don't think that will be a problem, Doctor. She hasn't said a coherent word since she got here."

"I'll be there as soon as I can."

"Thank you, Dr Standage. Sorry to disturb your evening off."

I put the phone down and took another bite of the now rapidly congealing pizza. I signalled to Leo, who thankfully saw me this time, that I had to go out again and went upstairs.

Why do people tend to put full-length mirrors in places where they capture every lump and bump? Why not put them behind a door so you can choose, or not choose, to see yourself in all your glory? Well, I was one of those people who did the former. I now stood staring at a massive orange blob on my shirt and a bottom that just squeezed into a size sixteen jeans. The blob matched the orange of my untameable hair that sprung from my head with reckless abandon. It had been the bane of my life since I was small. My friends could wear theirs in bunches and pigtails tied with pretty ribbons, but I looked like I regularly stuck my finger in an electric socket. My dad jokingly called me Einstein. He would say I had his brains, and his hair. I don't have his brains I can tell you, especially lately. Some days I can't string two thoughts together, never mind understanding the theory of relativity. I looked down and I knew I would have to change my shirt before I left for the station. I didn't think anyone would take a psych opinion from a tired, lumpy, old woman with a suspicious stain on her right boob. They would, however, have to settle for a tired, lumpy, old woman. That part I could not change.

I quickly decided on a pale pink shirt. Checking I had a light coloured bra on. I once wore a black one to work, under a white shirt. The client spent the whole time I was with him staring at my breasts. You couldn't blame him really when I looked like a pole dancer. I went with pale pink, as it's a non-threatening colour. It's something I learned in training. If you go into a potentially volatile situation wearing bright orange or red it could be seen as confrontational, and could add fuel to an already raging fire. It's something I always have to think about, before I launch myself headlong into the fray.

By shuffling things around in the over-stuffed dressing table drawer, I found my lipstick hiding behind a packet of tissues and a packet of antacid tablets, but as I got closer to the mirror to apply it, I noticed the crows' feet I'd had around my eyes since I was in my thirties, had grown six pairs of legs each and were marching down my face. God I was tired. I dragged 'Rose Blush' over my lips, puckered, blotted and swept the full to bursting laundry basket into my arms. I left the room laden. Not only with the washing, but with the worry that I couldn't keep this crazy pace of life up for much longer. I had been on call for the last two weeks, due to the other permanent Psych being on maternity leave. Now, I was going back in on my only night off. It couldn't be helped. That was the nature of the job. Someone was in hotter water than I was right now, and needed my help. No matter how I felt.

I came down the stairs tentatively, peering over the basket for hazardous obstacles such as Dinky toys and stray Lego bricks. I forgot to check on the way up, as I was in a rush, but luckily I'd made it safely. I nearly came a cropper once, due to my grandson Charlie using them as a garage. I had skidded on a row of saloon cars and fell down the last four steps. There I was, on my bottom in the hall, rubbing a very sore ankle, getting an earful from him, in his three-year-old way, for messing up his parking. I poked my head round the door to the lounge and waggled my fingers at Leo and Gina.

"Bye mum," he called. He was so used to me going out at all hours, leaving in the middle of film night, or halfway through dinner. I said goodbye, but they were laughing at Whoopi Goldberg's imitation of a medium, so I left them to it.

I always wonder what I'm going to encounter when I go to Winston Green police station, but I've been doing it so long, that these days nothing really surprises me. I mean, if they've called for a psychiatrist it's never going to be a walk in the park is it? I try never to judge a situation without the full SP, but had I known what was going to transpire and how much it would change me. I wouldn't have responded to the call.

As I hauled myself into the car I thought to myself, 'Please don't let me have to section her tonight, or I'll never get home.' It wasn't meant as a selfish thing. It's just that this was supposed to be the one night this week that I got to spend with my family and it was already late. Leo and Gina would have gone to bed by the time I got home. I took a deep breath and rubbed my temples. My limbs felt like dumbbells and a dull ache started to lead an assault up my neck. "Come on, old girl," I said to the crow's feet in the rear view mirror, "get a grip," then I started the car. Pushing the button for the radio, I hoped for some nice relaxing classical music. Something that would set me up for dealing with whatever I would be walking into at Winston Green. 'The Ride of the Valkyries' blasted forth. Well! If anything could have woken me up, that did. I let the music wash over me as I drove, but I seemed to hit all the red lights on the Edgerly Road right by McDonalds. The massive yellow M was a magnet to my grandson, but to me it meant more brightly coloured toys for me to trip over.

The traffic jam seemed to tally with my life right now. Stop and go. Well more stop than go really. It's hardly surprising, with work the way it is. I can't remember the last time I had coffee with friends, or went round the shops for anything other than food, and it had been nearly seven years since I had a date. Quite frankly I think I'm too old for all that now. I'm four years off retirement and wishing them away. In my brain, I bounce between sixteen and eighty. The latter happens mostly when my arthritis plays up. The sixteen-year-old me was fun and energetic but she hadn't visited in a while, whereas the eighty-year-old me seemed to want to hang around like a damp cloak. I'm not naive. I know that I'm on the wrong side of sixty and I can't do things as quickly as I used to. Also having Leo, Gina and Charlie full-time now means stretching myself even further. I'm not complaining, I love having the house full again. It's not their fault they were gazumped and that Gina was made redundant all in the same month. They'd had an offer accepted on a lovely two-bedroom place about ten minutes from me, which would have been ideal, but someone swept in at the last minute with a cash offer and took it right from under their noses. Anyhow, I digress. I must admit the rousing music did its job and I felt better for the time alone in the car. My headache had retreated from behind my eyes and was waiting at the back of my head to resurface later. Which is just as well, because the woman in there deserved the full service, not parts and labour. I pulled into the space reserved for the Staff Psychiatrist and parked up.

I could hear screaming as I walked through the double doors, but had to wait for a couple of minutes for someone to buzz me in to the inner sanctum. A fight had kicked off in the cells and the officers were dealing with the aftermath. I knew instinctively, that the keening noise down the corridor was coming from my client and not from down in the basement. It had that desperate, unhinged quality to it that I was all too familiar with. The sound kept stopping abruptly, before starting again a few minutes later. With the racket coming from below decks, however, it was difficult to hear what was what. Somehow, I got the feeling that she wouldn't be fit for interview tonight. I'd just got my phone out of my bag to let Leo know it was going to be a late one, when I was let through the inner door by a harassed looking officer with a scratch on his cheek and blood on his collar.

"Thank you for coming so quickly, Doctor. Sorry about the wait before you were buzzed in. As you can hear, it's been a busy night."

As we walked together toward the interview rooms, he told me what had happened.

"Just as we were booking your lady in, all hell broke loose in the cells. We had to call an ambulance."

"For your lot or the suspects?" I asked.

"A bit of both. Sergeant Neal has a broken arm and lacerations to his nose, and one of the suspects of a burglary had an earring torn out and his jaw busted by his best mate. We misguidedly kept them together in the corridor while we were sorting out the cells. Someone was sick in six, and we couldn't put them both in one cell, it's against procedure. Apparently one's been copping off with the other's missus and he let it slip half an hour ago. Yours is in there. Go right in. Sergeant Thomas is in there with them."

"Thanks Officer...?

"Kemp Ma'am, he said blushing, the scratch on his cheek reddening. I was the one who phoned you before."

"Sorry," I offered and smiled at him. "I have a head like a leaky sieve. Of course, I recognise your voice now." I noticed he was quite handsome despite the long spidery scratch and I wondered to myself if it would scar. I liked scars on men, it made them more attrac... What was I thinking? It was my turn to blush and I noticed a smile creeping to his lips.

"That's OK, Doctor. I don't remember my own name sometimes, especially on nights like this. It's all go in here."

"Megan," I said to him." My name is Megan."

"Alfie," he replied sheepishly, his face scarlet now. Just then, the door to my patient's room crashed open and the WPC assigned to her appeared. "Can I get some help in here please? We're running out of cups."

"Vicki. This is Doctor Standage, she's the psych standing in for Dr Harrison. While she is in the room I want you to stay with her but not get involved unless she asks you to, all right?"

"Righto," replied Vicki, turning back into the room.

As I entered, the woman stopped screaming immediately. I stood on the periphery for a moment, listening to the soothing tones of the person sitting next to her. As my client calmed, I took a chance and walked slowly to the table. The scene was of two desperate people, amidst a mound of white, reminiscent of the Alps. Tiny pieces of paper littered the table and the floor. The woman's friend, whom I now know to be Miriam, pointed to the blizzard and said, "It keeps Sal a bit calmer, so we kept the cups coming." Tears tracked her cheek and she brushed them away. I smiled at her and touched her on the shoulder. Poor lady. I bet when she put her clothes on this morning, she never thought she would be in the middle of a nightmare like this. Her eyes tracked to the person sitting beside her. Behind the ever-increasing mound of paper, was the like of which I had never seen before. Covered in blood, skin as white as alabaster and hair like a wraith was Sally. But Sally wasn't in. I moved slowly up beside her, being careful not to touch and said in a quiet, voice.

"Hello Sally, my name is Megan. I'm a doctor and I'm here to help you."

Sally

There was lots of noise when we got to the police station. It buzzed in my brain like an angry wasp and I couldn't make out what Miriam was saying to me. It seemed to get louder and louder and it hurt my head. I tried to put my hands over my ears but I still had Larry's blood on my fingers, so I put them down again. I pressed myself against her for comfort and she wrapped her arms around me. There were men moving about behind the glass and I wanted them to stay there and not come out, because I wasn't sure if any of them were called Larry. In the end I braved the blood and rammed my fingers in my ears to block out the sound, but the angry male voices coming from everywhere still filled my brain. I lost it then. Miriam said later that I tore away from her arms and bolted for the door. I have no recollection of that at all, though I do remember pummelling my hands against the cool panes over and over, trying to get away from all the Larry's. Outside, through the rain-streaked window, I could see cars and trees and open spaces floating through the hazy yellow floodlights. I felt sure I could break the glass. I couldn't of course. Another thing I was useless at.

Miriam came over and pulled me gently back into the room. She held me for a moment and I calmed down a little. We followed Vicki down a long passageway with doors on either side painted battleship grey. They looked like rotten teeth in a huge mouth all set to swallow me whole, but Miriam was with me as I kept moving, pressing myself between her and the wall. I felt safer as the loud went to a whisper, so when one of the rotten teeth opened up, I was brave enough to go inside. As soon as Vicki shut the tooth, there was absolute silence. I was glad the wasp had gone, but I didn't want to be here either in this smelly room. I couldn't leave here. I couldn't go back to when I was watching *Coronation Street*, before I opened Larry's little black book and I couldn't see anything beyond this night. The truth of the situation poked me hard in the chest, knocking the breath right out of me. I was waiting for a doctor who could put me in the nut house for the rest of my life. Or, a policeman who could put me in jail and throw away the key, and all because of Larry. Even having Miriam beside me couldn't stop the fear taking me over. I began to scream then, as the enormity of what I'd done to myself hit home. I was thrust onto a chair, my arms held in my lap. "Calm down, lovey" I think Miriam said. "Don't do this to yourself." I tried to make eye contact with her, to get the reassurance I needed, but it was just too hard.

Vicki brought us some water in paper cups. They won't give you plastic. People slit their wrists with it. They let Miriam stay with me the whole time we were waiting, because every effort to prise me from her, made me feel as if I was losing everything and was powerless to stop it. Then I lost control. Killing someone will do that to you.

It stands to reason something like that would hit you like the proverbial sledgehammer. I tried to take my mind back to earlier when we were in the police van, when Vicki and Miriam were holding each of my hands just the right amount of tight. I remembered feeling that I was sitting between the only two people in the world that wanted to help me. My breathing slowed and the keening noise crept to a whisper in my head.

It had been warm in the van. On the Edgerly Rd, McDonalds 'I'm Lovin It' had loomed large to my right. The big gold letter, blurred by the rain on the windows, looked all fuzzy and soft-edged. Welcoming. I longed to be sitting there eating a quarter pounder with cheese and a side salad, and I remembered that I used to go there with Miriam, when The Cakehole had closed for a few weeks for refurbishment. Larry would have put a stop to it straight away if he had found out, but the times spent there with my friend, amidst all the hustle and bustle were special to both of us. I knew that the situation I now found myself in was far from yellow and fuzzy. It felt cold and hard and iron grey. I wondered if they had steel bars in prison now. I didn't think so. I saw a documentary just last week about prisons. They kept the inmates in plastic boxes with sliding doors, controlled by a guard from a huge panel in another room. The only time the inmates weren't gawped at, was when they went behind the screen to go to the toilet. I wouldn't like that. Imagine every aspect of your life controlled, examined, ridiculed every day. Come to think of it, would it be so different from the life I have led up till now? I didn't think so.

The plastic cages in the documentary reminded me of a rat I had as a child. The school's pet had had babies so they farmed them out to anyone who would have them. He was black and white, with a greyish pink tail that reminded me of a dried-out worm. Mother never even knew I had him. She never went into my bedroom. She had somewhere else she would rather be. I didn't name him so I wouldn't be sad when he died. I'd already lost Barney so I didn't want to have that feeling again, whatever it was. I remember him trying to scrabble up the side of his plastic box in a bid for freedom I guess, but his little feet kept sliding back down. I understood hopelessness even then. He looked so pathetic doing that day after day and never getting anywhere. So I let him out on the floor once in a while. He would run here and there, loving the freedom. That is until Mother's cat got in and killed him. I don't think she did it on purpose. Cats will be cats after all.

Back in the room I began to rip the paper cups into the tiniest pieces I could manage. Having something to do with my hands, other than shoving a knife in someone's chest, calmed me. When I ran out of cups, Vicki brought more. The shushing sound as I was tearing them was rhythmic and soothing. Miriam gave me her 'It's OK' face and at that moment I'd never cared for her more. It had been her on the other end of the redial. She had held me tight when I was naked and covered in blood. She'd been by my side all through school, begged me not to marry Larry, and she was here with me now going through the same kind of Hell as I was. Well almost. She could get up and leave anytime she wanted, go back to Brian, to their cosy little house, to warmth and company. It was something I never had, not really. I began to rip faster. The mound of paper on the table was growing and beginning to spill over on to the floor. It was reminiscent of the snow in a snow globe, the pieces floating gently down without a care in the world and I would have given anything even for a moment, if myself, Miriam and Vicki too, could be cocooned inside the glass, safe from all the Larrys in this world.

Miriam hurriedly pushed the last of the paper cups at me as the door opened. It startled me and I paused mid rip. I could feel my body going rigid again and I wrapped my arms around myself for extra protection. I kept my head down. I had no way of knowing who was coming in, or if they were someone else who just wanted to hurt me. A soft perfume wandered into the room and I knew it wasn't any of the Larry's outside. I felt brave enough to take a quick peak out the corner of my eye, as a rounded figure walked up beside us.

"Hello, I'm Megan and I'm here to help you." I think that's what she said.

I stared at the blizzard in my lap. I remember thinking that if I was to stand up and bolt for the door, all the paper would fall to the ground and that would be the second mess I'd made tonight. One red mess, one white. Still, a mess is a mess. I glanced at Miriam who nodded and smiled, so I stayed sitting down, even though I wanted to press myself into the nearest wall and become invisible. Why did the doctor want to help me? There has never been anyone except Miriam, who even cared enough to bother. Still, I would try to tell her what happened to me. I wasn't a great talker. I suppose that stemmed from having no one to talk to where I lived. It was as if I didn't exist, until they wanted something from me. Miriam would help me, if I couldn't find the words. Talking is something she does very well. She got used to filling the silences when I had nothing to say as a kid and she's never got out of the habit. Brian jokes to Miriam that he can't hear her anymore because she's talked his ears off, but I have been so glad of her incessant rambling over the years. It got me through the dark all-consuming grey, that had threatened to kill me over and over again. I would go as far as to say, her enthusiastic chatter saved my life more than once.

It's strange isn't it? The thoughts that go around in your head when something big happens to you, and let's face it, a huge thing was happening to me right now. You think nonsensical things like, have I turned the gas off? Or, did I feed the cat? In my case, as I haven't got a cat anymore my thought was, 'Oh God, I didn't pick up Larry's shirts from the dry cleaners! A part of me was panicked because I knew what he would do to me, but most of me felt smug. No doubt he would have worn one of them to wine and dine that Audrey Brown. It might have got stained with her lipstick, and as Larry had to have everything spick and span, I would have had to take it back to Ahmed's in the precinct and get it cleaned all over again. He's a nice man Mister Ahmed, I must remember to ask after his mother. I hate Audrey Brown. She scored an eight.

I realised the doctor was talking to me through the haze of shirts and mothers and other women. Her voice was quiet and had no sharp edges, so I felt it was safe to come out from all the rubbish in my head. To come back to the land of the living, pardon the pun.

"Sally?' she said in a soothing voice, 'we are going to the hospital in a few moments all right? I'm leaving the room for a little while, but when I come back in, we will take you, and Miriam to the Infirmary. You can rest there and we can have a little chat if you feel like it. Does that sound OK?" I quickly met her eyes, nodded once and looked away.

"It'll be much better for you there, lovey, and I won't leave you until you're settled I promise," said Miriam in her 'everything in the garden will be rosy' voice. I began to shiver so Miriam got up and wrapped me up in her safe, familiar arms.

"It's time to be brave now, Sal," she whispered in my ear." I think Doctor Megan can help you, I really do." I looked up at my only friend and held her gaze for as long as I could, but just before I looked away, I saw a big fat tear roll down her cheek and plop onto a tiny white island in a sea of paper.

Miriam

It was still raining when me and Sal got to the police station. The downpour only made the situation feel worse, if that was possible. Plus, two seconds out of the van and me perm made me look like our Garry's cockapoo Raquel. When we got in the warm, we were taken to a desk in the foyer. Sal was formally booked in, but Vicki said they had to do that as it was police procedure and Sal could have been in the queue at the post office for all she knew. Inquiries were still going on to find out what happened at that house tonight. I gave the booking in bloke Sally's details. She wasn't able to on account of her being on another planet. But me eyes were on her. She looked like she were about to bolt. She was! She had her fingers so far in her ears her knuckles went white. She started swaying and spinning around as the yelling in the station ratcheted up a few notches. Poor Sal flew at the window and pushed herself against it as if she was trying to smash it, but with her body weighing as much as my left leg she didn't have a hope in hell. When I'd peeled her off the glass, we were taken to what looked for all the world like a little front room. Me and Sal must have been left in there, with Vicki by the door, for at least half an hour. It smelled greasy and strong, like sweat, fried egg and something sweet I couldn't place. Not a nice sweet neither, a dirty sweet and If it were up to me I'd sack the bloody cleaners. I was afraid to put me hands on the table and our shoes made a spluckety spluck sound when they touched the floor. I know it's mad thinking about bleach and a scrubbing brush when my friend was going doolally, but believe me the whole situation was on the finishing end of barmy.

I wished the doctor would blinking hurry up. I was wondering what film Brian would have watched and whether he'd eaten all the biccies. Ooh I would've given anything to be with him right now. Vicki kept giving me small smiles every time our eyes met. She was trying to reassure me I expect. Nice of her, but it wasn't working. Sal kept going from dead quiet to howling and I would shush her, and give her the paper cups that people use for water so she could rip them up. Never mind the water I thought to meself, I could have done with a couple of stiff gins right about then. The cups were running out and I hoped they had more. Vicki must've had the same idea, because she opened a little cupboard in the wall and got the last packet out. That would keep Sal going for a while longer. She was certainly making the most of them. The table looked like that picture of the mountains on the wall in the dentist's surgery on Isle street. That, in turn reminded me that Brian had an appointment to get a new set of uppers fitted. Oh Lord. I know me mind's wandering again but I'm still that shook up, if I was a bottle of champagne, I'd have popped my cork long since. Anyhow, I told Sally I was popping out to ring Brian, but that I'd be right outside. When Vicki went to shut the door after me Sal started to scream so we had to leave the door open. How she could see me with Vicki stood in the gap I'll never know.

When I got out of the room I had a little meltdown of me own. I turned me back so Sal couldn't see me crumble. I was meant to be the strong one, but me legs were like jelly and me heart was trying to leave me chest. I went to phone home, but for the life of me I couldn't remember our number. I was surprised I could remember me own name with everything that was going on. I had a rook in me bag for me little address book, and hope I'd written it in there. I had, thank the Lord. Brian picked up on the second ring, bless him. He'd stayed up all this time waiting for me. He worries about me you see, I'm very lucky like that. I told him in a nutshell what happened. I don't think I could've given him chapter and verse right about then, even if my life depended on it "Flamin Nora," was all he could manage. "I'll pick you up when you're ready," he said, "or do you want me to come down there?"

It was lovely of him to want to help me, but I told him to go to bed and get some sleep because the police would bring me home. I didn't much want a panda car outside me house, but hopefully the curtain twitchers would all be in bed at that time in the morning.

"No," he said. "I'll come and get you. Just give me a ring and I'll get in the van."

I snapped at him a bit then, because I didn't know where I was going to be, or even what the hell was going on. I could be a couple of hours, or all bloody night. "Fine," I said, "I'll phone you when I'm ready," to which he replied,

"Don't get involved, Miriam." Which is bloody silly really, seeing as I was standing there with Larry's claret all over me coat, and a mad woman tearing paper in the next room.

"She's me friend Brian and she hasn't got anyone else. I know you two aren't bosom buddies, but if the shoe was on the other foot she'd be there for me."

"But," Brian jumped in, "the difference is you wouldn't want to kill me."

I thought to meself at times I wasn't too sure, but I mumbled, "No, of course I wouldn't. Look love, the police are going to want me to make a statement so I have to go. I'll see you later." I put the phone down before Brian could say another word and looked past Vicki at Sal. Larry came into my mind unbidden, black winklepickers pointing to heaven. I thought to meself when the lift to the pearly gates came for him, he'd be going down to the basement if you get me drift.

I went back into the sticky room and sat down in my seat next to Sal. I still couldn't get me head round the fact that she'd killed him, but there we were, in a police interview suite with only the constant rip, rip, rip of paper cups to keep us company. We were running out fast now. I quickly rummaged in me bag and took out two little packets of tissues. I always have some on me, you never know when you might need them. I thought if worst comes to worst they would have to do. Just then the door opened.

I'd expected the doctor to be a bloke in a suit, all stuffy and self-important, like the one I went to see about me shoulder, but I was completely wrong. It was a woman and she reminded me of me Aunty Vi. Dr Standage had the same sort of crinkly red hair shot through with silver.

I expect in her job she had seen a lot of things that would turn your hair grey eventually. I'd always wanted auburn locks like hers. At school a girl called Randi Abernathy had red hair down to her bum. Titian they call it. Mine was a kind of mouse and straight as pump water, I had eyes the colour of a muddy puddle to boot. The doctor's eyes were a twinkly green with just a hint of mischief and I thought to meself, I bet she'd be fun at a party. I felt better straight away knowing she was here, I didn't know what was going through Sal's mind when the door opened, although she did stop screaming. There was something about this lady that made me think Sally wouldn't be just a number on a form and I wished with all me heart that would be true. She came over to the table and smiled at me, She didn't try to shake hands, but touched me shoulder as she moved very slowly toward the table.

"Hello," she said softly. "I'm Megan. I'm a doctor and I'm here to help you." Sally stopped ripping and looked, just once, at her. I moved in me seat, just to get comfy and Sal's arm shot out and grabbed me. "I'm not going anywhere, lovey," I said softly. "Isn't that right, Doctor Megan?" The doctor nodded and smiled at Sal. She told her gently that I could stay till she was comfy. As she came closer to us, I could smell lilacs that got stronger when she moved. I loved lilacs. Me granny always had them on the window sill when I were a kid. I'd love to have them in my house, but every one I'd ever bought, I killed with kindness.

"We will be taking you both to the nearest hospital so you can get some rest for the night under sedation," said the doctor. I asked if I could have some too, only half joking. She smiled at me again and even in the midst of all this madness, it met her eyes. She told me quietly, that when Sal was settled I could go home. I don't mind telling you I was so relieved. One, I would be seeing Brian. I couldn't wait to have a cuddle. Two, I could leave this room and all its sadness and shower the stink, and Larry's blood away down the drain. I knew Sal was going to be safe and taken care of. I wasn't worried about that. Of course the madness was all going to start again in the morning. I'd have to do me statement. Something I never thought I'd be doing in a million years. I'd hadn't even been in a police station before, except to hand in a wallet I found in Tesco's car park once. I wondered if Sal would be Sal enough to do hers, or if she'd taken up permanent residence in cloud cuckoo land.

They took us to the hospital in an ambulance. There wasn't the urgency we had before. They drove at the speed limit and Sal looked to be asleep. I don't mind telling you I was knackered an' all, rung out like an old grey dishcloth. I was glad Sally's eyes were closed. I didn't want her to see me flagging. When we got to the Infirmary, Sal was wheeled in by a sour-faced orderly with glasses too big for his face. He kept looking at Sal in the wheelchair then at Vicki, who had volunteered to come with us. Lord knows what was going through his mind. Thinking the worst I expect. The nurses were better, but there was none of the banter we had with them before when we came in after a beating. I expect they didn't think this situation called for it. They were told we were coming and why. They did their jobs, but there weren't much warmth in it. The handcuffs on the bed didn't help, I suppose. Sal wasn't chained up or anything. Doctor Megan said they were there just in case she got out of control again and tried to hurt herself.

I sat by Sally for that long the chair moulded to me bum. It came with me as I stood up, but I managed to put it down quietly. Sally had just gone to sleep. Doctor Megan said she would be out for the night now, as she was under heavy sedation. So when she said I could go home I was the one to lose it. When I started to sob, she came over and folded her arms around me and I let the tears come. God, I needed it. When we parted, I dried me eyes and went over to the bed. I kissed Sal on the head and whispered, "I'll be back in the morning, lovey." Even though she couldn't hear me, I felt better that I'd told her I was going. Then I left the room to ring Brian. He came for me in Garry's truck, because our car was still parked outside Sal's house at Mulberry Crescent. When we came together in the car park, he took one look at me, said, "Bloody hell girl, that better not be your blood." Then he grabbed me and held me tight while I broke me heart.

Megan

After sitting with Sally, reading police reports and filling in countless forms, I finally walked through my door at 7.30 a.m., only to have Charlie fly into my arms. I wasn't ready, so my tiredness and the velocity of a three-year-old in hyper mode pushed me back into the wall.

"Nanny!" he exclaimed, his huge blue eyes shining with delight that I was home.

"Hey Charlie Bear," I said softly, squeezing him to me as if my life depended on it. I nuzzled his hair with my nose taking in the sweet scent of shampoo, crayons and toothpaste.

"I've been really good today," he said jiggling up and down in my arms.

"He's only been up half an hour," said Gina laughing.

I gave him another squeeze and released him. "I'm very proud of you, Charlie, keep it up."

"OK Nanny," he giggled, running into the kitchen for his breakfast. I followed him into the bright sunny room and Gina shoved a cup of tea into my hands.

"Bad night?" she asked gently. I sat at the kitchen table and rested my head on the cool, hard surface.

"Not good, love. I have to go back to the hospital later today to re-assess a lady who was brought into the police station. She's sedated at the moment." Gina knew from experience that I was bound by a confidentiality agreement and couldn't give any personal details, so she didn't ask. Instead she rubbed my back and said, "You need some sleep. Go to bed. I'll keep Charlie amused. He can do some painting, can't you, son?"

"Yippee!!" yelled Charlie. "I'm gonna use red and blue and green and purple and orange, and I'm gonna paint you a rainbow, Nanny. Would you like that?"

"I would love it, Charlie Bear. Just what I need to cheer me up."

"Don't be sad, Nanny," he whispered, climbing onto my lap and kissing my cheek. The tears threatened to come then. For me because I was beyond tired. For Miriam, because she had been suddenly thrust into what could only be described as a nightmare, and especially for Sally, who'd been through one of the worst nights of her life, and would no doubt have to cope with the aftermath of her decision to pick up that knife for many years to come. I wondered, if I would ever be able to get her to trust me enough so she could tell me what had transpired. I quickly swept my thumbs over my eyes so Charlie couldn't see me cry and said, "You know what, Charlie Bear? I'm going up to bed now as I'm very sleepy, but when I wake up, I'm expecting the biggest rainbow I ever saw! Can you do that for me?"

"Yes!" said Charlie. "I'm good at big rainbows."

"Then let's do it," said Gina, "say night night to Nanny."

Charlie giggled. "You're silly, Mummy! It's not night time, the sun is shining."

"Well then, I'll pull the curtains," I said, giving him a kiss on his downy blonde hair.

Upstairs I tugged the blackout blind down and pulled the curtains. The instant dark soothed me as I lay on my bed and waited for oblivion, but sleep evaded me for the moment as my mind began to go into overdrive. What could have happened in Sally's life to reduce her to the person I saw in the safe room at the police station? What had her childhood been like? I could only guess at what she had to endure in her life with Mister Wilson. Larry I believe his name was. The only information I had available to me was what Constable Thomas had gleaned from Miriam at the scene. I would hopefully get the full picture in the morning when I spoke to Sally, though I understood there was domestic violence repeatedly throughout her marriage.

My mind jumped again, this time to Charlie and I made a vow to myself there and then that while I had breath in my body, he would never be ridiculed and made to feel small. He would never know violence, only love and understanding. So when he grew up, he would give his family the same. He would never know coldness or indifference in our household. I couldn't shield him from outside factors, but he would always have someone to talk to. Always. I must've slipped into sleep then. I didn't dream which I was thankful for, but instead, slept like the dead. I awoke to a knock at the door. Gina popped her head round and said that it was noon. I sat up in bed, awake in an instant, only to see a very large rainbow marching in the door with two little hands and two little feet the only part of Charlie I could see.

"It's KHUGE ! Do you like it, Nanny?"

"Like it, I love it! It's made me very happy," I said, and then the tears came.

"They're tears of happiness, Charlie," said Gina before he could get upset. "Aren't they, Nanny?"

"They are, Bear. They really are. I shall pin it up right over there," pointing to the large wall above my chest of drawers. "So that every time I feel sad, I will look at it and feel happy again. Thank you, Charlie." He pushed the painting into his mum's hands and climbed on the bed with me. I cuddled him and silently thanked God for him, for Leo, and for Gina. I knew that Sally had never felt safe in her home which was incredibly sad, but I knew, even though my job scared me at times, I was as safe as houses here with people who loved me. I hugged Charlie once more and said in his ear, "I'm hungry. Let's go down and get some lunch."

"Yippee!" said Charlie. "Can I have sketti on toast?"

"Of course you can, and I might have the same."

"Yippee!" said Charlie again bouncing off the bed. "Come on, Nanny, let's eat." Gina chuckled and said, "That boy will be the death of me!"

I smiled and replied, "We wouldn't have him any other way."

Sally

Isn't it weird how people's perceptions of you change when the shit hits the fan and the tables are turned? I've been to the hospital quite a few times over the years and I've come to think of it as my sanctuary. Somewhere where the hands that touch you aren't out to hurt you. The nurses always treated me as a real person, albeit one that was fragile and a bit broken. If my nose began to bleed someone would rush over with a clean soft pad to stem the flow. If my lips were swollen and sore, there would always be cool water to soothe them. The staff had time for me, even though they were always busy. The coming and going of the doctors and nurses was like a dance I thought, it relaxed me, made me feel safe. Here I knew what to expect, I'd done this before. This time it was different. The small pinched man that wheeled me to my room scowled at me. He kept looking at Vicki then back at me, anyone would think I had murdered someone. Miriam smiled and patted me on the hand and said, "It's OK, lovey, things will be all right, you'll see."

Somehow, for the first time I didn't believe her. Her voice has been a constant in my life for a very long time, either in person or on the telephone and has always been one of calm and reason. She always dropped everything when I needed her, even though Brian always moaned about it. My life wouldn't be worth living if it wasn't for Miriam, I'm certain of that. The nurses kept giving clipped glances at the handcuffs on the bed rail, knowing I had been suspected of killing my husband. It can't have been the only time someone had come in with a police escort. Megan had insisted on no cuffs being used unless It was for my own safety. What she probably meant was, it was for the safety of everyone else! No one wanted an hysterical mad woman who'd rammed a knife in her husband's chest on the loose in a busy ward, did they? The doctor on call, who was actually nice to me, kept calling Vicki the FLO, which she later explained meant Family Liaison Officer. Did I need one when the only family I had, besides Miriam of course, had been taken to the morgue and was now lying right underneath me? It unsettled me a little, knowing that we were still, after all that had happened, sharing the same space. He couldn't get to me, could he? I didn't think so. The morgue was a long way down. He'd be in a drawer, wouldn't he? They'd lock him in, wouldn't they? One thing I do know is they only give you an FLO when your world crumbles around you, when you're worried about bodies rising from drawers, or when someone goes missing, or dies in mysterious circumstances. I didn't need Vicki though. I had my best friend.

There was a rustling sound in the corridor and I noticed movement near the door and I grabbed Miriam's hand as they came toward us. Because of the medication they gave me my eyes had trouble focusing. Who were they, and what did they want from me? My instinct was to bolt but my legs felt screwed to the bed.

"Don't worry, Sal," I think she said. "It's only Doctor Megan. She came in her own car, remember? I expect she got stuck in traffic by McDonalds, It's always chock a block." She moved as close as she could to me, sitting on an ugly orange chair that squeaked like a dolphin every time she moved. She sat stock still, trying not to add to the cacophony of the busy hospital. That was just like Miriam. Never one to make a fuss. Why are the chairs in a hospital always so rigid, so unforgiving? I used to know a man like that. I don't anymore. Megan came into the room and smiled at us. "Sorry, I was a bit behind you, there was an accident on the Edgerley Road by McDonalds and there was a traffic jam."

"It'll be fine now, Sal, You'll see," Miriam said, patting my arm. I wasn't so sure. Will it ever be fine again? Well it never really has been, so I guess I'm used to it. There is always hope, I suppose, but, due to experience, I'm a glass half empty kind of gal. The thing is, when you've killed someone, whether you meant to or not, fine is not a word that comes to mind. Peace. Silence maybe? But definitely not fine. Larry is dead. It'll never be fine for him. Or for Audrey Brown who must be missing him by now. At Mulberry Crescent, the new carpet in the hall is ruined, the walls will have to be repainted and the swing bin will forever remind me of Larry, so nothing is fine there either.

An agonizing scream from the next room brought me back to the blinding whiteness of the ward. There's a kind of Yin and Yang about a place like this, isn't there? There's hope and sadness. Loud and quiet. Life and death. There was a loneliness about it that made me feel helpless, God

I knew that feeling. Focusing on Miriam, I tried to rise from the bed and tried to use my eyes to ask her for help. She gently pushed me back down, whispering to me that she was here and I was safe, but I fought against her and lost the plot. It was then that I realised I was as mad as the screaming woman in the next bay, that the loony ward was the right place for me. It was overwhelming, it was the beginning of the end. Megan saw what was happening and spoke quickly to a nurse. The next thing I knew, all these people were holding me down. I felt a needle pierce my flesh. I cried out and tried again to get off the bed, Miriam sat stock still, tears rolling down her face.

"Go with it, lovey. I'm here," she said, although her words had a muffled quality like she was talking through a black velvet curtain. I could hear Megan saying relax, take it easy, but I was scared that if I went with it I wouldn't wake up. It was too soon. I wasn't ready. I tried to focus on the green light of the CCTV camera that was standard for loony rooms, but as it got bigger and greener and more fuzzy and soft, I let it consume me.

When I woke up and tried to open my eyes, everything was in soft focus. Smokey. I felt like my body had been hit by a mac truck and I couldn't move. My mind began to race like Red Rum in the grand national. Thoughts and pictures were streaming by so fast. Colours were merging, sounds distorting in my ears. I panicked. I didn't like it! I tried to call out for help and in my mind I was roaring, but all that came out was a pathetic, raspy whisper. I felt very small again. Very beige. Rustling coming from somewhere on my right gradually got louder and began to drown out the din in my head. Slowly I came back into the room.

A sound, like ripping paper, took me back to yesterday. To that little room and the mountain of white. The sound stopped abruptly, and then more soft rustling. I struggled to make my head turn. My body rigid with fear. A veil like softness still covered my eyes but it wasn't soothing. When you can't see your enemy, but know he's there. If he's hiding round a corner or say behind a door, your survival instinct goes through the roof. I got ready to run, only in my mind of course. I couldn't have got off the bed if my life had depended on it. Did it?

"Hey Sal. You're awake. How are you feeling, lovey?" whispered the source of the noise. "I was just rooking in me bag for a mint, me mouth tastes like our Garry's slippers. Shall I get a nurse?"

My body instantly relaxed. "You've been asleep that long, Sal, it's the afternoon. Still you've had a good rest. Things will be clearer in your mind now, you'll see." I didn't want things to be clearer in my mind. I wanted more drugs to send me back to black. I didn't want to think about Audrey Brown, or Larry or how his blood had seeped into everything, tainting everything. Tainting me. I realised Miriam was still talking to me, so I pulled myself away from Larry, back to safety. I tried again to keep my eyes open and at last, the smoke began to clear. "Doctor Megan will be along in a minute Sal, and I'll leave to it, so you two can have a chat." I must have shown her something through my eyes, because even though I couldn't tell her with my voice, she knew being without her would scare me, so she said she would be right outside the door if I needed her.

"Can you sit up, Sal?" I gave it my best shot but had to wiggle my head again. No.

"Not to worry. I'll help you. You don't weigh more than a fag paper these days. Come on." Miriam put her arm round my shoulders, braced herself, then hauled me up in to a sitting position. All at once the room began to spin and I knew I was going to throw up.

"There there lovey, get it all out," soothed Miriam, holding a cardboard pot in one hand and rubbing my back with the other. I wished I could. I wished I could vomit all the hurt, the betrayals and the poison out of me, but most of all, I wished I could go right back to the beginning and not have been born at all. Miriam wiped my mouth, pulled a comb from her bag and dragged it through my lank brown hair. I looked down and noticed the blood had been washed from my body. All traces of Larry erased like chalk from a blackboard. I didn't want to think about what happened. My mind had been assaulted enough for one day, but still, it played images like a film on speed. I saw me in the freezer aisle in Tesco's looking for sea bass for Larry's dinner. Flash to him drunk, mocking. The knife, his lips grey, the room red. Flash to Miriam's concerned face. Then I realised the worried face was real. That was my fault too.

"You're safe now, Sally," Miriam said, seeing my confusion." Don't worry, love. Oh now! Look who's here."

At that moment Megan arrived. Her lilac perfume took the stink of chemicals and boiled cabbage from the room as she pulled up a chair next to Miriam. "Hello Sally. How are you feeling? Are you up for a little chat now?" she said quietly. Should I put my trust in this person? Could I spill all the secrets of my forty-five years on this planet to her? I wasn't sure. I had no idea what would happen in the next few hours and days, but it was fight or flight time. Shit or get off the pot, Sally, what are you going to do? My eyes went to the door. They had anticipated my response though, because Vicki stood in the doorway preventing escape. Should I try to take the flight option? Even if I had the strength to run from this place, where would I go? Miriam rubbed my arm and told me for the millionth time today, that things were going to be all right, and if I couldn't trust her, who could I trust? I lay back on the pillows and willed my mind to make yellow. It's the hardest colour to keep around and that's because I never really had many days when I felt at peace, felt able to think straight. I made the decision to fight. For now.

Miriam

I don't mind telling you I was bloody shattered when I finally got home. Brian went to make a cuppa but I couldn't keep me eyes open, so we went straight to bed. I fell asleep as soon as me head found the pillow, thank God It meant I didn't have to run the whole thing through me mind again. I'd already done it a thousand times at the hospital. Sitting there in the dead of night staring at Sally as she slept. Afraid to leave in case she woke up. Afraid to stay in case she woke up. I had stay though, didn't I? I was her friend, the only one she had at the moment, and I would be there for her, warts an' all. The next day I woke up late. I was like a bloody zombie before Brian gave me a cup of tea and a couple of party rings, he kept for me from last night. Bless his cotton socks! He'd only gone and saved me favourites too. Milk chocolate digestives. If I ever had to escape from a burning building, I'd take two things. My Brian and choccy digestives. I didn't get to have them yesterday though did I? Because one did a nose dive in me tea, and I didn't get a chance to fish it out and dunk another one, because this whole nightmare started. I had me breakfast and a shower and felt more like meself again. Brian kept moaning about me going back to the hospital, but I said nothing was going to keep me from being there for Sal, so he'd better get used to it. He drove me there in our Garry's van, hardly saying a word. Garry and Jamie, his mate, were going to pick my car up from outside Sal's later on. When we got to the hospital, I didn't give him a chance to get his two penn'orth in. I planted a kiss on his cheek, got out of the van and told him I would ring when I was ready. "When will that be?" he asked, in a sharp tone.

I told him he knew as much as I did, and said again that I would phone him later. I shut the van door and walked towards the entrance. I didn't look back. I didn't want to see the disapproval on Brian's face. He could look like he was sucking a lemon when he were cross. I love my Brian to distraction, but I were getting a bit fed up with him sulking like a five year old because I wasn't at home feeding him tea and biccies. I were needed elsewhere. Besides, my mind was on Sally. God only knew what state she'd be in when I got there?

My life has always revolved around Brian and Garry. It's lovely to have friends and I like to help them where I can, but me family mean the absolute world to me, even if one of them was throwing his toys out the pram at the minute. Our Garry has got a new girlfriend and he'd be moving out soon to get on with his own life. Grace had a little girl from her last relationship called Sarah and they made a lovely little family. I couldn't wait to play Granny and spoil her, but it was early days yet. I was biding me time.

When I got to Sally's room she was still asleep. The nurse I spoke to said she had had a comfortable night and that I could sit with her for a while. She told me that a policewoman would be with us in a minute, and I should take a seat in that ruddy orange chair. Well! That minute stretched to ten and was still stretching and I wished she would hurry up. I'd had peanut butter on toast for me breakfast and me mouth still tasted like a mouldy sock, so I rooked in me bag for a mint. I don't know if you ladies have the same problem, but it doesn't matter what size handbag I use, I fill it, then I can never find anything I'm looking for. It's a ruddy bottomless pit. I found me mints in the end, right down in the corner, ripped the packet open and stuck two in me gob at once. When I looked up from the rubbish in me bag, I noticed Sally's eyes flickering. It was like they were glued shut and it was taking all her effort to unglue them. I was a bit nervous about being alone with her now she'd started to wake up to tell you the truth. I didn't know if she was still crazy, or whether she was Sal again. Mind you she's always been a bit on the strange side. All through school, and again very recently actually, she'd find the nearest wall and press herself against it whenever she were upset, or worried. I found it a bit odd to tell you the truth. It seemed to calm her though, and when she was ready she would peel herself off and be Sal again. She was trying hard to move her neck, to see where the racket was coming from I expect. She wasn't very successful, I could see it was hurting her. The bruising was coming out now and looked like one of Sarah's paintings. I spoke quietly to her, saying that I was glad she was awake and that I was just getting me sweets out of me bag. She calmed down straight away and the weird eye twitching stopped. The poor love didn't look too comfy though, so I asked her if she wanted to sit up? She nodded as best she could. I got me arms round her and pulled her up so she could see the room. She was sick then, even though she'd had nothing to eat for hours. I think I got her up too fast, bless her. I wiped her mouth, plumped the pillows, even though they felt like ruddy concrete, and she settled back. She kept trying to say something, but it came out in a whisper and on account of a burst eardrum when I was three, I couldn't hear a bloody thing she said. The policewoman came in then and I was so glad to see it was the girl from last night. Vicki, If I remember rightly? She looked smart in her uniform, but tired round the eyes. I wondered if she got any sleep after the horror of yesterday. Mind you, I suppose she was much more used to seeing dead bodies than I was. I'd only ever seen one before Larry and that was me Gran. She'd looked just like she was sleeping but she died of old age, and not with a ruddy great knife sticking out of her chest. Vicki pulled a chair up next to the bed and she asked how we both were. I said I felt like I was in an episode of the twilight zone and she said she knew what I meant.

I knew I couldn't stay at the hospital all day, as I'd got to go and do me statement at the police station, but I wanted to wait until Doctor Megan turned up. She told me last night she would get back as soon as she could and I felt safe leaving Sal with her. There was something about the woman that I trusted. She would help us make sense of all this madness, I could feel it in me water. Vicki touched me on the arm and turned towards the door just as Doctor Megan walked in. I knew I'd have to leave soon, but I'd hang around for a little while, just to make sure Sal could cope. The police station wasn't going anywhere and I needed to know she was settled and calm enough to answer Dr Megan's questions, without her losing it again and taking the last train to Nutsville.

Megan

When I left the house the next afternoon to go back to the Infirmary the sun was shining, a welcome reprieve from yesterday's constant rain. I was slower today. Ploddy. The damp weather we'd had for weeks now was playing havoc with my arthritis, and my eighty-year-old self had seemingly come to stay. I know, I should have booked that appointment with the rheumatologist, but the thought of being an invalid for four to six weeks sends shudders through me. I am not a good patient at the best of times, and I must admit I am scared of going under the knife, even if the end result affords me two new knees. Hobbling down the drive, I hear a tap at the window. I turned to see Charlie, nose pressed up against the pane tongue out, eyes crossed his fingers making rabbit ears. I pulled a face back at him and his giggles followed me all the way to the car. I tried not to wince as I got in the driver's seat. Charlie didn't need to see that. I hoped my medication would work soon. Sally needed me on full beam, not sidelights.

As I turned left towards the Edgerley Road, Shakin' Stevens rendition of 'Green door' whispered out of the radio. It was a marked difference from 'The Ride Of The

Valkyries' and I kept it low, so I could concentrate on the road. My painkillers were on board now, but I was still sore and I didn't want to take any chances. All of a sudden Shaky suddenly petered out and a new voice made me turn it up.

"This is Amy Roberts at WG FM with tunes you want to hear. We'll be going back to the music in a moment folks, but now we go over to the news desk for a 'Newsflash' with Raun Nixon."

"Thank you, Amy. A report just in. A forty-nine-year-old man has been found dead at his home in Winston Green. Police have declined to comment at this time but enquiries are on-going. We will update you as more information becomes available. We'll have the full weather report in a few minutes and it's looking stormy out there for the next few days, so brollies at the ready, but for now it's back to Amy in the studio."

I was glad the news report didn't mention any names. It would be hard enough getting Sally through the interview without fighting off hordes of reporters baying for blood on the steps of the police station. I got out of the car at the hospital and stepped gingerly onto the tarmac to test my joints, hoping for the best. The anti-inflammatories I'd taken had begun to kick in and I felt more ready for what was to come. Famous last words! As I was still the psychiatrist on call, it would be my job to assess Sally again, and determine whether or not she was now fit for interview.

She did look a bit better when I walked into her room. The blood had been washed away and she had a pink, hospital issue gown on her waif-like body. Her skin had taken on a more normal, healthy, flesh tone but her eyes told a different story. They looked haunted and so dark, they seemed bottomless. Her friend Miriam sat beside the bed chomping on what smelled like humbugs. She smiled at me and I returned it as she offered me a sweet. Vicki Thomas, the FLO, sat at the side of the bed nearest the door. I nodded a hello and approached the group.

"Hello Sally. Do you remember me? I'm Megan. I was at the police station last night. I'm here to make sure you are all right. I'd like to have a talk with you about how you are feeling when you're ready, if that's OK?."

"I killed Larry," she offered in a robotic tone. "I killed him. He's dead." It was difficult to hear what she was saying as her voice was croaky, her lips cracked and dry. Miriam got up and held a cup of water to Sally's mouth. She drank greedily and sank back into the freshly plumped pillows.

"I need a few minutes with Sally if that's OK?" I asked of Miriam. Vicki would stay as liaison officer but would retreat to the back of the room, to be there if we needed her.

"Of course," Miriam said. She smiled at me again but there was worry in her eyes. She patted Sally's hand and smoothed the sheets. "I'll be right outside, lovey. You will be fine with Dr Megan and Vicki. I'll see you in two shakes of a lamb's tail, OK?" Sally nodded, but her eyes tracked Miriam all the way to the door which shut behind her with a loud click. The empty sound seemed to echo all around the room, like an approaching thunderstorm, then it stopped abruptly, rendering us at the mercy of the ever ticking clock. Sally met my eyes and an involuntary shudder coursed through me. What must this poor woman have gone through to end up here in this hospital bed?

What must it have been like, to think that the only way out she had was to plunge a knife into someone's heart? I wanted to prepare her for what was to come, but for the first time in my professional life I couldn't find the right words. Instead I asked, "How are you feeling, Sally? Are you injured anywhere?" She shook her head, but as she did so, I noticed a dark red mark on her neck and a huge bruise on her left shoulder, as her gown slipped down over her bony frame. I didn't ask about them. I figured there would be plenty of time for that. Instead I ran through the usual questions we ask to test for lucidity. Sally passed with flying colours. I sort of wished she hadn't, so she would have more time to rest before the onslaught of interviews, fingerprints and photographs. I hoped, when she had had time to breathe, she would be able talk to me about what led up to the tragic circumstances surrounding the death of her husband. No one should keep that sort of horror to themselves. It eats away at any chance of coming out the other side. I knew nothing about Sally Wilson or her life, but I did know she needed help.

I'd decided I would like to take her on as my client when she left the hospital, if she wanted me to. I felt invested somehow. Something in me felt there was more to this lady than met the eye. I wanted to try and help her, regardless of the outcome of the police enquiry. I couldn't do anything about whether or not they would charge her, but what I could do was help her make peace with it all. No one could bring her husband back, and no one could do anything about the life she has lead up to this point. But going forward I would do my best to show her there is better to come, even if it did begin with a spell in a psychiatric hospital, or even prison...

…Much later, as we approached the police station in my car, Sally stiffened and stopped dead. Vicki, who was beside her, spoke gently. "It'll be all right, Sally. All you have to do is tell them what happened and sign a written statement. It won't take long then we'll go and get something to eat. You must be hungry?"

"Where's Miriam?" she asked, still standing in the same spot, her eyes flitting like a butterfly on a leaf.

"She's here" said Vicki quietly pointing to the annex of the huge building. She's giving her statement right now but you will see her as soon as we've finished here."

"Don't worry, Sally," I said in a practised voice meant to soothe a child. "Vicki's right, Miriam will be waiting for you when you've made your statement and had an interview. You'll be able to talk to her then, I promise. In the meantime, I'll be there if you need me." Sally started towards the same doors she had entered last night, walking head down between us through the maze of cars. Every so often, she would do a kind of rocking motion, taking one step back, then continue walking normally again. I noted it, and would ask her about it later, though I wasn't sure if she was even aware she was doing it. There were a couple of reporters milling about the entrance to the police station, but as no names, or photographs had been released we sailed past. As we got inside, Sally began to visibly shrink. Her shoulders met her ears, hunched like she had aged fifty years. Her head moved quickly from left to right as if she were scanning for anything that might hurt her. She was terrified. Vicki and I took her freezing hands in ours. This seemed to calm her. She stopped twitching and we proceeded down the same corridor she had travelled only eighteen hours and a lifetime ago.

Sally hadn't yet been formally charged with anything, as the police were still conducting their enquiries, but she had been arrested on suspicion of manslaughter last night. That was just a formality. The forensic team were still at the house in Mulberry Crescent, gathering evidence that would shed light on what had happened there. A file would then be sent to the CPS, who would make a decision as to what, if anything Sally would be charged with. She hadn't even registered the arrest at the booking in desk last night. She wasn't compos mentis. Who would be? I know I wouldn't. In the tiny interview room, the duty solicitor sat with Sally, advising her of her rights. I wasn't sure if she was taking anything in. Her head hung low and she was all curled in, making herself as small as possible I noticed she kept trying to scoot her chair nearer the wall, so I reached over from my seat in the corner and touched her left shoulder. She flinched slightly, but allowed my hand to rest there. She stopped scooting and began to relax. Her head came up to meet the officers on the other side of the desk for a split second but it was a start.

In certain circumstances, an appropriate adult can be present in an interview. If the suspect is under the age of sixteen, or is deemed be unable to understand the questions put to them. Sally's situation was delicate and she was still in a fragile state, so in cases like this, an appropriate adult is called in to give comfort and moral support. Because Miriam was a witness, she couldn't do it, so I stepped in to the breach. Sally wasn't the manic hysterical person of the night before, but she was still terrified and subject to bouts of sustained silences, which in an interview didn't bode well. I was there to encourage her to tell her story. There were two detectives in the room, making five persons in all. I don't know about Sally, but I felt claustrophobic and under scrutiny and I wasn't even the one in the hot seat. The tall one with kind eyes was very gentle with her, coaxing the answers from her rather than using the clichéd good cop, bad cop, which would have been disastrous in Sally's case. The other, more rotund one looked as if he would rather be anywhere else than here. They kept us there for over an hour, but in the end they had all they were going to get.

As they left the room, I heard the bald, more bored looking one of the two say that getting information out of Sally was like scraping gum off the pavement. Nigh on impossible. He obviously had no idea how traumatised she was, how difficult it had been for her to relive that night, there in that stuffy little room. To be honest, he couldn't have cared less. I was the lucky one. I got to go home to my wonderful, chaotic family and have a cuddle from Charlie. Where would Sally go? That was still to be determined, but I hoped it wouldn't be prison. In my opinion, that was the worst place imaginable for her. At the end of the interview I had a few minutes alone with her. She seemed calmer, but flatter, as if she had a slow puncture. She had begun to retreat again. I noticed her staring intently at a wall the colour of baby poo, as if her life depended on it. I got up from the chair that was bolted to the floor and knelt down facing her. My knees were screaming at me to stop and my face said as much, but I looked into her frightened face and said, "No more questions now, Sally. I know it's hard to tell a stranger things you have never told anyone before, let alone one with dodgy knees, but if you want me to, I'd like to try to help you." I smiled at her then, and she looked at me, really looked and I could see the years of pain and suffering in the depths of her eyes. Brown, black, tired, scared. "If it helps," I gently told her, "you could write it down. Many of the people I help do that. Sometimes seeing things in black and white helps make sense of them." She just nodded as if her speech had all dried up, turned her head, and gazed toward the door.

"Let's go and find Miriam, shall we, Sally?" She nodded again and then she did something totally unexpected. She took my hand.

Miriam

I was sitting opposite the officer that was taking me statement and me legs were like jelly. Being shut in a room no cleaner than the one last night, spilling me guts to a stranger, was not on my bucket list, I can tell you. He wanted to know everything but the colour of me undies. I told him, I might not have been there for the whole thing last night, but I knew Sally, and I know she must have been scared to death that Larry was going to finish her off to do something like that. She could never hurt another person unless she was in fear for her life, I was sure of that. I put that in me statement too. I told him I always thought it would be Larry that would do for Sally. I made sure the officer knew the nightmare she had lived for the last twenty-five years. Too frightened to leave, but scared witless almost every day she had stayed. I know Brian thinks she plays the victim a bit, but he didn't take her to the hospital umpteen times with cut lips, black eyes and nose bleeds. Or when she's had that many bruises on her thighs the poor mare couldn't walk. He says if it were that bad she'd have dobbed Larry in by now. We did that a couple of times, Sally and me. We talked to the police, but she would never press charges. She knew if she had, Larry would have bloody killed her. She must have been desperate to do what she did. I could only imagine what was going through her head, bless her. She must have panicked and felt she was fighting for her life. Which truth be told, she was. I know in me heart that if she hadn't done what she did, whatever the rights and wrongs of it, she would not be here today and that's a fact. I knew she would tell me what happened when she could, and I know that whatever she did say would be the truth. I would support her through whatever came next anyhow, that's what friends do. I prayed that Doctor Megan would be able to get Sal to open up. Get her to make sense of the ruddy mess she found herself in.

I could only guess at the life Sally had before I met her. She told me snippets, I know she lived with both of her parents and they weren't the joy and sunshine type, but she has never sat down over a cuppa and given me chapter and verse. I know it wasn't good. Sometimes, even now, I catch her with her head down staring at the floor with the concentration of a sniffer dog, obviously reliving some horrible childhood memory. It does look odd and a bit creepy, but I think I'd be left of centre if I had to live with crappy parents all my young life, then to cap it all off, get saddled with Larry. Our Brian drives me round the bend sometimes, but I wouldn't swap him for the world, well maybe when the snooker's on the gogglebox for days on end. I could happily swap him for Jill and Mandy then, just for a while. I'd be able to watch something that wasn't sport with me besties for once. Seriously though, I really don't know what I would do without my Brian, even when he is driving me scatty.

I remember the day I first clapped eyes on Sally. We were eleven years old and were both starting Winston Green Academy. I was new in the area and hadn't made any friends like the other kids. They all knew each other from primary school and had formed cliques. Me family moved here from Leeds, from a council estate that was as rough as coarse grade sandpaper. Mum and Dad wanted a better life for us, so they got an exchange up to Winston Green. It was a different world. There were trees and birds and houses that weren't built on top of one another. Me Mam said we would all be the better for it. Our Mick, along with his mate Kevin, had got in a spot of bother with the gangs down there. Mam were having none of it. She said we all needed a new start, so move we did.

Over by the bike racks, I saw some girls laughing at something and not in a good way. They were pointing at a tall, skinny girl, with long brown hair, and egging each other on to throw the next insult. That girl turned out to be Sal. She had her back to the playground wall, pressing herself against it for all she was worth. The more they made fun, the flatter she got. She looked scared to death. I thought about going to get a teacher, but instead, I went over and stood next to her, so neither of us would feel so alone. I felt the urge to protect this girl I'd never met, so I began to talk incessantly about who I was and where I was from. She turned her head and glanced at me in snatches through a long fringe, then looked down at the ground again. It was as if eye contact was an effort for her. Eventually the witches lost interest and moved on. I didn't ask any questions about what they said to her, I just gabbled on. Little by little she began to relax as she listened to me nonsense. Brian is always telling me I talk too much, but this time, it came in handy. We looked like little and large standing there with our backs to the wall. Me, small and dumpy. Sal tall and so skinny, a stiff wind could have blown her away. From a distance we must've looked like the number 10.

From that day on we stayed together. We didn't care if we weren't popular. We were happy in our own company, although, at times, I would've liked a few other friends, just to ring the changes. A girl did try once. She was a bit lonely and wanted to hang about with us, but Sal was as cold to her as me mam's chest freezer. On the days that Sal didn't come to school, and there were a fair few, I went round with Hannah. What Sally didn't know wouldn't hurt her. I told her I was sorry about Sally shutting her out. She said she didn't mind. I loved her company. She was funny and generous and she sang like a songbird. Hannah understood that Sal had a few problems and needed me more than she did. She was happy to take a step back when required. Anyhow, halfway through that term, Hannah found a boyfriend. Luke were lovely. I were glad for her and it meant I didn't have to split meself in half anymore cos she was too busy snogging behind the bike sheds. Despite my presence, Sal still bore the brunt of the playground jibes from time to time. I stuck up for her then, and I bloody well will now.

I told the policeman what I saw when I got to Sal's that night and he wrote everything down on paper. I also told him that Larry was a monster and treated Sally like a slave. He used to smack her one, when she was a bit slow, laughing at the poor mare when she showed she was scared. I told Officer Kemp about the time she had a panic attack, because the bus from Winston Green was five minutes late. She knew she wouldn't be home at the time Larry told her to be. You should have seen the poor girl, shaking like a leaf she was. I thought she were going to keel over right there and then. That night I had to take her to the hospital. Larry had given her a right going over. Although I pleaded with her to press charges, she wouldn't, she couldn't, because if she had, she knew it would have been the last thing she ever did.

I told them everything I could about Sal's life with that bastard. I tried to make them understand. I'd done my bit, now I just wanted to see her, make sure she was all right. I was worried what they were going to do with her and what, if anything, they would charge her with. I wanted to give her a ruddy medal. Not for killing him you understand, but for finally growing a backbone and fighting back. I just wished it hadn't ended the way it did. I wish she'd just found the courage to leave him instead. It would have been easier all round.

After I'd signed me name on the bottom of the statement. Officer Kemp showed me to a little waiting room with a few magazines on a little corner table. He said he was sorry that he couldn't offer me a drink, they'd run out of cups. He said I was to wait for Sal there, that they would be finished shortly. I asked if Doctor Megan was with Sally in the room and he nodded, though I could swear blind he was blushing. I told the police that Sally would be staying with me until we knew what was happening. I gave them me address and whatnot. They knew where she would be, so they were happy to send her home with me and I know Sally couldn't ruddy wait to get out of the place. When she came into the room with Doctor Megan, I gave her a big hug and said, "Let's go home." I didn't yet know how long she'd be staying with us, or how bloody hard it would prove to be.

Sally

I don't want to have to do this, to put my life on paper, but I need to try to make someone understand me. I have never told Miriam any of this, because if I had, I may have lost her and that would be the end. So, here goes. You asked for warts and all. Here it is from the beginning. As a child I used to pull the wings off flies. The desperate fizzing sound they made calmed me for a while I suppose. There is something surreal about watching someone, or something else panic, isn't there? I guess it could be because it wasn't me for once. It was like watching a flickery silent movie. You know, the black and white kind, where colour is something they haven't invented yet. I would stand over them watching, not helping, just watching and when they stopped moving in manic circles they became like ink blots on the table. I squashed them then, they had no point anymore. I understood that. In fact I don't ever remember a time when I didn't feel insignificant, or for that matter, used. Whenever I looked in the mirror, which wasn't often, my eyes reminded me of a fly's body. They were round, and so dark they were almost black. I wore my hair long, with a fringe, that I would close like curtains to hide my soul from people. I never used to fit around others, well, until I met Miriam, that is. I could sit for hours with Mother and Father coming and going around me. *Where's the brat?* They would ask and I'd be right there, right under their noses and I'd laugh to myself at how stupid they were. I liked being invisible, it made me feel safe, so I began to find places to hide. I figured no one would notice nor care, so I would cram myself into the smallest spaces imaginable and try to become part of the house. There is something comforting in bricks and mortar. Something stable. People have a habit of letting you down, of jeering at you, hurting you, but a wall is solid. You know where you are with a wall. I used to walk around my bedroom trailing my hand along all four of them. Touching, feeling, remembering all the bumps and cracks, so I would know where I was if I ever went blind. My dog went blind. My father shot him. Barney couldn't walk in a straight line anymore, he would stumble around, bumping into things and in the end he became helpless, like the flies. My father said he would rather spend the money on other things more important than taking Barney to the vet. Instead he took him into the back garden and blew his brains out with an air rifle. He didn't even get a decent burial. My father threw him on the bonfire when he was burning an old pear tree that was rotten from the ground up. The tree wasn't the only thing that was rotten. I hated my father more at that moment than I ever did, and I'd hated him with my heart and soul since I was old enough to be either ignored, or ridiculed. I hated my mother more if that was possible.

Talking of walking in a straight line, it's something most people take for granted, isn't it? One foot in front of the other, but for years after Barney, I didn't find it so easy. He was the only thing in my childhood I ever had any good thoughts about. I can't say it was love, because to feel love, you first have to receive it. I didn't know what the feeling was, but I knew that I missed him. So I got into the habit of taking four steps forward, one for each of Barney's legs, and one step back, as if I was unsure of where I was going or what would happen when I got there. There was a part of me you see, that always held back just one step. There still is if I'm honest. If I could go back in time and talk to my then six-year-old self, I would give her a heads up. Warn her that life wouldn't get any better. Give her the courage to protect herself from people's cruelty by any means possible, and not to marry someone called Larry.

I understand the way I walked did look a bit odd. Father would drag me along as if I was doing it to be awkward but I wasn't. I remember it did get worse for a time, when I started jumping over the lines in doorways. Again, I don't know what I thought would happen if I stepped on them. I was always too scared to test it out. Thinking about it now, what could possibly happen to me that hadn't already? The odd walking went on for quite a while, well into my late teens. I could hear people in the street saying things. Whispering in groups while waiting for the post office to open, or queueing for the sales. You know, it's funny when someone talks behind their hands. They actually think it muffles the sound of their jibes, but of course it doesn't.

"There she goes, that Sally Jones," they'd say. "She is a weird one. Shame really. She's quite pretty when she's not hiding behind her fringe. It's a wonder she can see to walk at all." Or my particular favourite. "She's an odd'un that one, always on her own. What she needs is a fella, that'd sort her out."

I never said anything back to them. Never defended myself, and at those times I remembered having that kinship with Barney and the flies. I knew what it was like to be unimportant in people's eyes.

I used to think a lot about having a boyfriend, but who would want a freak like me? Oh I got over the walking thing, well almost, but I was still reserved and distrustful of people. They weren't always what they were supposed to be, I had a lot of that growing up. I realised, if I kept myself to myself it would be safer. If I didn't put myself out there, I couldn't get hurt. Self-preservation was the most important thing to me. The grey is descending, so If you don't mind, I will save the rest for another day. There's a lot more to tell, but It's tiring, isn't it? Dragging all the injustices I've ever suffered back into my head. I am glad you suggested writing it all down though. I had my reservations at first, but It's quite cathartic in a way. It's like you can say all you ever wanted to say without recriminations, because everything I write for you is confidential. These letters will be my testament. The last full stop at the end of a long novel. The last brick in the wall.

Miriam

Sal's been a bit brighter since she's been doing what Megan said and getting everything down on paper. She even smiled yesterday. I didn't think she would ever smile again after what happened with Larry. I haven't asked her about what she's writing. I expect she'll show me if she wants to. I told her she could talk to me anytime, but truth be told I'm dreading the day she does. Brian asked me again when she was leaving. He asks me that a lot lately, but I haven't a clue meself to be fair. Megan says the house is nearly ready after being specially cleaned of all the claret, but I'm not sure Sally wants to go back there just yet, if at all. I'm feeling a little bit claustrophobic if I'm honest. It's just that everywhere I am, Sally is. I can't have a minute to meself. I know she takes comfort in being near me, but it gives me the willies having her up me bum all the time. Oh I understood it when it was all raw, and she couldn't go five minutes without remembering what had gone on that night. I spent ages cuddling her through all the screaming and the muttering, telling her things would get better. Now, two weeks on, I'm trying to keep me distance a bit, let her try and work things out for herself. Brian tries his level best to avoid her, which is ruddy daft when we live in a two up, two down, with a garden the size of a postage stamp and a shed you can just about sit down in, if you didn't move your arms. I've seen him skirt around her, pressing himself to the cabinets in the kitchen to avoid having to touch her. It's like he thinks he might catch whatever ails her. She's the same with him. She turns her back to the nearest wall when he comes in the room. Sal's always done that though. Ever since we were kids. It's some sort of comfort to her I suppose. A place of safety, but it's like a Mexican standoff with the pair of them and there's me, always stuck in the middle. They've never been what you'd call friendly, but now they are downright hostile to one another. It ain't half awkward, because when Sally is attached to me skirt most of the time, he won't come near me either. So he's always somewhere else. The only time I get to spend with him is at bedtime and by then, he's usually in such a grump about something Sally's done, or didn't do, that a cuddle is out of the ruddy question.

We can't go on like this. I'll have to talk to Megan tomorrow. Sal is seeing her at two o'clock. She comes here, which is great for me because that's when I do me shopping and whatnot. I've asked Brian to come with me, but he'd rather paint himself blue, and stand on the Winston Green roundabout whistling Dixie, than be seen dead in Tesco's. He thinks men and shopping shouldn't mix. He still gets our Garry to buy me birthday and Christmas pressies. HIs old mam, God rest her soul, had to buy me engagement ring, because Brian wouldn't go to the precinct to choose it himself. She hadn't a clue what size I was, so it ended up being two sizes too big.

I had to keep me fingers in a fist for fear of it falling off till I could get into town and get it resized. I don't mind going on me own. Shopping is a couple of hours respite for me, and for Brian. He retreats to the shed and sticks his nose in the latest Dean Koontz. He has to be careful when he turns the pages though, or he bangs his ruddy elbows. He's obsessed with horror books is our Brian. Weird really when he can't cope with what Sally's done, even though it was in self-defence. He told me last night, there's nothing to stop her killing us both in our bed if she had a mind to. I told him not to be so melodramatic. I know Sal. She would never hurt me and mine, that I'm sure of. That's why Brian likes horror fiction, I think. You can go there, without ever really going there if you get my drift. It's safe for him, bless his cotton socks. Sally brought that world a bit close to home for Brian's liking I reckon. I hope she'll feel like going back to Mulberry Crescent soon. I miss seeing me other friends Jill and Mandy. We'd always meet on a Wednesday. We wander into town for a bit of window shopping then a cuppa and a sticky bun. I haven't seen them at all for a fortnight and I'm starting to go a little bit stir crazy. Jill thinks I'm barking mad having Sal at our place. I saw her brother in Marks and Sparks the other day and he said she's worried about me. Bless her. I told him to tell her not to worry, that it wouldn't be long until things went back to normal. I were crossing me fingers behind me back when I said it though, cos I wasn't sure what was going to happen meself. We still don't know whether or not Sal will be charged with anything, but until then she hasn't got anywhere else to go and I won't see her out on the street. Brian keeps saying things like, "She's a bit clingy, Miriam." Or "What's happening with the case?" I have no bloody idea what to say to him, so I repeat, "It won't be long now, love," and pray, for all our sakes that it's true just to stop Brian from moaning. I told him divorce will be on the cards if he asks me again. Trouble is Brian knows I don't mean it so it doesn't stop him. Megan will be here in half an hour. She'll know what's going on…I hope.

Sally

Miriam took me in. I knew she would. I feel safe here. Protected. I've never really felt like that before, except when I was with Miriam's family after school thirty odd years ago. Just having someone to talk to without being shouted at is a gift and I hope I can stay for a while. I'm still waiting to hear from Detective Sergeant Whalen, the lead officer in the case, about what is going on. I have no idea what will happen to me or when just yet?

At least they let me out of the police station on bail and home to Miriam's, which I've taken as a good sign. Megan was the one who talked to Miriam and Brian about me staying with them and Miriam didn't hesitate to say yes. I bet Brian wasn't best pleased. She would have overruled him though, because she loves me.

I think both Megan and Miriam thought it would be better for me than being admitted to The Chimes, which is the local psychiatric hospital for rest. If you can call being drugged to the eyeballs so you don't become a problem rest. My grandmother went in there. She never came out. Oh, I didn't care about her, I never really knew her anyway. I just didn't want to end up like her, in a tiny room, all alone waiting until I met my maker.

Megan thought a home environment would be much more comfortable. It would allow me to process things and help me to come to terms with what happened that night. I already had, but I didn't tell anyone. Once I'd got over the shock of nearly dying myself, it was easy. Larry was dead. End of. Miriam thought I was still worrying about it. She said stewing about it all was making me too thin and could I do with a bit of tender loving care. I knew she'd listen if I wanted to talk, not that I would of course, because she's a good friend. Brian's still a bit of a problem though. He never liked me and I have to say the feeling is mutual. He keeps asking Miriam how long I'm going to be there. I'll stay as long as I want, he'll just have to put up with it. We've never seen eye to eye, even in the early days. Oh I liked the way he protected Miriam from anything he deemed dodgy. He always had his arm around her, like a shield of sorts. I was a bit jealous of that sometimes, because Larry was as about as far removed from Brian as it's possible to be in the protective stakes. Once, when Patrick Bodie put his hand up my skirt at a dance, instead of knocking his block off, which is what Brian would have done if it happened to Miriam, he laughed and said that he could cop another feel for a fiver. I should have heeded the warnings then, shouldn't I? Miriam told me to ditch him. She saw straight through him. Back then though, I thought it was better to have somebody than nobody, and I had no other offers. I was awkward and not very attractive according to my mother. Larry was always telling me I was plain or 'interesting' and not in a good way, that I should put a bit of make-up on, be more like the other girls he hung around with. When I did, he would call me a tart and tell me to wash it off. I began to resent all the insults, I'd had enough in my life already, but then again I suppose I was used to it, so I let him get away with the name calling. Then, of course it escalated. As I said at the beginning of all this, sometimes I felt like killing him.

Funny isn't it? How things turn out. When I think of that night. What happened to me, to Larry. All I see is that little book. The black one with the green ribbon that marked the pages. The one where everyone in it is better than I am. I have one particular memory that sticks in my mind, because it rams home just how insignificant he thought I was. We were celebrating his thirtieth birthday at a restaurant in the precinct. I would have liked to go to the new Italian place just outside Winston Green, but when I mentioned it, he went mad and said he wasn't spending that amount of money on spaghetti. I got a slap for that one so I didn't mention it again. Anyway, he was sitting across from me, but his eyes were anywhere but. Scanning the room, his eyes settled on each woman in turn, looking her up and down like a cow going to market. What he saw must have pleased him, because he carried on doing it all the time we were there, no doubt wishing he was with anyone of them instead of ugly little Sally. The only words he said to me that night were 'pass the salt'. Oh I know now why he stayed with me. No one else would be stupid enough to take what I took from him day after day, but I was used to being a slave, and a nobody, so my life carried on pretty much as it always had.

I'm doing my life story for Megan. I didn't think I could ever find the words in person, so she thought my writing it down may help her to help me. I think I'm a bit past help myself, but putting things down on paper, no holds barred, is a good thing, isn't it? Maybe I'll be able to shed some of the load I've been carrying my whole life and walk away from it. Leave it for Megan to make sense of, God knows I can't. Miriam is going shopping when Megan gets here. The first time she went out, I was a bit worried she wouldn't come back. I had to remind myself that she hasn't had the life I've had. She would come home when she'd done what she needed to in town, because she wanted to and not because she was on a timer. She wouldn't be beaten if she was late getting in. If Brian ever moaned about her being a bit long at the shops, she would tell him that if he wanted Hobnobs with his tea he would have to put up with it. Then they would giggle, give each other a cuddle and that would be that. I must admit a little of the old jealousy has been creeping in again lately, well, more than a little really.

Megan

As a psychiatrist I've seen a lot of sorrow, anger and even indifference in my time, but reading the first letter from Sally, I have to say I was stunned at the lack of any of that. The matter-of-fact delivery and the absence of any emotion at all chilled me to the bone, and broke my heart in equal measure. If Charlie had not been leaping about the lounge in a pirate suit two sizes too small, giggling away to himself I would have wept. He came bounding up to me as if he knew I needed cheering up. He kept waving a plastic cutlass in my face and saying, "Pieces of cake, pieces of cake." I hadn't the heart to tell him the parrot in the story was saying pieces of eight. Explaining that to three-year-old Charlie, with all the questions that would arise, was, quite frankly, beyond me at the moment. Reading about the flies particularly worried me. I pictured their wingless bodies lying on the table waiting to be turned into something reminiscent of a Rorschach test, and wondered what had happened to her that made her feel so insignificant. I will ask Sally about it when I see her later today, but I will have to read carefully. Something about the way she writes is very telling of her mental state, fragile to say the least. Not ever being seen, or listened to as a child, meant that for the briefest while the flies, in their desperate state, mirrored her helplessness and she wasn't alone. A big part of me said tread carefully Megan. Once you open Pandora's box, you can never shut the lid. Why didn't I listen?

Charlie, fed up of being a one-legged pirate for the moment, came up to me and snuggled up next to me on the sofa. I quickly pushed the file down the side of one of the cushions. Why I did that? I haven't a clue. Charlie can't read yet, but In my own way I suppose felt I was protecting him from seeing evidence of a life that, for the most part, was empty of warmth and love.

"Are you OK, Nanny? You look sad."

"How can I be sad when I have my favourite pirate to keep me company, Charlie Bear?" I replied in an upbeat tone I didn't feel. I hoped it would be enough for him to move on to another topic. It worked, because he pulled at my arm and said, "Nanny, look what Mummy's got for us." It turned out Charlie was right all along. Gina came through from the kitchen with two huge pieces of chocolate fudge cake.

The sugar brought me solace. The chocolate smoothed out the edges and gave my brain a much needed boost. I was able then, to read the rest of Sally's words in a clinical, more objective way. It was my job after all. A big part of me felt sorry for Sally, but I didn't lose sight of the fact that she had killed another human being. She had suffered years of physical and emotional abuse from this man, I realise that, but taking another person's life, whatever the circumstances, was never the answer. She has hinted at even more horrors to come and if this is only the first letter, what other things would she divulge? I vowed that whatever it was, I would try to help her make some kind of peace with the past so she could move on with her life. She was still young enough to start again. To fill her life with good people and she has Miriam, as well as me to help her with that.

Charlie finished the last morsel of cake and then licked the plate. He turned to me and my heart melted at the sight of his beautiful blue eyes shining out of his chocolate -covered face. Suddenly it came to mind that life is a kind of seesaw. That all the awful things that happen to people in life can be balanced out by wonderful moments like this. I swept Charlie into my arms, which was quite a feat as he was getting heavy, and held him tight.

"You're squishing me, Nanny," he said in that sing-song voice that was home. My heart and soul belonged to this little boy. He would ground me as I navigated my way through Sally's life. Charlie, with his happy outlook on everything would keep me sane. Tears came and for once I didn't brush them away. Charlie tracked them with his finger. "Nanny," he said quietly, "you're raining."

Sally

It wasn't until the first year of secondary school that I met Miriam. She was alone, like me, because she had just moved into the area from Leeds. She spoke in an accent I'd never heard before. It took some getting used to. She said the same about me funnily enough, but we managed and she became my friend. In some ways she was my path through the dark grey that some days would just descend on me. It was like walking with a constant cloud above my head that would turn from purple to black depending on what had happened between the hours of 4pm and 8am.

When I was with her and her family, sometimes, a little bit of blue sky would peek through the bruise above me and I would feel a glimmer of what Miriam called happiness. Her childhood was very different to mine though. She would tell me stories about her parents, her five siblings and where they used to live. I didn't offer much information about mine and Miriam, sensing I couldn't talk about it, didn't ask. That was one of the things that made me grow to trust her. She never pried. She knew when I was down and would fill the void with chatter about the latest family saga. I liked the one where her brothers Ben and Tom went scrumping and had to stay up the tree for hours, because the farmer's dog had positioned himself at the bottom and wouldn't leave.

She never wanted anything from me except friendship and although I must have been hard work at times she and I rubbed along well. We were a unit. We didn't need anyone else muscling in. Miriam couldn't help noticing the way I walked sometimes and did ask about it. She never normally asked questions, so I told her a little bit about Barney and how it just became something I did after he died. I said it usually happened when we had to face the bullies, or something from where I lived had upset me. Though I never went into detail about what happened when I wasn't with her, she just accepted the silly walk as part of how I coped with things. She had her little habits too. Like nibbling all the chocolate off of a wagon wheel, then pulling the mallow up and licking the jam. It took her at least ten minutes to finish one. The last part would be the biscuit which she broke into four pieces eating them one at a time. It was then I realised everyone had their idiosyncrasies, so I didn't feel quite so awkward when it came to mine. We became like bookends really, always side by side, but left on the shelf when it came to be chosen for anything, especially where boys were concerned.

Miriam made my life more bearable, because I knew that whatever was going on where I lived, I knew I would be seeing her the next day and she would be full of the ins and outs of Bullen family life. Full of belonging to a crazy gang. Full of normal. Life between the hours of 4pm and 8am was a minefield for me. I tried to avoid the incendiary devices that were my parents, mainly by keeping myself close to something solid, namely a wall. I thought that if I stayed on the periphery of things, they would go about their business and leave me to my many jobs. It didn't always work. I knew I was safe with Miriam and her large, messy, happy family. They were my wall, *because when I was with them, I counted. My mother was a drunk, there was no other word for it and I was nothing to her. I was eleven, about to start puberty and all that entailed and she couldn't have cared less. The only thing my mother loved was a fella called 'Jack Daniels'. She'd fallen into drink when my brother moved away. He was her light, her only son, her reason to get up in the morning. His name was Jim, never James or Jimmy and no middle name. She used to delight in telling him he was named after one of her favourite bands in the sixties, 'The Doors'. The lead singer, Jim Morrison, had a dark sultry quality according to Mother, that used to give her delicious chills. He was only twenty-seven when he died, Morrison that is, not my brother. I don't know what happened to him. He could be the CEO of a global company, or a drug-addled alcoholic, living in a commune in Tewkesbury. I don't know and I don't care! I was glad to see the back of him. I wondered, when he left, if it would make her notice me at all. It didn't. Mother always had a strange fascination with Jim, always stroking his face. She watched him constantly and I often wondered, if that was what made him do those things to me. Maybe if I'd told Mrs Bullen about Jim she would have stopped him. Perhaps Jim was leading by my mother's example. I was never sure if she did anything, but I saw, and heard enough to at least think it. He left the minute he was sixteen and I haven't seen him since. He ran away in the middle of the night.*

The next morning Mother took to her bed. She started drinking even more than usual to help her fall asleep after crying and wailing all day. Then it snowballed. She would drink anything she could get her hands on and my father supplied it. He wanted her out for the count, so that he could go and do whatever he did outside the house. I didn't know what he did or where he went, but it took him away most days and I couldn't have been more glad about that. He was elsewhere and that was enough for me. He shot my dog and he must have known what was going on with Jim and everything, but he chose to ignore it. He knew that Mother had hated me from birth. I suppose she saw me as something that would take time away from her beloved son. Father couldn't care less about me either. He had as little to do with me as possible. I didn't mind. He wouldn't save me.

Mother showed her disdain for me in lots of ways right from the start, not least with my name. Jim got 'The Doors', but I was originally called Agatha after some smelly old aunt of hers that she hated the sight of. I think in her mind, it was the worst insult she could come up with at the time, but Father said no to that. Not because he wanted to save me the embarrassment in later years, but because he said he wasn't putting the name Agatha on the catchment area waiting list with the Emilys the Susans and the Marys, so it was relegated to second position and Sally was hastily chosen. It was better than the alternative I suppose.

On the odd occasion Mother deemed to rise from her bed to use the bathroom, or to get another bottle of good old JD from the wardrobe she would weave around the furniture on shaky pins, using the walls for support. I understood that, but I resented her touching them, the walls were mine. Before she retired to her room again, she would stand at the top of the stairs wobbling about for what seemed like hours, although it was probably just minutes, her eyes fixed on the bottom. I used to think about what would happen if she fell. Every so often I wondered what it would feel like if I pushed her.

Miriam

I'm done in. I've been running about like a blue-arsed fly today. I could do with a coffee but I've got a few things to do until I meet Jill and Mandy. Jill's just texted me and said she was on the way, but she'd got a bit waylaid. Her David hasn't been too well, but he's on the mend now, bless him. I've always liked him. It's funny cos Brian's been a bit out of sorts lately an' all, a bit tired and whatnot. I didn't want to leave him today, but when Megan came, she said she'd make him a cuppa, so I managed to get to Tesco's and get the bits we needed. Something strange happened when I got to the precinct though. I went to get a key cut in the dry cleaners. They do all sorts in there you know, you can even get your shoes mended if you had a mind to. Well. Mr Ahmed, that's the owner, came over with an armful of shirts and dumped them on the counter, covering me door key completely.

"Mrs Wilson hasn't been in to collect these and I wondered if she was all right?."

He clearly didn't know about Larry being dead, or about Sally doing him in, because the names had been left out of the paper and all the news reports on the radio, thank the Lord. I couldn't tell him. A, because I wouldn't do that to Sal, even though she'd been trying my patience lately, and B, it would be all over the precinct by teatime. Mr Ahmed could gossip for England.

"I expect It slipped her mind," I said. "Sal's up to her eyes with all sorts at the mo. I'll take them for her. Is there anything to pay?"

"Oh no. Mrs Wilson always pays when she leaves the garments with us. She knows she will get a good service. She was going to bring her husband's shoes in to be re-heeled but if she's been busy…"

"I'll be sure to remind her," I cut in, a picture of Larry's shiny winklepickers entering me mind. I could feel me face getting red, it blushes to the roots of me hair it does. Brian said I couldn't tell a lie if I wanted to, me pink face always gives me away. "She'll pop in soon," I said, grabbing the bag and stuffing the shirts in willy-nilly. Thanks, Mr Ahmed."

I got out of the shop as quick as I could and half walked, half jogged to the coffee shop where Jill and Mandy were waiting. I were all out of breath and hot under the collar. I'm never running again, I'm telling you that.

"What the Hell's happened?" Mandy asked. "You look like the devil himself was after you."

I just told her I was worried about being late for our chat, as I didn't have much time and left it at that. I didn't want to talk about it. If I had, I would have wept I was that het up. I decided I was due a ruddy great doughnut with me coffee, with fresh cream and jam an' all after the morning I've had. I realised that looking after Sally was draining me. I really didn't want to go home, and that is the first time I ever felt like that. It was like walking on eggshells with her. She's started going out on a Tuesday morning. Normally I would be happy that I could spend time alone with Brian, but as I said, he'd been a bit green around the gills lately. He doesn't really want company except for Dean Koontz and Stephen King. They weren't constantly feeling his forehead or making him drink bucket loads of water. "You're drowning me, woman." His words. When Sal comes back from where ever she goes, she's always in a mood. When I ask her what's wrong, she never makes much sense. Keeps going on about Lycra, books and the number eight. I feel it best to leave her to it when she gets like that. This situation couldn't go on though. I hoped the police would hurry up and do what they'd got to do. That Sally would either be charged, or could go back home. I didn't want her to get in trouble you understand. She didn't deserve that. I just wanted me house back so me and Brian could get back to normal. To being us.

Megan

Sally's letters are proving difficult reading. I knew even before she began putting things down on paper, that she must have suffered both physical and emotional trauma as a child, indeed all through her life to date. After nearly forty years on the job I could tell. She always hung her head rather than make eye contact with me. It was as if any kind of gentle human interaction would pierce a hole in her soul and all the guilt, pain and shame would pour out for all the world to see. She gave very little detail about the abuse from her brother Jim, choosing to skirt round it, but wrote at length about how her parents had named them. How Jim's had been picked with love, hers being the opposite. That clearly still hurt her deeply. The way she wrote about her life back then, brooked no argument. She was saying loud and clear, that she had never counted, had always been something to be used, then discarded, like a snotty tissue.

As a psychiatrist, I am supposed to be dispassionate and level-headed with my patients. It's a requirement of the job. If you took all the terrible things you hear home with you, you would probably end up in their seat. With

Sally it's harder than most. To read such horrific words, written in such a cold detached way and not want to cry for her is a feat in itself. The letters are telling in one respect, but on the other hand, she's revealing very little detail of what actually happened in that house. It's clear the balance of her mind is disturbed, but I hope in time, she will come to terms with it all and move on.

Learning about the nasty things people do to each other never gets any easier, but as a psychiatrist you are supposed to be able to compartmentalise, It's not that easy. Some things do stay with you, no matter how much you wish it to be different. The first ever abuse case I ever had to deal with, comes to mind every time I read Sally's letters. The cases were strikingly similar. A husband and wife still living together, despite many attempts by the woman to leave the marital home. After a particularly vicious beating rendered the woman in a coma for a week, she plucked up the courage to see me in secret. She was gaining strength and courage and was, at last, going to leave him, to have a chance to make a life for herself and her children, one without fear. I had arranged for a local women's refuge to take her and the kids in until a suitable home far away could be found. She had just finished packing and was leaving to get the children early from school, when her husband came home sick from work. After beating her senseless, he strangled her to death using the belt he'd hit her with. I have never forgotten that poor woman. She was on the cusp of changing everything, but would now never know what it was like to be free. That man took her life without a moment's hesitation, leaving three children to be taken in by strangers. Larry had his life taken too, I can't forget that. But I think it was an entirely different set of circumstances that made Sally do what she did that night. I believe it was the classic fight or flight response born of panic. She just needed to get away.

Psychiatrists often have the great debate amongst themselves about nature versus nurture, and for a long while I sat on the fence. But due to the things I've seen and heard in my job over the years, I have changed my position. I am now firmly on the side of nurture. If you are never loved or made to feel safe as a little one, you see the world as something to fear, to shrink from. You run and hide from people in case they should hurt you and that is what Sally did all her life, until Miriam. I finally gave in to my feelings and could feel wet on my cheeks as I read. I think having Charlie around me full time has softened me up, to the point that I ask myself whether I should still be doing this job. I've never cried over a case before, not even when that poor woman died at the hands of her brute of a husband. I think I was too shocked if I'm honest. It was my first case, and I was as green as grass, but I thought I'd toughened up since then. Sally didn't need some gibbering wreck. I wouldn't be any good to her, if I carried on like this.

I can see why she needs Miriam so much. She was the only person who showed her any kindness or acceptance at all. I think Sally writes so matter-of-factly about things, because she truly believes her lot in life was to endure, to accept. In all her correspondence to me to date. She has never referred to the house she was brought up in as home, or spoke of her parents with any warmth or feeling. All of her life she seems to have been displaced, never really feeling safe anywhere except with the Bullens. At the moment she's living at Miriam's and although Sally is happy there, there are problems and it can't be permanent. We are looking at getting her back into Mulberry Crescent soon. I don't know how she'll feel about going home, but if she can't do it, she may have to spend some time in The Chimes until she is properly better. I have a clinic there sometimes and as psychiatric hospitals go, it's a good place. The police are still processing evidence from the house to present to the CPS, but I think, well I hope, that when the investigation is over, they will conclude it was self-defence. Sally would wither in prison. Being separated from Miriam for a long period of time would be devastating for her. No one really knows what they would do if they were faced with the horror Sally had to contend with that night. To kill or be killed. What would you do? I saw her today and asked her about the flies, about Barney but she wouldn't be drawn. I suppose the fact that she's is writing it all down is enough for her and maybe it is for now.

Miriam Is still finding it tough having Sally there. It's been nearly a month now and it must be awkward having another person in your home all the time. Brian hasn't been well either and it's a lot for one person to carry. She tells me Sally has been going out regularly on a Tuesday. Initially I thought it was a good thing, but now I'm not so sure. Miriam says she is jumpy and snappy for a while when she comes back. I don't feel I can ask her outright, because as long as she follows her bail conditions, she is free to go where she pleases. The fact that it's the same time, on the same day every week, is concerning. It's something I need to try and broach with her, but it's difficult because Sally is still refusing to engage with me properly. Miriam has tried talking to her, but she can't really help when she doesn't know the half of what has gone on. She hasn't read the letters. So far Sally hasn't wanted her to and I am bound by a confidentiality clause, so I can't show her anything.

I put the file away and climb the stairs still on the lookout for obstacles, and quietly open Charlie's bedroom door. He lay, bathed in a golden light, with the occasional spaceman glancing across his face. I'd never seen anything so beautiful. I bought him the night light for his birthday and he loves it. The gentle images floating across the ceiling lull him to sleep, to dream of astronauts, shooting stars and the odd Black Hole. Charlie is obsessed with space, particularly Black Holes. At dinnertimes he pretends his mouth is a bottomless void that all food must be sucked into. I gently remind him that whilst his mouth may be a black hole, his tummy certainly isn't and would at some point send the contents of the void back out into the universe. I go in and brush a stubborn lock of hair from his face. I remember doing the same thing for Leo when he was small. I smile at the memory, kiss Charlie's cool forehead and leave the room. My own room was pitch black. I had no nightlight guiding my way through the darkness. I couldn't help but draw parallels with my job at the moment. I was trying to help a woman who was at best mentally ill, or at worst, a killer and I was truly scrabbling around in the dark. I would put in my report and the CPS would decide what to do. I knew the outcome Miriam and I wanted, but it wasn't up to us.

Sally

I've started going out on my own. Only on a Tuesday and only for an hour. I found out quite by accident, that was when Audrey Brown left for the gym. As I was lying in bed in my tiny box room the other night, Larry's little black book came into my head, as it often does. Normally I shove it away in its virtual drawer and don't open it, but that night, my mind picked it up and turned to the page that had changed my life as I knew it. I moved the bottle green ribbon and let it dangle over the spine. I could see the list in blue ballpoint pen, with the scores by the names, but I could only focus on one. Audrey Brown! She was at the top. She was special to Larry and it was torturing me. I tried to picture her from his description, but all I could see was her neck that somehow kept morphing into a swan. What had she got that was worthy of such a score? I had to find, out so I focused my mind back to that night and read, not only her name in the virtual book, but where she lived as well. The police had taken the actual book into evidence so I wasn't sure if I had the number quite right, but I was sure of the name of the road. It wasn't far from Miriam's which was a bonus, so I went the next day, a

Tuesday, and I was in luck. Larry's notes detailing Audrey Brown's bodily charms fit the woman walking down the path of a house in Nightingale Terrace. It could only be her. Her bag, all neon and diamanté, swung back and forth as she bounced along the road. I hadn't intended to follow her, but something in me wanted to know more about the person, who had occupied so much of Larry's time when he was alive. In retrospect, I should thank her. At least, when he was with her, he wasn't hurting me.

I followed her all the way to the leisure centre just outside town. I learned she was fitter than me because by the time we got there I was sweaty and struggling for breath. She was as fresh as a daisy. As she approached the double doors, she draped herself around a guy that wouldn't have looked out of place on the world's strongest man. Her breasts were barely contained by the lime green Lycra she was almost wearing, and her buttock fitted nicely in one of his huge hands. A part of me looked at her as some kind of cliché, a typical example of the other woman, but another part, a big part, was angry that someone as trivial as this could give my husband what I couldn't. Well I probably could have, but he wouldn't let me. Maybe if I'd plastered makeup all over my face and squeezed into clothes a size too small, he may have paid me more attention. Oh, not the kind that bruised or made me bleed, but the gentle more loving kind.

Audrey Brown disappeared into the cavernous building and I should have gone back to Miriam's there and then. I didn't. I waited until she came out and followed her back to Nightingale Terrace. I watched her walk up the drive and close the bright yellow door of the house behind her. I vowed that would be it. I'd seen her now. I still didn't get why Larry had scored her an eight. I personally think she is more of a five and that's being quite generous. It didn't matter what he thought now anyway. So, as I said, that, should have been that, but I went again the next week and the next…

I have been working hard at writing everything down for Megan. It's so much easier than saying it out loud. I haven't shown Miriam the letters and I don't ever intend to. I'm afraid that if she does get to read them, she won't look at me in the same way again She's been busy with trying to work out what's wrong with Brian anyway. Oh she knows that I haven't had it easy, but she doesn't know what happened with Jim. In fact I don't even think she knows I had a brother. I would have thought, knowing her as I do, that it wouldn't make a difference, but I can't take that chance. I can't have the one person in all the world that's on my side turn against me. I'd rather die than be totally alone. Miriam and I are meant to be friends for life, however long that may be.

I did it again! I can't seem to help myself, It's like a drug. Just say no! I hear you cry but, as you may know, when you first take a pill it helps, but after a while you need more and more to get the same feeling. It's just like that. I've got closer to Audrey Brown each time, but today, I was practically on her heels. It gave me a weird sense of power, knowing I could reach out and touch her and she wouldn't see me coming. I suppose it's because I blend into the background. In another life, I always fancied myself as a private detective, I'm at good hiding in plain sight, as you know I've done it all my life, It was safer that way. As my relationship with Larry went on, I started to wear clothes that were non-descript, mostly shades of beige. I figured that if Larry couldn't see me, he would be less likely to shout and scream and hurt. I suppose when I think about it now, It didn't make any difference whether I wore brown or red. He simply didn't see me, his wife. He saw his own personal slave, his punchbag. I think it made him feel big when he was making me feel small. He found fault with everything much like Mother had done when I was a child, and punished me accordingly. It was probably me, just being beige that turned his attention to brighter, more colourful playthings I guess. Audrey Brown looks like mutton dressed as lamb, but that is probably what attracted Larry in the first place. That and the fact that she would open her legs whenever he asked her to. Larry had said often that having sex with me was like humping a fallen twig, and had stopped all overtures years ago. I tried initiating it once a few years ago. He just laughed at me.

I'm going to write the next letter for Megan in a moment. I'm getting to the part about Larry. The part where I feel I lost me completely, if I was ever there to begin with. Would I ever find the real me? What if Megan can help me? What if I do eventually come face to face with my true self and wish I hadn't?

Miriam

I'm that worried about our Brian. I don't know what's going on? He looks pale, like a ghost at Halloween. I said I was going to make an appointment at the surgery and he told me to stop fussing, but I can't get him to eat more than a mouthful at dinner times and that's just not right. Brian loves his food I can tell you. He's a right glutton for puddings. I bought a glazed doughnut yesterday and he wouldn't even look at it. Brian would normally do anything for a cake. That's how I got him to plumb in the washing machine and rewire the bathroom light. A sticky bun, or a nice chocolate éclair dangled in front of him always worked. It was like the story of the carrot and the donkey, but not now. If nothing changes in the next couple of days, I'm ringing the surgery. Dr Kelly is a love and has been our doctor for years. At first Brian felt iffy about seeing her, what with her being a lady an' all. Anything personal he would prefer a male if you get me drift, but he wouldn't see anyone else now. She's been great with his blood pressure and that, and sees Brian regular, every month.

Sally is still going out on a Tuesday. I'm not bothered

anymore. I'm finding everything a little too much if I'm honest. I have enough with looking after Brian, without worrying about her an' all and she's acting weird, or weirder than usual. I had a word with Dr Megan about it. She said she thought that it coincided with her putting her story on paper. She told me that Sal was working through stuff, that it had brought up some memories that might make her a little distant, just till she gets her head round it. I told her that when Sally is at home, she is far from distant. She wants to be with me all the time and gets twitchy when I leave the room, but when she comes in on a Tuesday she's different, she goes straight to her room. Any other time she's like a second skin and I can't breathe. It's not that I don't care for Sal, you understand. It's just that it's been six weeks now. I didn't realise she would be here this long, or how much work it was going to be juggling the two of them. I might not have told her she could stay at all if I'd known, but we are all ruddy wise in hindsight as me husband is so fond of telling me.

I'm still right worried about Brian, and with me Sal -shaped shadow ever present, it feels like the walls are closing in. Me sister Linda can't understand why I'm moaning. She said that Garry is staying with Grace, so she can't see how the house should feel claustrophobic. I replied, in a tone less than friendly, that her husband and kids lived in a massive apartment in New South Wales. She wouldn't know what cramped was.

Dr Megan said she'd talk to the police and see if Sal could go back to Mulberry Crescent. The sooner the better as far as I was concerned, because I was nearly at the end of me rope. Sally's me mate, but at the end of the day family comes first. Brian is poorly and our Garry won't bring Grace and young Sarah to ours when she's here. They say you never know a person till you live with them and that is so true. I didn't realise Sally was quite so odd, or so needy. I suppose I did do a lot for her when Larry was alive and that is why she feels safe with me, Back when she was at Mulberry Crescent she needed the hospital a lot, and she doesn't drive, so I'd have to take her. I felt so sorry for her because she went home to the brute afterwards. It was like ruddy groundhog day. The nurses at the infirmary would patch her up. They would call the police. Sally wouldn't press charges because she was afraid of the consequences. I'd take her home and the whole thing would play out again a week or so later. It didn't feel so suffocating at the time, because I got to be with me family between the visits to A&E. I wouldn't see Sal for a week or two back then, but we spoke on the phone and whatnot. I would check in once or twice a week, just to make sure the bastard hadn't killed her. Funny how things turn out, isn't it? Larry's toes up, our Brian's poorly. Sally's a ruddy basket case and I'm hanging over a cliff by me fingertips. Things have to change, and quick.

Megan

Miriam wanted to talk to me in private when I got there on Thursday she looked drawn and was just about hanging in. She asked me if the police had finished with Sally's house, I said they had. I was going to broach the subject with Sally this morning. I was concerned she wouldn't want to go back, that it would cause her to break down again. We both knew she would find it very hard to leave the safety and security of Miriam's house. For six weeks she been cared for and fed well. She was putting on much needed weight and her colour was beginning to return. But all the attention she'd received, seemed to make Sally need Miriam more than ever. I sensed that this was what had tipped things in the wrong direction. Far from making Sally feel more confident, it had had the opposite effect and the weight of it was making Miriam ill. I could see the conflict playing out in her kindly face as she was talking to me. She felt responsible for Sally's wellbeing and cared for her deeply, but of course, her family had to come first and Sally's behaviour, especially towards Brian, had become difficult to say the least. Miriam felt sure that it was partly to blame for Brian's malaise. I understood completely, of course I did. The strain on the both of them must be immense. I explained to Miriam, that if we did have a chance of getting Sally back to Mulberry Crescent soon, it would have to be done gently, so she wouldn't see it as a rejection on Miriam's part. She sighed deeply and thumped down heavily on one of the plump comfortable chairs in her cosy lounge. We hadn't long to talk. Sally was out in the kitchen making drinks. I could see Miriam straining her ears to hear how long we had got. When we heard the stairs creak, she quickened her speech.

"We haven't got long, Doctor, she's just gone up to give Brian his tea. It's three o'clock, she always makes the tea at three. It's bloody hard if you need a cuppa at half past four, because you have to run the gauntlet with her. It makes her mad. I suppose she only wants to help, that's probably when she had tea back in Mulberry Crescent. I understand it's something Sal feels she can be in control of. Lord knows she hasn't had much of that in her life, but it's driving us to distraction. I need me house back! Our life back! I need to have a cuppa when I want one, Dr Megan. It's been really hard on me and Brian, what with him not being well and me not being able to see me son, it's getting too much." The tears began to fall, running rivulets down the new lines and creases on her soft kindly face. I knew, in that moment we had come to the end of the road as far as Sally staying here was concerned. I held Miriam's hand while she patted her eyes with a crumpled tissue. My heart went out to her, to Brian, to all the family. I hadn't fully taken into consideration the strain this would put on all of them, but at the time it was any port in a storm. I didn't want Sally to go to The Chimes, nor did Miriam. We believed it would be too much for her straight after the events of that fateful night. I should have realised, it would tire Miriam out because I understand how she feels in that regard. With everything I have to juggle, I get worn out too. The difference is that I took Leo, Gina and Charlie in because they are family. Sally is the proverbial cuckoo in the nest. Miriam had been so sure she could manage, but then we only thought it would be for a couple of weeks at most. We were wrong.

I saw Miriam stiffen suddenly and low and behold the door opened, and Sally came in with the tea tray. She flicked her eyes in my direction, then looked at Miriam. I wish I knew what was going through her mind at that moment, because the look on her face was unreadable.

"Is something wrong?" she asked Miriam, ignoring my presence.

"No lovey, I'm just a bit tired, nothing to worry about," Miriam replied with a strained smile "Let's have our cuppa and I'll leave you to your session. I'm just going to tell our Brian I'm off. I've got to get to Tesco's and whatnot. It's fish and chips for tea." When Miriam left the room, Sally and I settled on either side of the coffee table. She shifted in her seat and produced the third letter out of a large pocket in her beige and brown skirt. When she handed it to me, it seemed to cross from her hand to mine in slow motion, as if she was reluctant to divulge the secrets it held. I decided to skate over it, for the moment.

"How have you been?" I asked her.

"Fine, why do you ask?" she said abruptly. "Why was Miriam so upset?"

"She's just a bit worried about Brian, Sally. He doesn't seem himself at the moment, does he?" I ventured. All of a sudden she screwed up her face as if she had tasted something bad.

"Oh that," Sally said through clenched teeth. "I don't think there's much wrong with him. He's taking up a lot of Miriam's time. She's busy anyway, but with her being at his beck and call, I hardly get to spend any time with her."

That was almost the exact opposite of what Miriam had just told me. I kept my face calm even though my mind was racing. I sipped my tea to give me time to think about how to handle it and decided that diversion was my best shot. I said, "Thank you for the letter. How are you finding writing it all down?"

"Oh I haven't written everything," she spat. "I have to keep some things back, you know, just for me, until the time is right of course. I have tried to remember the order of things, but some may be out of sequence." Her cold, clipped, tone gave me the shivers and her eyes bored into me like a hammer drill. I was taken aback by the intensity of her stare. I normally had a hard time getting her to look at me at all. I wondered just how much she was leaving out and how much the parts that weren't there would change everything?

"The order doesn't matter, Sally," I said as gently as I could, though I was still feeling cold all over. It's best to write down as much as you can, I'll read it and then we can talk about it, when you feel comfortable of course."

"I'll…" Sally didn't have time to finish her sentence before all hell broke loose…

Miriam

Garry looked so tired. I told him to go back and get some rest, to and see Grace and Sarah but there was no way he was going to leave me and his dad, not at a time like this. We gripped each other's hands over Brian's bed, trying not to look up at his ashen face. The beep-beep of the machines were constant like water torture, but at least it took the stillness from the room. I felt meself singing in me head to the constant beat. I couldn't help it. I bet if Brian could've heard the song I was singing he would laugh. It was 'Show me the way to go home'. The ever present blip-blip was intrusive, frightening even, but if it were to stop, me and Garry's life as we knew it, would be over. We'd been at the hospital for the last twenty-four hours. It was Friday night now, although I couldn't tell you what time it was. The room, our whole world at the moment, was dimmed, to let Brian rest and I couldn't see, or hear the clock. I was glad of that. Could you imagine the tick-tick of the second hand as well as the beep of the machines, I'd go as mad as Sally.

They'd sedated Brian, so his body could recuperate. His blood pressure kept going sky high, then back down to nothing. The doctors thought that that's what had caused him to have two heart attacks in four hours. They were doing test after test and we were waiting to find out if his life would be forever changed by it. I thought to meself, I would rather have a changed Brian, than no Brian at all, but I know it would be the beginning of the end for him, if he couldn't do the odd job in the house, or sink a few pints down the pub. Jemma, the landlady of the Lamb and Flag keeps telling me that Brian and his mates Alan and Col, fund her family's trip to Lanzarote every year. Well, they'll have to go to Brighton next time, cos Brian will be cutting down on the booze I can tell you. If he pulls through.

Being in this place now, takes me back to a few weeks ago, when I was sitting beside a different bed, in a different ward. Beside Sally. We didn't have the beeps then, of course, but the waiting around to see if there would be any change was almost the same. The big difference is, this is me family. Brian me beloved hubby, Garry and me, all together in a ten by twelve room, watching, waiting for silence, knowing that your world would end if it happened. Sally will have to leave when we get Brian back home. The only thing that matters is getting him well again. She'll have to look after herself from now on. I can't get me head round how my life has changed so quick. One minute I have everything and the next it's all balancing on a ruddy knife edge, praying you won't fall off.

Yesterday, when Dr Megan had come to talk to Sal, I went upstairs to tell Brian I was off to Tesco's. I expected to be told to stop fussing, but instead he was gasping for breath, grunting and clutching his heart. Then, he went limp. I must've screamed blue bloody murder, because the next thing I knew, Doctor Megan had flown up the stairs, elbowed me aside and felt for a pulse. Straight away she started banging on his chest. People say that when something awful happens, things go into slow motion. I didn't believe it could happen. I do now! I could see Doctor Megan blowing in his mouth trying to keep my Brian alive. I could hear the cars going past in the street. The thud of the clock on the bedside table got louder and louder and it felt for all the world like I was in that film that our Garry likes, *The Matrix*, where that bloke moves so slowly, it looks like he freezes in time. All of a sudden, Sally's eyes peered round the door frame. She just stood there, staring at Brian on the bed, at Doctor Megan trying to save him.

"Call an ambulance," Doctor Megan shouted. "Tell them it's a category one." Sally turned and started down the stairs. I couldn't move. My Brian was dying and I felt useless. I was there in body, but it was as if me mind was spinning through space, and life, as I knew it, was about to change forever. I could hear sounds, but they were all muffled, as if we were all under water. I tried to focus on where they were coming from. It was Dr Megan, and she was talking to me.

"I've got him back for now, Miriam. The ambulance is on its way. I can hear them. Sally will let them in. Try not to worry. He'll be in the best of hands."

I nodded at her but I couldn't speak. It felt as if me throat was stuffed with an old sock and I couldn't form the words around it. Just then two men burst in and took over from her. She quickly explained to them in medical jargon what'd happened, then they got Brian on a stretcher and in to the ambulance quick as lightening. I climbed in beside him, and before they closed the doors, the last thing I saw was Sally standing in the road staring straight at me, and Megan's, arm pulling her gently back to the pavement…

They put something called a stent in Brian's heart and, within two days, all his colour came back. It was a bit of a shock at first, after a week of tombstone grey. The blushing pink looked like he'd been sunbathing without factor thirty but, bloody hell, was I pleased to see it. We brought Brian home almost two weeks after the heart attacks. Sal was still there, but Doctor Megan had made it quite clear to her that she would have to go back to Mulberry Crescent until the CPS had reviewed the case and made their decision. We were doing the right thing. It would be far too much for me to look after one that was poorly in the body, and one that was poorly in the head. I did feel bad, because Sally had been a rock when my Brian was in hospital. She cooked my meals, she did all the housework and she held me while I cried. She said that we would always have each other no matter what and I was grateful for that. With all the things going on in her own life, she was there for me. She seemed to be more upbeat too, but I expect she did that just to chivvy me along. She's been going out more now, in fact she's hardly been here this last week during the day. It's been lovely having the time to sit with Brian, even though he was showing his grumpy side cos he had to stay in bed. I still wondered, where she could be going every day. I made a mental note to ask her about it. Sal's never needed a key to our place, as I'm usually in, but with all Brian's hospital appointments and whatnot, I put one on a string and hung it inside the front door just in case. I know it isn't the sensible thing to do, but I'm banking on the fact that we won't get burgled anytime soon. The insurance company wouldn't pay out if we did. One of me neighbours, Tam, caught a burglar coming out of the back of her house last year. He'd nicked a marble statue, an iPad and a six-pack of cheese and onion crisps. She whacked him on the head with her umbrella over and over, as the bloke cowered in the corner, Tam's husband Duke came out and sat on him till the police came. No one's tried anything since. Tam's the head of the neighbourhood watch now, so I don't think any would-be burglar would chance it. The posters pinned on the trees all along our street have a picture of an umbrella on it with the words, 'This is a neighbourhood watch area, don't even think about it.' It always makes me chuckle.

Sally is back to being weird, especially when she comes in from her walkabout. Even when she does talk, she doesn't always make a lot of sense. Her thoughts don't seem to connect to anything. It seems to be all random words. When she is speaking, her face looks as if she's going through every emotion known to man in the process of five seconds. I'm worried she might be depressed or something, which is perfectly understandable with what she's been through. I might ask Dr Megan whether Sal should see her GP. I don't hold with tablets as a rule, but he might be able to give her something to lift her mood. She still hasn't told me what's in the letters she's been writing, but in a way I'm glad she kept it just between her and Dr Megan. What with worrying about Brian and Garry, and remembering to put me clothes on the right way out every morning. I don't need anything else to think about at the minute. I'm worried about how she'll cope on her own when she goes back, of course I am, I feel terrible about it, but I want Sally gone.

Sally

The day I met Larry it was my sixteenth birthday and until lunchtime that afternoon, nothing special had happened. I got a card and a bracelet with my name on from Miriam, but nothing from my parents. Oh don't get me wrong, I didn't care, as it was hardly anything new. They thought it was fun to ignore the day I was born. I guess they did it to make me feel even more insignificant than I did already. The birthday snub was almost certainly Mother's idea. She loved to think of new ways to torment me, well, this one was hardly new. I suppose her whisky-addled brain prevented her from thinking of anything else, so she just repeated the slight sixteen times. I got out after that. My father didn't care enough about anything so trivial as birthdays, or anything else for that matter because, as I said, he had his own life to think about. The mere trifle of his daughter's sixteenth was far too unimportant to bother with.

I used to wonder what my father got up to in all the hours he wasn't at our address, but I'm glad I didn't get to find out, I had too much to juggle, hiding from people, keeping safe, and doing the housework. He used to have this one friend, George, who would call for him sometimes. He was slimy, like a greased pole. If I answered the door, which I usually did, as no one else deemed it their job, he would talk to my chest and not to my eyes. What with me being skinny and with a bust that didn't even push my jumper out, I wondered what he found to talk to. I used to excuse myself as quickly as I could and call for my father. The door would then slam shut and they would be gone, thank God. Anyway, Miriam had suggested we have a meal in the local cafe, her treat. She was meeting her boyfriend Brian later, but wanted to do this for me first. She knew I liked the veggie burgers from The Cakehole in the town centre. We'd been going there since we started at Winston Green Academy five years since. There were two men sitting opposite our table and one of them kept smiling at me. I say men, but they were at least a few years older than us. Miriam ordered our food and went to the toilet. As soon as she had disappeared from view, one of them came over to me, said hello, and our fates were sealed.

Larry appeared to be everything I wasn't. Popular, outgoing, unapologetic and I felt different when I was with him. It was like wrapping myself in a clean white towel after being grubby for the longest time. It seemed then that Larry was the only person, besides Miriam, to actually see me. All of my life most people had treated me as if I was invisible, except when they were yelling at me or using me, and so Larry, who treated me with kindness, at least in the beginning, was a breath of fresh air. He took me places and showed me that things could be fun, though at times, I would hold back that one step, when I found situations a little overwhelming. Crowds, noise, too many colours, would make me nervous, but Larry would pull me along anyway. It took me back to when I was a child, being dragged places when my feet weren't ready. Miriam didn't like Larry and the feeling was mutual. Looking back, I should have listened to her and realised that she had my best interests at heart. She still does. She always will. You know how it is *though, when you're young and naive. He showed an interest in me when no other boy ever had and I was taken in. I think, looking back, that Larry didn't want me, Sally. He wanted someone malleable, someone desperate to be loved, who would do whatever she was told. He could be kind and loving, but there was always an edge to it like the teeth of a circular saw. He would show his displeasure with me by saying things like 'why are you so dumb?' and 'You're with me because no one else will have you', and all manner of things that kept me in my place. It was a familiar place I guess, so I didn't let it bother me.*

It's funny how a person can know in her soul that something is very wrong with the way she's treated, yet won't do anything about it, even if she could. Sometimes, it's better the devil you know, isn't it? The alternative may be much, much worse. Of course, that didn't turn out to be the case, did it? There were always quite a few things about me that Larry wasn't happy with, but the subtle way he changed them didn't register at first. He didn't like my hair long, said I hid behind my fringe and it made me look weird, so I had it cut short, even though I felt less and less safe with every snip of the scissors. Miriam said it made me look like her brother Ben and said she hoped it would soon grow back. It did take me some time to get used to it, I will admit, but it made Larry happy and that was the main thing.

One of his other big bugbears was Miriam. He said she was too nosey and took my time away from him, that he wanted to be with me as much as possible. I thought it was nice that he seemed to care that much, but she was the only friend I had and I couldn't lose her. She and I met without my telling him for all those years, until I killed him of course. No need to hide our friendship now is there? I don't know what would have happened if he had discovered us together back then. I wondered if he thought about who took me to the hospital all the times he beat me black and blue. I don't suppose he cared. He just upped and left and went to the pub, leaving me bleeding, spilling all shades of red on the carpet. If he ever found out I had defied him, I would be the one in the morgue.

I left Mother and Father's house as soon as Larry found us a little flat. It was miles away from them and for the first time in my life I was truly happy. Getting away from the place that shackled me for seventeen years was the greatest feeling I had ever had. Would ever have. I didn't realise then of course, that I would be exchanging one set of handcuffs for another. Larry and I were together for quite a while before he proposed. I'll be honest, Miriam begged me not to do it and I did have a few reservations myself. He was quite controlling, but in a way that made me feel cared for, most of the time. His true colours had yet to surface, and, when they did, they were black.

Miriam came to my wedding. I told Larry I'd bumped into her on the high street the week before and felt it rude not to invite her. In fact, she had been with me every step of the way. Buying the dress, which we had seen in a charity shop in Winston Green, sorting the flowers for my bouquet and getting a small cake from The Cakehole which in the end, the proprietors had given to me as a wedding present. A thank-you for all the veggie burgers I had consumed over the years no doubt. I had wanted Miriam to be maid of honour, but Larry said I'd spent enough on my dress. I tried telling him it was only twenty pounds from the British Heart Foundation on the High Street, but he said it was silly to fork out for a bridesmaid's outfit for one day, especially since I hadn't seen her for years. Having kept that one secret from Larry all this time made me feel powerful. Something just between Miriam and me. Something he couldn't sour.

She brought her boyfriend Brian with her to the wedding.

They were the only people on my side of the church. My father didn't even know I was getting married, I didn't bother to tell him. He wouldn't have come anyway and my mother was dead by then. She fell down the stairs. You could see Brian worshipped the ground Miriam walked on. I knew that I would be seeing a lot less of her now, what with me about to be a married woman, and Miriam and Brian getting serious, but I knew in my heart she would always be there if I needed her. I should have taken heed of Miriam's warning, when in the grounds of the church, minutes after we had tied the knot, Larry looked Miriam up and down in a way that made her feel very uncomfortable. He told her that now she was 'getting some', it somehow made her more attractive. Miriam stood her ground, which is something I never did. Holding Brian at bay, she reminded Larry that it was me he had just married, and to pay any compliments he may deem appropriate to his wife of all of ten minutes. Larry just laughed at her and walked away.

Miriam had told me repeatedly over the years that he was eventually going to stray and I suppose deep down I knew she was right, but I wanted a fresh start. I was now Mrs Sally Wilson instead of invisible Sally Jones and I thought to myself that now things would change for the better. We moved into our forever home in Mulberry Crescent a year after we were married. It was a nice area, but it wasn't like the street where Miriam lived. There, everybody knew everybody else, it was a real community, but I barely even saw my neighbours to speak to, and when I did, most of them were curt to the point of being rude. Nevertheless, I hoped that Larry and I would settle down there and I would eventually learn to fit in. Maybe then the turmoil that was my old life would be a thing of the past. How wrong was I?

You know the point when fluffy white towels begin to go a bit

grey and bobbly? Well that is what happened to my 'new life'.
He got angry a lot and I was, for the most part, used as a skivvy
and the occasional lay. He said by now I should be pregnant,
that I wasn't even woman enough to give him a son. I didn't
point out that it took two to tango. Besides, we weren't even
having sex that much. We know why now, don't we? I could
see, even then, that history was repeating itself. I would never
be anything in his eyes, but was too weak from what happened
in my childhood to challenge him. Perhaps I wasn't meant to
have a life like Miriam had with the saintly Brian. They say
what you never had, you never miss and maybe that's true,
but it doesn't stop me wondering what it would be like, to be
anybody but me.

It was when we came home after the honeymoon that it first
got violent. I dropped a towel on the bathroom floor and before
I could bend down to pick it up, he drove his fist into my face. It
knocked me clean off my feet and my head connected with the
sink. I registered the blood, but was in shock. It was the first
time he had actually hit me. It wasn't the last by any means.
Why is that people think you can read their minds, then scream
at you when you get it wrong?

"Get me my blue shirt," he would say. "Not that one,
you idiot, the one with the green stripe." He found fault
with everything I did and started staying out later and later,
sometimes not coming home at all. I didn't mind him going out.
It was peaceful when he wasn't there. I began to hug the wall
again and tried to stay out of his way. I grew my hair long to
spite him and began to hide behind my fringe a lot. It was safer
in there. I began to hate him. I knew I should leave, but that
would take courage I didn't have, anyway, where would I go?
I could stay at Miriam's, but that would be the first place he'd
look. He'd never let me leave. Never let it be that easy. Nothing

with him ever was. There was always a twist, a consequence. Miriam said more than once that he would kill me in the end. Turned out I got there first.

Megan

Sally's case is taking up a lot of my time these days. I only see her twice a week at Miriam's, but she is never far from my thoughts. I keep going over her letters, there are three to date. I could probably recite them word for word, but I want to be sure I truly understand what she is saying about her life, not only with Larry, but also what she went through before she met Miriam. By her own admission she's not telling me everything and that is her prerogative, so I'm reading between the lines, trying to catch all the little nuances she's not aware she's revealing. The inferences, the mood behind the words. That is just as important as the writing itself. It gives me an insight into her state of mind. I'm finding, more and more, that my arthritis is a problem though. Sometimes the pain is so great, I have to read them over and over, keeping copious notes, Even then I worry that I've missed something. Miriam is struggling too. Up until a couple of weeks ago, I hadn't had to worry too much about Sally being taken care of, but with poor Brian having had two heart attacks in the space of a couple of hours, it's pushing Miriam to breaking point. God, I was so glad I was there that day, because quite honestly without prompt intervention and my medical training kicking in, Brian would almost certainly have died. I am so worried about Miriam. Her radiant smile has died. I can see she's losing weight and has circles under her eyes the colour of thunderclouds. If Miriam went under, poor Garry would have a lot on his shoulders, with both his parents, and his young family to worry about. It had been revealed to me that Grace was expecting Garry's child, and poor Miriam was so upset, because she hadn't seen them all together in weeks. She really misses little Sarah who is the sweetest little thing in the world, except Charlie of course.

Winston Green Police have been in touch to say the CPS have still not given a decision as to whether or not Sally was going to face charges, but Officer Kemp told me that her house had been professionally cleaned and she could go home. I had explained gently to her that she was to go back to Mulberry Crescent in the next few days. But as soon as the words had left my lips, her body became ramrod straight, her eyes, like lasers boring, through the lounge wall. She stood stock still in the same position, for a long time, then turned on her heel and left the room. I felt it was important for her to face things head on so I followed her into the kitchen. I spoke softly to her, like I did when I wanted Charlie to understand something important. I told her I would go to the house with her, that it would only be a short visit, Just so she could look around and see that with Larry was no longer there. I hoped she would see that she could start again, without the fear of violence. She was scared, I could see that, but I thought it was a positive step forward when she said that if Miriam came with us, she would try.

On Saturday I had a rare day, off so I was spending it with Leo, Gina and Charlie. He wanted me to make a fort with a couple of double duvet covers and the dining chairs, so Leo arranged them in a square and Charlie and I tried to drape the duvets over the top. They kept collapsing in the middle and everyone was laughing. All except my Charlie Bear, who was getting quite irate as the roof caved in on him time and time again.

"Ah," said Leo with a smile in his voice, "I have an idea. Wait there, mate." He sped off to the kitchen and came back with my new mop and bucket and my grandma's old peg bag. He cleverly propped the middle up, using said mop and bucket as a tent pole and clipped the duvet to the chairs with pegs every colour of the rainbow. Instantly, Charlie was happy. He invited us all in to 'Fort Bimble', named after his much loved teddy. It was a bit of a squeeze, but it was one of those moments that would stay with me forever. Gina with Charlie on her lap, and Leo, with his six-foot-four frame bent almost double, in order to fit. Me, I got as close as I could to all three of them. A snapshot of life, laughter and love. There was safety in that fort, covered in duvets printed with pictures of the night sky. We were all together. A happy family.

It was bitter sweet because, I knew Sally didn't have a family to help her readjust to life in Mulberry Crescent, but there were people in place who could help her with the day-to-day things, like shopping and cooking, just until she felt able to manage by herself. I would still be having regular sessions with her and would encourage her to keep writing the letters. She'd still be in touch with Miriam, by phone initially, then coffee occasionally. Miriam needed a complete break, but she knew the importance of reassuring Sally that she was still there for her, at least in the beginning. When she got stronger, Miriam would ease off, allowing Sally to have control over her own life.

As the day of the visit to Mulberry Crescent drew near, Sally began acting weirdly. Miriam told me that she stayed out for much of the day every day now and they still didn't know where she was going. I needed to hear more about this and I wanted to check on Brian anyway, so I went to see Miriam at home.

As soon as she saw me, she rushed into my arms and thanked me for the millionth time for saving Brian's life. I reiterated that anyone with a bit of first aid training could have done the same thing, but she said that without a doctor in the house at the right time he might not have made it. I was glad of my medical degree that day, even though I had gone down a completely different route after my finals. My interest in psychiatry had been peaked when I was a junior doctor doing rotation on the wards. I had become aware that some of the consultants saw just the injury, or the disease, rather than an actual person lying in the bed. Most of the doctors had a great bedside manner, but a small number looked at the patients as 'the kidney stones in bed five', or the 'pneumothorax in bed three'. I didn't ever want to see another human being in that way. I learned how the mind can have a massive effect on how we heal. How having a healthy outlook on life can take days or even weeks off a patient's recovery time. That is what led me to nearly forty years as a psychiatrist. A long time in anyone's book.

Miriam sat me down with a cup of tea and a homemade chocolate brownie and suddenly everything she had been holding in gushed out like a tsunami. I got up and held her until the torrent became a trickle. Mopping her eyes, she told me that she was getting increasingly worried about Sally. That since they brought Brian home, she was back to being aloof and prickly. She would mutter to herself and couldn't sit down for any length of time. In fact, Miriam had become quite scared of her erratic behaviour. She couldn't seem to get through to Sally to find out what was wrong without her blowing up and leaving the room. I said I would speak to her and try to get to the bottom of what was going on when I saw her the next afternoon. Miriam seemed happy with that, especially as I told her the walk-through of Sally's house was booked for Friday. She said she would be there, that Garry was going to sit with Brian. I got up to leave, but I'd only got halfway out the front door before Miriam ran up the hallway, slid on the rug and skidded to a stop beside me.

"That ruddy mat will be the death of me," she puffed. "I nearly forgot, Sal has left you another letter." She thrust it at me, crumpling the corner as it reached my hand. "I suppose you will want to read it before you see her tomorrow." I could sense, by the way she wanted rid of it, that poor Miriam needed to push her worries about Sally on to me to solve so she could concentrate on Brian. I understood, of course, it was my job after all. I took the letter and promised I would read it when I got home.

"See you on Thursday, Miriam," I said and hugged her goodbye. She was reluctant to let go, so I gave her an extra reassuring squeeze, then as I turned towards my car, I couldn't be sure, but over the road, behind a particularly splendid hydrangea, I thought I saw a pale face with lank brown hair peeping from the bright pink petals.

Sally

I saw Megan leave from across the road. I don't think she spotted me, as Mrs Bronstein's shrubbery was the largest in the street and afforded me cover. I'm not sure why I hid from her. It was probably because I was sick of being psychoanalyzed, having my every move watched for signs I was losing the plot. I didn't need anyone to tell me that. I knew already. When she turned to hug Miriam for the longest time, I got a prickly feeling up my arms. The pink started churning in my gut and was rapidly turning to orange. I didn't like them touching. Miriam was My Friend, my yellow in all the grey. Megan was My Doctor and that was that. She was already making me leave here. Sending me back to the place where the end came. I hadn't even packed my bags, and there was Miriam already replacing me with somebody else. The person who saved Saint Brian no less. He's still there, still an annoyance. He was always taking time away from Miriam and me. Oh I know I'm out a lot at the moment when I could be with her, but I have other concerns in the form of a Lycra-clad home wrecker. Miriam seems happier in Brian and Megan's company than in mine anyway. Megan wouldn't give her a minute's worry if she was her friend. Not like me. I'm damaged. An emotionally devoid drain on her patience.

The orange turned to red and began to burn. I could kill Megan at this moment. She was the interloper. I was the one who'd known Miriam since childhood. I knew her inside out. Megan would never be able to understand her like I do, love her like I do. I waited until she had driven out of sight before coming out from my hiding place and crossing the road. When I got to Miriam's front door, I pushed my hand through the letterbox and pulled the cord. Miriam didn't even hear the door close behind me. She was banging about in the kitchen. It was curry night. I must admit I was looking forward to it. She made the best chicken tikka I had ever tasted. When I got to my room, my place of safety, I let out the breath I didn't know I was holding and closed the curtains. Day became night instantly. The darkness, black as my mood crowded in on me. I lay on my bed and tried to calm down, but images of the hug still flashed before my eyes and all I could see was betrayal. Whatever my head tried to replace it with, the embrace lingered in the forefront of my mind. The anger was still red, still fizzing, threatening to boil like an over-filled kettle. I was unwanted, I knew that for sure now. It hurt, but I had a plan. It would all be over soon and we would have each other again, just Miriam and me. Just as it's always been. Just as it as it should.

I'd got so close to Audrey Brown today that I could smell her cloying perfume, the one Larry always stank of. Sandalwood and patchouli were the worst smells ever, except lavender of course. I only had to be in the vicinity of that to get a headache. People who wear so much scent that it taints everything within a hundred yard radius should be shot in my opinion. I was down wind as well and It was so thick I could chew on it. The day before, a Tuesday, I hadn't followed 'Miss I scored an eight' to the gym, instead, I stayed on the corner out of sight. I'm getting better at lurking. She didn't even look in my direction when she sashayed down the road at precisely ten am. I had been following her for weeks now, but I hadn't seen her in the same outfit twice. Her hennaed hair looked newly tangoed and as false as the eyelashes she wore. I got pleasure from the fact that she wouldn't know who I was, even if she looked me straight in the eye. She had no idea that I was at the bottom in Larry's little black book, while she came top in his eyes. She probably didn't even know there was a book keeping score of their sexual exploits. I wonder what she would do if she found out.

When she disappeared into Oak Street, I knew she would be gone at least an hour, so I crossed the road to her gate. I was only going to have a look round the garden to see if I could see in through a window, to see why Larry had wanted to spend most of his time there. She'd left the kitchen one open at the back a little way and something must have taken me over, because before I knew it, I was jumping down from the sink unit into a large kitchen diner. As I slid off the sill, I knocked a few things off the draining board, so I picked them up and put them back. Hopefully in the right places. Her colour scheme was bright and harmonious. Very different from the bland box Larry and I used to live in. I poked my nose into the sitting room, but my curiosity, however, led me straight to her bedroom.

As I opened the door, I was bombarded by images

of sex and affection. Of Larry kissing, touching, loving this woman, scenes my mind created to torture me. I was powerless to stop them as one by one they came in at warp speed, It was overwhelming. Suddenly, I was violently pulled back through time to my childhood, to the flickery movies, to the flies, to the shame. I must have gone into a sort of trance then, I would say it was to save my sanity, but we all know that ship has sailed. When I came back to earth, I glanced at the clock on Larry's side of the bed. The floral tissue box and a pottery owl on her side gave it away. I'd been here an hour. Where had the time gone? I made to leave, but as I reached the door my eye caught a silky robe draped over the back of a chair. Soft painterly flowers in pinks and greens flowed all over the delicate lilac fabric. I grabbed it, sniffed it, there was no cloying smell. I shoved it in my pocket and left the way I had come. Out on the street I felt euphoric. I'd finally taken something from someone who had taken so very much from me. I'd go again next Tuesday.

Miriam

I'm going to be a granny!! It was Tuesday. Garry and his mate Jamie sat in me kitchen with two mugs of tea and a full English, discussing how they were going to go about following Sally to wherever she had been going all this time. I could hardly focus, as all manner of baby stuff I'd seen in Tesco's was dancing through me head. Grace had phoned just before Garry turned up, saying he'd got something to tell me. Well! The way things have been going lately I thought straight away that Garry had a ruddy disease or something, but it wasn't that, thank God. Grace had a bun in the oven, a brother or sister for Sarah. I'd gone from nought to two grandkids in the blink of an eye and I don't mind telling you, I couldn't have been happier. I went straight upstairs to tell Brian. He was over the moon too. I had a job, but I turned my attention back to the matter in hand and listened to the boys as they sorted the details. There was no getting round it. Sally had been acting even more weird than usual if that was possible. I'm sure it had something to do with her going home to Mulberry Crescent next week.

The walk-through had gone badly. She hadn't wanted

to go in the door at all. She was doing that odd step thing she used to do as a kid but, with a bit of coaxing from Megan and me she stepped into the passage. I could see the cogs going round in her brain, trying to take it all in. God knows what she was thinking. What she did next was weird, even for Sally. She went to the fourth stair and sat down which wasn't the strange part, she did that all the time, but then a terrible noise seemed to come from the depths of her soul. I thought she was about to cry, but when it got louder I realised she wasn't crying, she was laughing and not just a giggle neither. She worked herself up to near hysteria and started rocking faster and faster. Dr Megan looked at me as if to say it's OK, leave her a minute, then it was as if someone had flicked a switch. The laughter stopped dead and the screaming started. I rushed over to her then, well, as fast as I could with me weight the way it is and took her in me arms. We got her out of there as quick as we could after that. I was torn in half, to tell you the truth. I felt desperately sorry for Sal but it was getting impossible at home. I missed me son and his missus and little Sarah. They still wouldn't come round when she was at the house. I'd only seen Grace the once since Sal came to stay. We met in the biscuit aisle in Tesco's, and had a natter but it wasn't the same as having a cuppa and a brownie in me kitchen. I wanted life to get back to normal, but guilt was the biggest thing keeping me awake at night. What if I was sending her back to the very place that would send her over the edge. With all the terrible memories locked up in that house, she was halfway there already. But, Sally was an adult at the end of the day and she would have lots of people around to help. She'd be all right. Wouldn't she? Course she would!

Sally

I can't spend too much time writing today as I have somewhere to be but here goes. The school years. Miriam and I stuck together all through school. There was something about her stout frame and thick accent that made the mean girls of the academy leave us alone. Well, for the most part. She was very much my protector then, and still is today. I needed to be around her as much as possible and I would take every opportunity to go to her house after school. Anything to keep the grey away and prolong going back to Mother's. Mrs Bullen would welcome us in after school and shove biscuits and a mug of hot tea into our hands. She would ask how I was, and actually listen to the answer. Of course I never told her how I was actually doing, or what life was really like where I lived. I often think now, when I'm waiting for Audrey Brown to vacate the premises, that if I had told her what was going on at the house, she would probably have tried to do something about it, but because I didn't want her to think that I liked any part of what happened to me, I never let on, even to Miriam. I'm only telling you about it because you'll keep poking at my wounds if I don't.

It's the next day now, and I've come straight to my room to brood over what happened yesterday at Audrey Brown's. Before you think about asking me about it in our next session, I'm not going to tell you. Miriam never asks about anything anymore, because she knows she won't get an answer either. It's not that I'm being awkward. It's just that some things should be just for me, shouldn't they? I know Miriam worries about me, I am the most important person to her after all. I have to concentrate on what is important and cut out the rest of the chaos in my head now, don't I? It's the only way I can ever have peace I suppose. That is what the letters are for though, to push all the nasty bits on to you. It doesn't matter what you think of me and the things that have happened to me. You're paid not to judge, although I suppose in secret you do. It's human nature isn't it? You can't say anything to Miriam though, I know that. It's some sort of oath you people take isn't it? I suppose you are like a big receptacle. People dump all their rubbish into it metaphorically speaking, but where do you dump it? I ask that out of courtesy, I don't really care that much. Have to stop writing soon. I only have an hour or two at the most this morning and that goes by so fast. Time is relative, isn't it? If you are early for something, time is your friend, but if you are running late, it can be very much your enemy. I've already got lots of those and don't need any more.

Looking back to my old life, I think my brother was the worst of my enemies, or was he? When Jim was poking his thing in me in every way imaginable, making me do unspeakable things, my father went on with his life as if I was invisible. So he was a candidate for enemy of the month, and the only thing Mother cared about came in a bottle. I take a bottle everywhere with me too. It looks like vodka but it is only water. Mother hated vodka, said it had no substance, no colour. I knew that feeling. Living the way I did for all those years, made me invisible to the monsters I lived with, but even though they acted like I wasn't there most of the time, I miraculously appeared to them when the housework needed doing or Mother wanted a punch bag. Which, incidentally got more frequent when her beloved Jim left forever. I don't know what was worse in the crap life stakes? The parents or Jim? I guess maybe they were about the same. Come to think of it maybe not, because it wasn't my parents that got me pregnant twice, and gave me a venereal disease. If they had been normal, loving people, like the Bullens, they would have called the police, or at the very least sent him away. They would have protected me from the demon that was my brother. They would have stopped him from taking his rage out on me three or four times a week. Of course my young body couldn't hold on to the slippery little things and I flushed them away. When I went to the STD clinic to get myself de-clapped, they told me I needed to tell my sexual partner so he could be treated too. Not a chance, let him rot from the inside out. I would stab him if he came near me again. I didn't have to worry about that though, he left for good the next day. To be honest, if I'd really stopped to think about it, I think Jim needed saving just as much as me. From Mother. He was the moon and stars to her. She dogged his every waking moment. Buying him expensive gifts, ordering his favourite food. I say ordering because Mother never cooked. Thank God she didn't, as the whole place would have gone up in smoke. Drunk in charge of an oven M'lord, guilty as charged. Come to think of it, a fire might have been a way of getting out. Of being free. Why didn't I think of that? I think Miriam's doing pork chops for tea, with apple sauce. I could eat a jar of that with a spoon, well I have done, but it gave me awful heartburn.

As I said before, I never got presents from Mother. If my name had been Johnny Walker, or Jack Daniels she might have paid me more attention, but as my name was Sally Jones, I didn't have a prayer really. I longed for Mrs Bullen's house, with its good-natured squabbles. Miriam would argue with Phoebe and Ella about who had done the washing up last, or whose turn it was to put the bins out, but they always worked it out between them. I never had anyone where I lived to be together with. That's one of the reasons why Miriam became the most important person in the world to me. Finally, I had my together person. An actual friend. Her brother Tom's friend Zac was there a lot too. If boys had a forever person, Tom would be Zac's. In him, I saw a little bit of me really. He needed the Bullens' warmth and their zest for life to boost his confidence too. When I wasn't there, I missed the sharing of games, clothes and confidences in their warm comfortable home, but I think I took enough from the times I was safe and wanted, so that when my brother was raping me I could go to the Bullens in my head and stay there until it was over. Audrey Brown had another new pair of trainers on today, and Larry got buried. I didn't go to the funeral. Why would I? I would have worried that the people in the funeral parlour hadn't locked the coffin properly, that he would rise up and say surprise! I'm not dead after all. I'm sure you think I'm crazy and I won't disagree with you. The police let me know where the plot would be should I want to visit and lay flowers. Lay flowers! If I were a man I know what I'd like to do on his grave, but you can't take your knickers down in a churchyard can you? You'd get arrested. Oh yeah! I've been there, done that! I still don't know whether it's freedom, prison or the funny farm for me and to be honest, I don't care, they are all the same.

Did I tell you about the little black book, Megan? I can't remember. My mind keeps skipping between the then, and the now and never seems to land. I can't get past what Audrey Brown has done to me, can't seem to swallow the humiliation.

Oh, I've tried, but it gets stuck in my throat like I'm choking on a piece of rotten meat. Although as I said earlier, I must try to draw a line under it once and for all. I have to walk away, and focus on Miriam. I will. In a little while. Remember! You can't tell a soul about what I've told you, but if you were to betray my confidence for any reason, please don't let it be to Miriam. That would be very bad.

Anyway. Back to Audrey Brown, not that I'm obsessed or anything, but, I took something that belonged to her. It gave me a sense of power, something I've had all too little of in my life. Oh there's been a couple of times over the years when I've come out on top, not least when I stopped Larry from ever hurting me again, but it's not much to show for the forty-six years I've been on this godforsaken planet. Larry had had six indiscretions in all including Audrey Brown. For the thirty-odd years I had been with Larry, I'd put up with being treated as subhuman. I took the slaps. The punches. The black eyes, that was my normal, but when I found the book that night, it took me right back to when I was nine, to having Jim's dick in my mouth, to feeling worthless and disgusting.

Larry, like Jim, thought I was just there to be used, something to take their frustrations out on, never really seen or heard. In other words, I was colourless. I was see-through. When I'm gone, you will no doubt find the book and you can have a laugh at the things he said about me. If Miriam is still around she can too. Oh, when I'm thinking straight I know she'd never do that. She'd be more likely to burn it and dance on Larry's grave than side with him. She is my best friend after all. I find it's getting harder and harder to be Sally these days. Well, the Sally that Miriam thinks she knows anyway. In my mind, I seem to take what I see with my eyes and twist and pull it, until it becomes something completely different. 'How are you?' becomes 'Are *you well enough to leave my house yet?' A simple conversation over dinner becomes an interrogation. I start to feel that they're poking around in my thoughts, prodding like you would worry a mouth ulcer with your tongue. I get up and leave the table then. I can't have their questions in my head, I have enough crap in there already. Oh I know Miriam isn't like that really and it's just small talk over chicken and chips, but I can't let the wrong things slip out. Saint Brian is making me angry at the moment. He can't wait to get rid of me. He thinks I'm a cancer to be cut out of their lives, but Miriam is on my side. I suppose if I really was a true friend, I would tell her everything that happened to me and trust that she would love me anyway, but I can't risk it. It's funny how people buy into the misconception that love conquers all. In my experience, love is something that someone only pretends to give when they want something from you. It's all Larry's fault that I don't know real love. Well, his and Jim's and Mother's and … Miriam though has always loved me in her own way. She has always trusted me and has never asked anything in return and I believe she would walk through fire to save my soul. I will have to make her understand just how much I need her and I know now how to do it. I think I'll leave the gut-spilling here for today. I'll save the rest for the last letter, for the end. It will come, and when it does, I will deal with it.*

Megan

I haven't had a chance to read much of Sally's next letter. It's been burning a hole in my file cabinet since I got back from Miriam's. I need time, space and quiet to really get under the skin of what Sally is telling me, or not telling me as the case may be, and Charlie singing 'wind the bobbin up' over and over in his sweet tuneless voice isn't conducive to a peaceful environment. It's my job to pick up the narrative she thinks she's left out, and to help her to face the things that still haunt her. It will be there if I look hard enough. I promised myself I would lock myself away in my office, which incidentally doubles as the dining table, for a few hours this evening when the virtuoso has gone to bed. Even though the pain in my knees has hit twelve on the Richter scale, I have no choice but to read it all as I have a session with her tomorrow.

The little of the letter I have read so far has struck a chord with me. I can relate to her mention of the mean girls, we had them at my school too. They were called Alice, Lucy and Sheila and most people kowtowed to them. Too scared not to, in case nasty rumours, all untrue I hasten to add, were spread about them. I was not one of those people. I refused to bow down to the vacuous coven, who thought that being beautiful gave you everything in life, including the right to torture others. To them, any imperfection, a mole, a scar or, in my case frizzy red hair was a source of ridicule and entertainment to them. I felt so sorry for the kids who weren't as strong as me and couldn't stick up for themselves. They were made to feel ashamed, that they didn't live up to the visions of perfection that the three witches coveted. Now, being a shrink, I could have a field day with those 'mean girls' and their now obvious insecurities. They made fun of others to hide their own problems and worries. I know that now, but back then, they were just mean. Mum took me out of the school in the end and sent me to a comprehensive a thirty-minute bus ride away. I'd been diagnosed with stress and anxiety, after the last bout of particularly vicious rumours had made me a pariah. At least Miriam's presence saved Sally from most of that kind of stuff. I don't think she could have handled that every day, on top of everything else that was going on in her life.

My new school was my saviour, not just educationally, but socially too. I made good friends and three of them are still in my life today. Annie and Jane have their own busy lives, but would drop everything to be there in a crisis, both are there on the other end of the phone even though they live miles away, but my best friend in the world is Moira. The one I turn to in the truly difficult times. We have each other's backs. Always have, always will and I love her dearly. Sally only had one person to turn to, but I'm glad she had someone. They do say that if you have one good friend in your life, you are a very rich person, and I hope that having Miriam with her, went some way to easing Sally's burden.

I had an idyllic childhood in every way, in that I had wonderful parents and we were not short of money. We went on holiday to Cornwall twice a year, a place I eventually want to retire to. I want to take the whole family and live right on the beach, to give Charlie access to the sea, the countryside and the fresh air that I thrived on when I was his age. Mum says she will sell the house she shared with my wonderful dad for forty-five years and move with us. She still dreams of crashing waves on craggy rocks and the call of seagulls. The only sound she hears now is the roar of the new ring road that runs alongside her once peaceful village. Since we lost Dad, I have been trying to get her to move in with me, but she says my tiny house is already full to bursting and she would be a burden. In Cornwall she'll have her own space. If she needs respite from our lively Charlie Bear whom she adores she can have it, but she can join in with us when she wants a bit of chaos. I was going to carry on working until my retirement date, get the proverbial gold watch, but I am tired and in pain and the pull of Falmouth is stronger than ever.

After dinner, Charlie made me read two rounds of *The Very Hungry Caterpillar*. I always have to make the poor little insect gobble my grandson up when it was already full of apples, ice cream and cake. I tried to point out that caterpillars didn't eat little boys, rather, they preferred a vegetarian diet on the whole, but Charlie insisted the more full the caterpillar got, the quicker it would turn into a beautiful butterfly. It was no use telling him otherwise, so I went along with it to keep the peace. When he went skipping off upstairs with Gina to have his bath, I knew I would have at least half an hour before his bedtime, so

I settled down in the huge, worn purple armchair in the corner of the room and tried again to digest the rest of Sally's third letter. The chair was my father's favourite all through his life, resisting many attempts from my mother to send it to the tip. She was more than happy to see the back of it when he died, but, I suspect, was secretly glad it was coming to me and not to the local dump. Her memories were all in her heart she told me, and if a knackered old chair held meaning for me and made me feel closer to my dad, then who was she to argue? Every time I sat in it, it brought back memories of when I was very small and I used to use the wing-shaped arms to pull myself onto his lap and be read to. The chair enveloped us both, snug and warm and to me, that big lump of grape-coloured velvet was priceless.

I'm sobbing into a hanky with smiley green robots on it. Having found it earlier, up the sleeve of Charlie's blue fleece hoodie when I sorted the washing. I'd taken up where I left off, with Sally telling me about the Bullens. I felt a profound sense of sadness, that something as simple as a cup of tea and a handful of biscuits, had helped Sally through one of the most traumatic ordeals imaginable. The love of the Bullen family, gave her a powerful shield against the violation of her little body by her brother Jim. She must have gone back to Miriam's house countless times in her head when she was lying there being stripped again and again of her innocence. How scared she must have been going home each evening, never feeling safe, knowing she was heading to a place that at best, was uncertain and at worst downright dangerous.

A lot of the letter is in her usual style. Short, staccato sentences that have no emotion in them at all. That is what makes me sad. She has systematically had any feelings she may have had as a child, had a lot of what made her Sally ripped away. She also swaps subjects at the drop of a hat, and states quite categorically, that she is only revealing these things, because I am bound by an oath of confidentiality and couldn't tell Miriam if I wanted to. She describes incest, brutality and miscarriage like she is giving directions on a map, then skips to what she's having for tea. The only time I feel any warmth at all from her, is when she is talking about the Bullens.

As I read on, something is stirring inside me. I think it's fear. Not of Sally, but of not being in the right mindset to catch all the clues to Sally's thinking. My life has changed so much over the last year with the family coming to live with me, which I love, I'm not complaining, but my health is not what it was and I worry that I am not enough for her, that maybe another psychiatrist would be a better fit. A few years ago I would have relished such a complex case, but I have been thinking for a while now that I should get a second opinion, just to make sure I am doing the best for Sally, and for Miriam. I don't want to make any mistakes. The price of that would be too much to pay.

This letter is much darker than the others. I think that writing things down on paper has opened the floodgates for her. I don't know whether Sally, in her present mind frame, realises that the words she's putting on the page are actually being read by someone else. It seems more to be a catharsis, a testimonial of sorts, rather than a cry for help. Her writing is more difficult to read now as the stream of consciousness spills across the page. Jealousy is rearing its ugly head and it seems solely directed toward Audrey Brown. Larry's adultery looms large in Sally's thoughts, which, no doubt, has brought back those feelings of not being enough, of being used. The problem is, now that Sally has told me she has entered her premises, she has actually committed a crime. Ms Brown might have already called the police and it may only be a matter of time before they link Audrey's name to the note book, then to Sally. I need to talk to her urgently this has to stop now. The problem is, she hasn't really bonded with me yet. She simply has no trust in anyone who isn't Miriam. She's locked into the idea that if she keeps the ugly truth from her friend, she will still love and protect her. In Sally's mind, telling Miriam everything will mean more rejection, then, what would be the point of living? That is why she feels she can write it all down. She knows Miriam will never read it.

The last part of the letter is very different. Random thoughts are flowing in and out of Sally's mind, like Piccadilly Circus in the rush hour. Miriam's son Garry wants to follow her in his friend's van to see where she goes. I think, under the circumstances, that's a good idea. We don't know Audrey Brown's address yet, and have no way of knowing what Sally's intentions are towards her. I honestly don't think Sally wants to hurt her. More, I think she wants to know what it feels like to be Audrey for a while, to be desirable. Possibly, by taking her belongings, Sally wants her to feel loss. To wonder where they went? Whom they belonged to now? It was important to Sally to have these little victories. She may have won a few battles against Audrey Brown, but she was all too aware, she had lost the war.

The lack of any emotion about Larry's funeral was understandable and I get why she didn't want to go. I attended however, with Detective Sergeant Whalen. It's usual to have a police presence at a funeral of an unexplained death and I went along, so that I could answer Sally's questions about the service if there were any. There weren't.

It was the strangest funeral I had ever been to. Three women sat one behind the other on the left-hand side of the church, all weeping into their tissues each trying to outdo the other. I was sure they were some of Larry's conquests. There were no other mourners. That made five people in all. Five! Well, six with the vicar. Not much to show for forty-nine years on this earth. It was telling of the kind of man he was. I saw for myself all I had read in Sally's letters. Even the Reverend could find little to say for a man who had thought himself so important. Larry Wilson was now reduced to a plot in the furthest corner of St Anthony's churchyard, amidst ivy clad, untended graves. Sally wasn't going to pay for a headstone. Even if she wanted to, what would his epitaph read? 'Here lies Larry Wilson. Wife beater, philanderer and all round shit.' I think it was enough that she knew where he was and that he couldn't hurt her anymore. She needed peace of mind not a bill for a granite slab. I hoped now, she would have the courage to start her life again and leave Larry Wilson far behind, but I also knew it was easier said than done.

Just as I was about to make notes on what Sally had written, a downy blonde head followed by an elfin face, peered round the door.

"Nanny! I forgot to tell you! I got my boot stuck in a cow pat on our walk this morning and Mummy had to clean it with wet wipes. I got it on my trousers too and she's washing them in the sink. She says she feels sick now and wants a cup of tea. Can I play with you instead? My train set has come off the track and it's my turn to be the driver. I have to go to bed soon so we have to go now!"

What could I say to that? I closed my computer and put all thoughts of Sally to one side. I could go there later. My grandson needed my attention and who was I to say no?

"Come on then, Charlie Bear. Let's play trains, can I be the conductor?"

Miriam

You should have seen our Garry and his mate Jamie getting ready to follow Sal that morning. You'd think they were a couple of detectives getting ready to go on a stakeout, rather than driving behind her to wherever it was she went every day. It was getting to be a kind of obsession with her and I didn't think it was healthy. If I suggested she stay in because it was raining, or asked her to do something in the house for me that was going to make her late, she would start getting all twitchy and then angry, so it was better just to say nothing. Garry had to get another mate of his to go with them, because they couldn't use his works van; she would have recognised it if she saw it.

I'm telling you now. What turned up in our drive, a couple of minutes after Sal had left, looked like a cross between a 1950s' camper and the ruddy mystery machine. You couldn't even look in to see who was driving cos of the blacked-out windows. Garry said he thought they were a good thing, cos it would be game over if she caught them. I'd have thought the object of the exercise was to blend in, so Sal wouldn't notice them, not stand out by driving around in something Scooby Doo would be proud to call home. The driver, Garry's other mate Keith, beeped the horn a couple of times and I had to chuckle to meself. It sounded more like our neighbour Helen's bicycle bell, tinny and sharp. I'd have thought the horn on a big van like that would have been deeper, like melted chocolate, rather than sharper than a ruddy jif lemon. Keith stuck his face out the window and told the boys to hurry up or they'd lose her, but since she'd only left two minutes ago and was on foot, I didn't think it would be a problem.

Garry carried the thermos and the sandwiches while Jamie grabbed a six-pack of water and enough pork scratchings to supply the local pub. "What the ruddy hell do you need all that for?" asked, trying hard to keep a straight face.

"You can scoff all you want, Mam but we need to be prepared. This could take all day."

"OK, love. Eat all you want. Fill your boots. I'll phone Grace and tell her you won't be wanting any tea, shall I?" Garry shot me a mock, menacing look as if to say 'don't you dare' and I winked at him as I waved them off. When I got back inside I laughed till my belly ached, tears rolling down my face. It felt both good, and strange at the same time. I couldn't remember the last time I had a bloody good giggle. It cheered me up, but then the thought struck me. What the bloody hell have you got to be laughing about, Miriam McDougal? Life was hardly peaches and cream. Brian was upstairs, still as weak as a kitten after the heart attack, and Sal seemed to be in a different universe most of the time like that Dorothy in the film *The Wizard of Oz*. That did it! The thought of Sal swirling round and round in a hurricane with a terrier under her arm made me laugh so hard I nearly wet meself. I made so much noise that Brian banged on the ceiling making the horrible lampshade jiggle.

"Is everything all right down there?" he shouted. I couldn't answer right away cos the laughter had turned to hiccups and I had to down a pint of water. Me old gran used to say that it had to be a pint, no less, to cure hiccups. I don't know about that, I just felt as if I was drowning...

...The boys gathered in my kitchen the day after the big stakeout. They'd had to wait until Sal had left before they could spill the beans. Then, Keith did literally, all down his crisp white t-shirt while eating a ruddy great fry-up. I'm used to it now. Any meeting in my house and I have to break out the streaky and the Cumberland rings. It's like a rite of passage. Cooking it all is a mission, but it's a small price to pay for having their company. They always manage to put a smile on me face with their banter and their stories.

Sally hadn't gone far they said, but what she did when she got there had the boys scratching their heads. They'd followed her in the van, staying back a bit all the time so she wouldn't cotton on, but because she was on foot, it made it all the more difficult for them. They had to follow the road, where as Sal could take short cuts. Jamie had a brain wave. He got out of the van and walked behind her, staying on the phone with Garry all the time to tell him where they were. They ended up on Nightingale Terrace. I never go to that part of town. It's where all the posh people live and it's in the opposite direction from the shops. What the bloody hell was Sally doing there?

The boys parked up on the opposite side of the road so they wouldn't look conspicuous but because of the blacked out windows she couldn't have seen them even if they'd parked right next to her, the silly sods. When Jamie got back in he shrugged his shoulders.

"She's a bit of a weirdo, that one," he said. All the time I've been here she's been flat to that wall. What the heck is she doing?"

"I haven't a clue, mate," Garry replied. "She's been doing all sorts of crazy shit since she's been at Mam's. God knows what she's thinking, I sure as hell haven't got a clue."

"Hang on," said Keith, poking Garry in the ribs, "she's moving."

They watched as a tall slender redhead walked down the drive of one of the detached properties at the fancy end of the street. Sally peeled herself from the wall and set off after the woman. It was as if Sal was going to tap her on the shoulder, as if she knew her, but when she got to the corner she stopped short and peered round it. The lady had disappeared. Sally looked as if she would go too, but she turned on her heel and headed back the way she came.

"Bloody hell, she's on the move again, we're going to lose her," shouted Keith. "Trust her to go walkabout now. I wanted one of your mum's cheese and pickle sandwiches, I've been smelling them since we left your house." He went to start the engine but a hand shot out to stop him.

"She's coming back this way," said Jamie. "Let's just wait and see what she does."

They watched as Sally retraced her steps from the corner, back towards them.

"Duck!" yelled Garry.

"She can't see us, you plank. That was the reason you needed the van, mate, blacked out windows," chuckled Keith.

"OK, you Muppet, I just got carried away," Garry replied, his face reddening.

"Never mind all that," hissed Jamie. "Look where she's going." Instead of leaving Nightingale Terrace. Sally turned up the drive of the very house that the posh woman came out of.

"Oh my god! Is Sally having an affair?" giggled Jamie.

"No way, mate. After what she put up with from her old man, I doubt she'd ever go near a bloke again," said Garry. "It's weird though?"

Jamie suddenly leapt out and ran across the road. He waited a minute, then quietly opened the gate that Sally had just closed behind her. As he crept down the side of the house, the other two were frantically waving their arms about, trying to bring him back to the safety of the van. Silly really when Jamie couldn't see in. Quick as a flash, he pelted back down the drive, jumped over the gate and climbed back in the van.

"I went in as far as I could, I can't go any further. It's all open and she'd have seen me. I didn't see her though, which is a bit odd."

"Never mind, mate. We'll just have to wait until she reappears," said Keith rubbing his hands together. "Right Garry, me old son, break out those sandwiches."

They waited an hour before Sal came back down the drive. They watched as she closed the gate behind her, walked straight past the van and disappeared into the park.

"That's the shortcut to Mam's," said Garry. "Go left, we'll meet her coming out the other end." They were just about to turn the corner, when out of the rear view mirror they saw the redhead coming back down the road. Sal had cut it ruddy close. Or maybe, she knew just how much time she'd got to do whatever it was she was doing. Who knew? One thing's for sure they were going to find out if it killed them. They followed her all the way home and drove on past. Keith dropped Jamie and Garry off and they all agreed to meet at my house in the morning for a debrief, daft buggers.

When the fry-ups had been demolished and they told me all that had happened, I didn't know what to make of it all. I was beginning to worry for Sal's sanity and what it would mean for me and Brian, what with her staying here an' all. Having thought about it all afternoon, I rang Megan and told her everything. She said she couldn't tell me what Sally had written in the letters, but she thought she could put a name to the redhead in Nightingale Terrace. She said she would be round tomorrow afternoon. She said we would put our heads together and try to sort out what to do next. It was Wednesday already and Sal was due to leave here on Monday. I didn't think she was in any fit state to be on her own yet, if at all, so it looked a spell in the The Chimes was on the cards. Poor Sal. Part of me could weep for her, but at the same time, I was afraid of what she might do next. I took a cuppa up to Brian, to have a cuddle and a little bit of normal. I can't say there has been much of that in the last few weeks. Well if I'm honest, none at all.

Sally

I'm sitting on Audrey Brown's bed. It's the place I go straight to every time I go in. It's like I have to torment myself with scene after scene of tawdry sex, letting the images play out in my mind like a second-rate porno movie. Watching the two of them fornicate for England on a loop, is like being tied to a mast and lashed over and over again. Oh I know what you are all thinking? That I should put it all in a box in my brain and bury it like they buried Larry and start a new life, but I've never really been very good at seeing beyond the now. You have to understand, for the whole of my life I've had to live in the moment, always had to be on my guard. I've always held grudges too though. Against my parents, Jim, of course, Larry and now Audrey Brown and I suppose, being honest, I take a kind of cold comfort in them. So choosing to flagellate myself with the injustices levelled against me, well, it's something in my life I still have control over. Let's face it, my memories have rarely been good, so grudges are the only things I'll ever have that are truly mine and have, for the most part, stayed pink. Lately though, any negative comment or perceived slight from anyone and my anger and goes straight to blood orange. There is no comfort in those, just cold.

Saint Brian has been the subject of my wrath too lately. I hate the way he whines to Miriam about me, about how long I'm going to be in his house, his space. I hear him say how I take up all her time and that he doesn't get a look in. I think it's the other way round. When he was in the hospital she hardly ever left his side. She would sit beside the bed until one of the nurses kicked her out, leaving me home alone. Well, when I wasn't at Audrey Brown's. He had all the time in the world with her then and what thanks do I get, Brian?! Megan has started poking around too much too. It seems she asks the same questions over and over, expecting a different answer. I'd have thought by now she would realise I can't give her what she wants, not in person anyway. I try to give her a bit of detail in the letters and I am getting bolder. The trouble with that is, the words don't flow as I'd like. They're not smooth. They are not nice, or kind. They are clumsy, lumpy, thick with insecurity and self-loathing. The other thing is, when the feelings come out, they don't stay out. They go straight back in. It's like sucking chicken noodle soup through a straw. Memories thick with hate and shame flow through me over and over again. I know Megan wants me use my voice as well as telling her in the letters, but when I write it down, I can separate things into neat, tidy bundles and offer them to her on a plate. If I was to open my mouth to speak, all the grey and black would spew out like lava and we'd both burn up in it. I think, in the end, she will lose patience. Would that be such a bad thing? If she gives up on me, it will be one less person to have to fight for Miriam's affections. Don't think I haven't noticed them getting all pally lately. The odd hug here and there, the patting of hands.

I can feel the anger in my gut boiling over now. Am I mad? Does the fact I'm telling you all the ins and outs of my life and I just don't care how it looks, make me dangerous? I think, dear reader, that it's safe to say these things to you, because you don't have the power to lock me in the nut house and separate me from Miriam for a long time. Megan, however, does. She's a psychiatrist and if she is worth her salt, she is as dangerous to me as I am to myself. As I write the letters, they unlock even more doors in my mind. Doors that should be locked and firmly bolted. So now, not only have I got Audrey Brown to worry about, but I feel I'm being raped all over again as the memories hit me hard. Something has to give. I need to stop obsessing about the things I can't change, and focus on the things I can. The serenity prayer comes to mind and I focus on it. I have to draw a line under the whole Audrey Brown thing. I have to end it. I know that. I will. Just not quite yet.

Miriam

When Sal got home the next afternoon, she looked like someone had poured a bucket of water over her head. The heavens opened just after midday and I think the whole ruddy lot was directed at her. It wasn't showing any signs of stopping neither and I wanted to pop to Tesco's

"Bloody hell," I said, as I peeled the coat off her back. "You're soaked to the marra."

I chucked her the towel that was on top of the ironing pile. Yes! Before you all roll your eyes, I iron towels, tea towels, knickers and hankies. I don't do socks. I used to. A great source of amusement to Brian and Garry, but now, I reckon life's too short to flatten them out, only to roll them in a ball and stick them in a drawer. So now I just pair them straight out of the tumble drier. Does anyone else have a sock goblin? Even when I know I've put pairs in the washing machine, somebody always loses his mate. I can't tell you the amount of odd socks I've had to throw away cos I can't find their partners. Brian say's it's one of life's mysteries, like why is belly button fluff always blue, but I'd like to know where they all end up, that's for sure. Maybe there's another world at the end of the pipe. Where hundreds of little folk walk round wearing odd socks. Bloody hell! Listen to me! It's no wonder I'm a bit potty, what with all that's happened here lately. I truly think I'm following Sally down looney lane.

"Go and get out of those wet things, then come and 'have a cuppa with me," I said, as I hung her coat over the radiator to dry. "I made chocolate brownies earlier on an' all. They're lovely, even if I do say so meself." Ten minutes later, with her hair in a turban and dressed in a pair of warm pjs Sally sat, head down, over a steaming mug of tea. The silence was deafening so I thought to meself, it's now or never. I said gently, "You don't have to tell me if you don't want to, but where is it you go every day, lovey? I can't help noticing that it's doing you no good. You always look upset when you come home and go straight to your room. You know you can tell me anything, don't you, Sal? "She nodded once and looked up, for once, not looking away. As she held my gaze, the orange light on the freezer door reflected in her deep brown eyes, giving her that red eye thing you get when someone uses a flash indoors. I'm sorry to say I had to look away. It made her look a bit freaky. A bit like a vampire. She moved ever so slightly then and it disappeared.

There was a long silence as both of us sipped our tea. Sal hadn't touched her brownie. I was on me second. I didn't think she was going to say anything, and I thought, I'd just have to tell Megan what the boys had found out instead when she piped up. "I found a book." I just nodded because I thought if I'd said anything, she might just clam up.

"It had names in it. Women Larry had been with, you know, instead of me." I nodded again, so that she would know I'd caught on. It didn't come as a surprise to me.

I always knew he couldn't keep his willy in his pants. I told Sal that, before she'd even married the swine. All of a sudden Sal's floodgates opened and everything came out in a rush.

"Audrey Brown was on the top of the list. She was his favourite. I just wanted to see what she looked like at first. But when I'd done that, it made me angry with her, and with Larry, but mostly with myself for being naive and stupid. I can't stop punishing myself for not seeing what was under my nose. I didn't know anything about these women. Life went on as normal. He was still his nasty bullying self. I was just so pleased that he wasn't at the house all the time. It was peaceful when he wasn't there. At first I just watched her, but then I started looking in her windows when she was out. Don't worry, no one saw me, I went round the back."

I knew that part was true, because it's what the boys had reported, but I also knew she wasn't telling me everything. They'd waited nearly an hour in that van, so I'm sure she did more than look in the ruddy windows.

"Once I peed on her patio," she said out of the blue "I felt stupid afterwards so I never did it again."

I nodded a third time, as if what she she'd told me was completely normal. Then, three raps on the kitchen ceiling from upstairs made the ugly lampshade do the cha cha. Sally's head went down again and I knew I wouldn't get anything else from her today. Every time Brian bangs for something, I remind myself I have to change the ruddy thing. It was here when we bought the house. It's purple and white in a swirly pattern, a nod to the sixties and Lucy in the sky with diamonds. I didn't like it then, I bloody hate it now.

"Have your brownie," I said to Sal, mainly because I couldn't think of anything else to say. Something to break the ominous silence that had descended over my cosy little kitchen. As I turned to pour Brian's tea, she scarpered up the stairs. I didn't see her again until teatime. Well! I didn't actually see her then, not really. She rushed into the kitchen, grabbed a plate of bangers and mash, and ran back to her room as if she was being pursued. In a way I suppose she was. Both Megan and me were on her case all the time, and if I were Sal I might want to run and hide too. It seemed to me that there was a war going on inside her. One part really wanted to tell me what was going on in her head, but another part, the biggest part, wanted to hang on to all her secrets, like she had done all her life. I think she wanted to spare me the vile things that had happened to her, as if knowing would be a burden to me somehow. It would, but I would gladly carry it for a little while. Especially if it meant she could rest easy. I know I've got my Brian to see to, but for old time's sake, I'd lighten her load.

I'll call Megan in the morning. She needs to know what Sal had told me. Peeing on someone's patio, whether they deserved it or not, was at best stupid and at worst downright crazy. Maybe Megan can get more out of her than I did. Maybe she could get Sal to write yet another bloody letter. She was supposed to be going back to Mulberry Crescent on Monday and to be honest with you, Brian and I were looking forward to it. It didn't seem likely now, going by what Sal said today. She wouldn't be able to cope and it would fall to me and Brian again. Maybe Megan could find her a room in The Chimes, just for a little while. I honestly think it's the safest place for her at the moment, and for that Audrey Brown an' all…

Megan

I've just had a very strange session with Sally at Miriam's. Right from the off, she seemed very twitchy, her eyes flitting about like a restless moth. When I asked her all the normal stuff, like how she was feeling etc, which is how we started every meeting, she kept looking at a non-existent watch whilst hiding behind her fringe, which had grown a lot longer in the last few weeks. Something felt off. Ominous.

"Do you have somewhere to be, Sally?" I asked quietly. Hoping she would tell me about Audrey Brown face to face, instead of on the page. I was to be left wanting.

"No," came the sharp reply.

"If you have, you can tell me and we can do this another time, but we do need to move forward. You are due to be going home on Monday and we are still aiming for that. We won't just leave you to get on with it, but I need you to start talking to me, Sally. If you don't, I will find it very difficult to know what to do to help you.

"Fine," Sally whispered. She tried to lift her head, to make eye contact. She didn't quite manage it. There was clattering coming from the kitchen, where Miriam was making the tea and singing tunelessly along to 'the power of love' on radio two. Out there, behind the knotty pine door, life went on as normal. In here, with Sally, things were far from fine. She seemed very uncomfortable. Scared even. What was she thinking? I could only guess. As she squirmed on her chair I could sense something was building. A volcano waiting to erupt. Was I keeping her from something? Was she planning to go to Nightingale Terrace? Because of Sally's letters, I knew exactly what she had been doing in Audrey Brown's house, but as I had a duty to my client. I couldn't tell Miriam. I felt bad that all this was going on, while she was left in the dark. She still thinks that all Sally's done so far is pee on a patio. Garry and his friends had discovered Audrey's address last week and it made me feel better knowing, that if things escalated, the police could get there quickly.

"Is there something you want to tell me, Sally?" I asked softly. "I know you prefer to communicate through your letters, but you and I need to talk about Audrey Brown." Suddenly Sally went rigid. I honestly think she saw the letters as her own private diary, to be locked away when not writing in it. I'd certainly struck a nerve. Suddenly her eyes went wide. She now knew for sure that I did read the letters in detail, that they were not just there to help to purge her demons, and that I knew all about Nightingale Terrace. "Can you tell me more about Audrey Brown, Sally? You do know that if you continue to go to her address, she will probably call the police if she hasn't already." I don't think Sally heard the word police. At the mention of Audrey Brown, Sally shot from her chair and made for the door, nearly colliding with Miriam bringing in the tea. She pushed past her and we heard the front door slam.

"What the ruddy hell was that all about?" asked Miriam loudly."

"I think I might need to phone the police, Miriam," I told her. "Sally is upset and not thinking straight. I asked her about Audrey Brown, the lady at Nightingale Terrace and she bolted."

"I have Brian's phone. Let me try her mobile a minute, see if she'll answer."

Miriam reached into the pocket of her chocolate-smeared pinny and brought out an ancient Nokia. She quickly dialled the number and waited for it to connect. All of a sudden, a phone began to ring in the hall. Miriam rushed out of the door and came back with Sally's mobile still ringing in her hand. "I don't think we have a choice, Miriam," I said urgently. "Can you think of anywhere she may have gone?"

"The only two places she ever goes are Nightingale Terrace, and The Cakehole down the road. We used to go there as kids. Very partial to their veggie burgers was Sal. Can we try there first? I don't want the police involved unless we have no choice. It's just that Sal's on bail and it won't look good if we find her you know where?"

"Let's get in the car and check both places before I call them, but if she isn't in the cafe I will have no choice. OK Miriam?" She nodded and quickly took her apron off.

"I can't go out in this, or people will think it's me what needs the men in white coats, never mind Sally." She forced out a chuckle but neither of us really felt like laughing...

We found Sally packed tightly in the furthermost booth in The Cakehole as close to the wall as she could get. Miriam went in first and slid into the seat opposite her.

"Fancy meeting you here," she said whilst reaching for her hand. Sally let Miriam take it, but stayed stiff and upright in her seat, using the wall for support. "I've brought Megan with me, lovey," she whispered while beckoning me over. Sally gripped Miriam's hand for support. I climbed in next to her and smiled across the table at Sally "I'm sorry you are finding all this so difficult, but there is nothing you can't say to me. I won't judge you, I'm just here to listen, OK?"

"Doctor Megan's only here to help, Sal, that's all. Come on. Let's go home. That is unless you want a veggie burger?"

Much later when I got home, I turned what had happened that afternoon over and over in my mind. It was as soon as I mentioned Audrey Brown's name that the already highly charged atmosphere changed to volcanic. I knew it was a very difficult subject for her, but if I couldn't get her to tell me out loud about her life, allowing me to challenge her about her thoughts and feelings, we would never get anywhere. From now on I had to push her a little further. Ask her why she felt she needed to go to Nightingale Terrace every day? Until she opened up I was powerless to help.

"Nanny. Where are you?" yelled Charlie from beyond the closed dining room door. "Mummy says you are working and I can't 'sturb you, but I can't make green and Mummy's cooking dinner. We're having chips. Yippee!"

My grandson needed me to make green. There was nothing more important than that. I realised my family life had never been so important to me. It grounded me as I navigated through the maelstrom of Sally's life. I thought back to yesterday. All my family sitting round the table eating together, trying to stop Charlie from bolting his food as if it was the last meal he would ever have. The laughter. The tantrums, all of it. I wouldn't trade it for all the gold in the world, and I felt sorry for people that had never had it, or had lost it somehow. Sally fleetingly came to mind. I pushed her away. Charlie needed me to make green.

"Coming, Charlie Bear," I called, and opened the door to a little boy with a purple smear on his cheek and a yellow earlobe, and I loved him with all my heart.

Sally

That was a close call today! Megan uttering Audrey Brown's name made my anger, or was it fear? turn straight to red, fizzing like popping candy all the way to my brain. I reacted instinctively and did what I always do. I ran. They were getting too close for comfort. Megan and Miriam both. I had enough to deal with at the moment, without explaining my innermost feelings to a total stranger. Miriam, of course, wasn't a stranger, but I didn't know how much she had worked out for herself. I was safe in the knowledge that Megan couldn't blab, but Miriam was far from stupid. She has always been able to read my moods, and may have picked up the odd clue here and there. I would have to be careful in future. When Megan came out with that woman's name, I realised she knew everything. I hadn't given a thought to the fact that she dissected every word I'd written. I thought it was just a tool these people use to make you confront things, so you are able to put the slights against you in order in your mind. I thought she would just lock them in a drawer or something, until I was ready to face them. Clearly I was mistaken. Now, Megan knows how much I hate Audrey

Brown, and Jim, and Mother, etc etc. I couldn't have that. I had to have some things that were just for me. I wasn't a book to be opened and read like an encyclopaedia. A. for abused. R. for raped, H. for humiliated and K. for killer. All my life I've had to keep things to myself, out of fear, and self-loathing and to stop Miriam finding out of course. Now all of a sudden, they want to disembowel me, to make me spill my guts of all I've held in for the last forty-odd years. Sorry. No can do! They both know what happened that night, and about Larry's conquests. What more do they need? I'm not going to tell them how ugly and irrelevant I felt. How I whip myself with the details every single day, Why should I? The Audrey Brown thing's got boring now anyway. Time to sweep up the rubbish. It's time to move on.

Megan was wearing red today. It didn't suit her. I have always thought that orange and red should never be worn together. She couldn't do anything about her curly auburn mop, but green or a nice turquoise would be far better for her complexion. I didn't care enough about her to suggest it, so I went on letting her clash. Audrey Brown wore a lot of red. I never could as a child, it washed me out and when I got older, as I said before, I stuck to the creams and beiges, not wanting to advertise the fact that I was in the room. On that last day at Audrey Brown's, I tried on a blue pantsuit. It had splashes of gold and silver shimmering through it like fireworks. Looking in the mirror was like looking at two different Sallys. The first, was the same as she'd always been mousey and nondescript, letting the suit wear her, the bright colours fighting with her pale angular face and blank stare. The second. The one standing in the middle of a shower of explosive stars, was rising, she could feel it. She would step up and be counted, even though the suit was a bit baggy in the bust. I liked that Sally Wilson best. She would never let people laugh at her, never let people see her as inconsequential. She would do something about it. When I took the suit off I threw it on the floor. The old Sally Wilson would have hung it back up for fear of reprisals. Sometimes, at Miriam's, when I wasn't thinking straight, I thought Larry might come for me if I left my clothes on the chair instead of putting them away. At night, I would lay stiff in my bed, thinking that I was back at Mulberry Crescent, and he would be coming through the door at any moment raging about the mess I'd made. Funny how sometimes you let your mind convince you of things you know can't be true, but they paralyse you anyway. I've done enough of that now. From now on my thoughts will be yellow and gold and warm, like the sun. Who am I kidding? I might manage a beige, or a cream but sunshine yellow is definitely beyond me at the moment. Even so, no longer will I let people, who think they are better than me, win.

I'm back at Miriam's now after the whole 'Cakehole' debacle. She says we are going to have a chat in a bit, she's pickling onions and is at a crucial stage. "If I don't get them in now, lovey, I'll have to sterilise all the ruddy jars again," she told me about twenty minutes ago. I'm glad she's busy. It gives me a chance to construct what I am going to say. I don't really know why I bolted to The Cakehole. I can see you're waiting for me to say it's for old time's sake. It's familiar, that I felt a connection to it. Oh! I used to feel that way, a long time ago. When Miriam and I would sit on the shabby baby poo-coloured draylon banquette, in the big bay window and watch the people of Winston Green go by. We'd make a coffee last as long as possible, delaying the inevitable minefield waiting for me at the house where I lived. Meeting Larry there was, I thought, the icing on the rather good Danish pastry they made there. But of course, as usual, I got it wrong. After a while, his controlling ways kind of put paid to any yellow feelings I may have had about the place, and over the years I've lost any shred of sentimentality towards it I used to have. After Barney, I found it hard to find warm fuzzy feelings about anything. Now, with all that's happened. I find it impossible. I think the real reason I went there today, is because it has a very solid wall at the back. There is only one table there and it's usually empty, because it's in a little dark corner by the loos. Aubrey and Beryl, the owners of The Cakehole have tried to brighten it up with a red pendant light and a sixty watt bulb. It's done little to lift the gloom. I think the scarlet glow bouncing off the table looks like blood. Miriam has finished pickling, and there is a dark stain resembling the map of Africa on her apron, next to the chocolate streak she got at this morning's baking session. I will miss the sweet stodgy brownies and in particular her devil's food cake when I'm forced out of here on Monday.

Now I've drawn a line under Audrey Brown, I feel free to focus on what is important. I don't think Megan and Saint Brian realise how fundamental Miriam is to my life. If they think I can leave here, go on about my business without her, they don't know how wrong they are, she has been my centre since the age of eleven. She fought my battles at school in lieu of absent parents. She warned me not to get involved with Larry from the start. She has wiped the blood, the tears, the snot from my face when he was at his worst and it's Miriam I need going forward. I can't do it without her, I won't let that happen. Oh I know she doesn't want me to leave. She's bowing under pressure from the powers that be. We rub along together nicely her and me. I feel something akin to what I felt about Barney for her. Perhaps I do have the ability to feel something after all, whether it's love? I couldn't tell you. On the other hand. Maybe the feeling I have towards her is one of ownership.

Right! I feel compelled to write another letter now. To give Megan more background about my life to date now I know she reads them. Maybe then she'll begin to understand who I am, what I've come from and why I do the things I do, and who knows? Maybe one day she will leave me alone.

Miriam

I'm sat here opposite Sal, and I realise I don't know her anymore. She looks the same but her antics today were, well, mental. I know she's been through the wars an' all that, and I know about Audrey Brown, but that's not much to show for thirty-odd years of friendship, and because she never tells me anything, I can't ruddy help her. I think I must have given her me entire family history over the years. Granted, a lot of what I shared was to fill the long silences, when what she called the grey descended on her, when she got so far down all she could see was black, I would take her back to mine, where the racket and the laughter made her feel wanted for a while. Sometimes, she would be so far gone, I wondered how we managed to pull her up at all. I never knew what caused it, because she couldn't, or wouldn't say. I've had enough now! This is Sal's last chance to talk to me proper. I'm losing patience if the truth be told. I have me own battles to fight and I can't always drop everything and sort her out anymore. This morning, in the caff, I'd tried to talk her round from whatever it was that was bothering her, but doing that took me away from me husband, who is still recovering, and a mound of ironing that would rival Ben Nevis. I know she's ill and, don't get me wrong, I feel sorry for her, but I'm starting to feel, that it's somebody else's turn to deal with her now. Sally's been with us for just over two months and in that time, instead of becoming closer, we are now poles apart.

I've made a pot of tea and cut a couple of wedges of devil's food cake. Sal's come down from her shower and is sitting at the table scribbling in her notebook – she's always doing that these days. Brian's asleep and I've finished me pickling. I had to do it today if I want them ready for Christmas. They take a good while to turn the deep golden brown colour they need to be to taste just right. Me Gran and me old mam used to pickle. In the war they would pickle everything they could get their hands on. Me mam was always partial to a pickled egg. Gran had her own chickens, so they never went short. Pickling them was the best way to stop them going bad. The eggs, not the chickens you understand. I don't think they ever pickled them, even when one of them stopped laying.

"OK Sal," I say to her, "you've got to talk to me, lovey. I want to help, but if you don't tell me at least some of what's gone on, what can I do? You're going home tomorrow, and we won't have as much time to talk then. Come on, Sally love, give me something."

Sally looked at me, really looked for the first time in ages. I could see the fight going on behind her eyes. She took a deep breath and said, "I had a brother. His name was Jim, he was five years older than me." I was just going to ask what happened to him when she said, "He raped me!" She was searching my face looking for understanding, for anything, but I was so shocked and sad, I squeezed my eyes shut tight to stop the tears from spilling over and Sally lost it. She started smacking her face and pulling her mouse brown hair out by the roots. "I knew you would hate me, that's why I never told you. I didn't want to lose you and now you think I'm dirty. I know you do."

She slid off the chair and went into the foetal position on me lino. The noise she was making broke me heart. I've never moved so quick in me life. I lay on the floor next to her and wrapped her in me arms. "Shusssh my love shussh, it's OK. It's going to be OK. I could never hate you. It wasn't your fault." We rocked together there on me kitchen floor, for what seemed an age. Me back was freezing and I had pins and needles in me bum, but I held on until the screech became a whimper. "Is that why you never told me about your life? Because you thought I wouldn't want anything to do with you?" She nodded. "That couldn't happen, Sal. I only wish you told me at the start, then me, or me mam could have done something about it. We would have helped you. We could have got you away!" Just for a minute, I saw the old Sal. A lonely little kid, that I now know was scared to death every minute of her life, having to put up with all sorts being done to her, all the while saying nothing to nobody. I have never felt so guilty in me natural born days. Why the ruddy hell didn't I guess that something like that was going on? And how didn't I cotton on she had a brother? The old Sal slipped away again, her eyes blank. I knew that was all I was going to get from her today. Bloody hell though, that was enough to get me head around, that's for sure. She got up quickly from the floor and made to run. I had a bit more difficulty, getting from me knees to standing, so I called, "Sally Ruth Wilson! Stay right there," and she did. I was a bit startled. I didn't expect her to listen to me, but I hauled myself up on the back of a chair and sat down at the table. "Your tea's getting cold, and I didn't cut your favourite cake for it to go to waste, come on, eat up."

Sally sat back down at the table and picked up her cup. She didn't drink from it, she just held on to the warmth as if her life depended on it. She assumed the usual position, head down. Closed off. I reverted back to when she did this at school. I started talking. I told her about me appointment at the chiropodist for me bunion. I gabbled on about when she came to our old house. Me mam giving us fistfuls of biscuits, and about my brother Tom and his family emigrating to Australia. Slowly but surely she turned to look at me. "I could never hate you, Sal. It wasn't your fault. You were just a kid. You couldn't have done anything to stop him, lovey. I just wish you'd have told me." I was just about to ask if she knew where he was now, when her arm shot out and grabbed my wrist.

"You won't ever leave me, will you?" she whispered. Now what the bloody hell was I going to say? Twenty minutes ago, I was going to do just that. Not completely you understand. I was just going to pull back a bit. Let her stand on her own two feet, but now? What the bloody hell could I do? I felt trapped if I'm honest, but I patted Sally's arm and because I couldn't answer the question without telling a fib said, "Everything's going to be OK, you'll see." I wasn't sure even that was true. We weren't kids anymore and we each had our baggage to carry. It's just that I'd been carrying Sally's, even though I didn't have a clue what it was, for a long, long time. It was ruddy heavy to tell you the truth and it was time to put it down.

Megan

I'm at home eating cottage pie with my noisy family. Leo and Gina are laughing about something to do with llamas, and Charlie is sitting here picking out all the carrots from a cottage pie. He says he is saving them for the very hungry caterpillar, because, ever since I told him that caterpillars are vegetarian, he's been using it as an excuse not to eat his vegetables. He'll go far my grandson. I called his bluff however, when I told him we were having fish and chips the next day.

"Yippee!" he shouted. He soon stopped, when I said that chips were made from potato and that potatoes were classed as vegetables. I told him that unless little boys ate all their veg, they couldn't have chips. We couldn't help but smile, when he shovelled those carrots into his mouth as if his life depended on it. "I think the very hungry caterpillar is full up now, Nanny," he said, gravy dripping down his chin. "Can I have chips tomorrow?"

"Of course you can, Bear," I chuckled.

"Yippee! yelled Charlie.

When my beautiful grandson was tucked up in bed, dreaming of chips no doubt, my thoughts turned to what had happened earlier in the day. I was getting a little exasperated at Sally's refusal to engage with me. Her little performance and subsequent escape had disrupted Miriam's day, and made mine a whole lot longer. After finding her at the cafe, it took almost an hour to get her back to Miriam's. I had to write it all up in a report while it was still fresh in my mind. Normally, I would take notes that would jog my memory, but today, I had to fly by the seat of my pants. There wasn't time to take notes. I must say Miriam did a wonderful job of talking Sally down. Obviously, she knows her much better than I do, and was able to say the right things needed to get her out of the cafe. The problem came when she saw my car instead of Miriam's. She pulled back as if to go back into The Cakehole, her eyes wide with fear. Again Miriam came to the rescue. She held her and talked quietly to her until she calmed down. I think she thought she wasn't going back to Miriam's, but instead I was taking her to The Chimes. It took another ten minutes for Sally to believe she was not entering the nut house as she called it and allow Miriam to lead her to my car.

When Larry was first killed, Sally was 'non compos mentis' and couldn't have cared less whether The Chimes was on the cards or not. But since then, she feels safe at her friend's and the hospital has become a real threat. More so than going to prison. Because, in jail when her sentence was served, she knew she would have Miriam to help and support her. Sally saw The Chimes as a place where families put people to forget about them. She had good reason. Miriam had told me a story just last week about Sally's grandmother being admitted there. It went like this…

..."When Sal's Granny went senile they found her a place at The Chimes. It was called the sanatorium in them days. Anyhow. On the day she was to go, Sal's dad pushed his old mam in her wheelchair into the reception thingy, turned on his heel and left her with all her bags. No goodbye. No cuddle. No nothing, poor love. The family never went to visit, didn't even send a card on her birthday. That's no way to treat a frail, potty old lady, is it? Bless her. Anyhow. She never came out of that place. She died there all alone and scared too, I shouldn't wonder. What a way to treat anyone, let alone a member of your own ruddy family. I wouldn't treat our Garry's dog Raquel like that. Sally's been terrified the same thing will happen to her an' all. She's petrified she'll be forgotten, and no one, namely me, you understand, will care if she lives or dies. It's the only story she ever told me about her family, so she must have been afraid of ending her days alone, even back then, poor love...

...Whilst I understand Sally's reluctance to relive her past, to have to put it all into words, I feel I have a duty to Miriam to try and move things along. To give her and Brian much needed time to themselves. I now know that I misjudged Sally's dependence on Miriam. For that reason I am stepping up my meetings with her to three times a week, but I'm taking them out of Miriam's home and into my office in Winston Green. As things stand I believe Miriam's presence, instead of making it easier for Sally to talk to me, gives her a reason not to, in case Miriam should overhear and reject her. Miriam told me that at the weekend, however, Sally, when put under pressure, told her about her brother Jim. It had escalated quickly. It ended with Sally losing it on the floor of the kitchen, and Miriam having to deal with the fallout. Again. So I decided it would be best for everyone if we took the meetings down town.

Sally seems to be fraying at the edges, which I can identify with in a way. I'm much the same after a hard week. But where I can reason myself out of my funk. Sally seems to be unravelling at an alarming rate. One minute she's lucid, conversing readily about things that don't matter, like the weather, or what she's having for dinner, and the next, it's like flicking a light switch. Her eyes turn hard and fixed and obsidian black, bringing to mind those wingless flies. She mutters to herself, all set to bolt if you dare to bring up anything she can't, or won't, talk about.

I've taken advice from Carolyne Speed, a trusted mentor I had when I was wet behind the ears. She's retired now, but is still there on the end of the phone and I trust her opinion more than any other. It was her who taught me to listen in a different way, to read between the lines and not make assumptions. I gave her an outline of the case, mentioning no names. She suggested I bring things to a head. Give Sally no choice but to expand on what she has written in her letters. She said I need to gently make it clear that if she won't talk to me, it could be taken out of my hands and a medical doctor would take over. I have been pussyfooting around her somewhat. I can see that now, but I thought, with all that she's been through, she could do with me cutting her some slack. That is clearly not working is it? If I'm going to help her, I need a different tack. The thing is though, it could take years to help someone like Sally just three times a week. A big commitment, even for a much younger person. Me?

I don't I have it in me. If she wants me to help her, she needs to start talking. Fast.

Sally

I'm sure Miriam keeps looking at me funny. She never did that before I let slip about Jim. Oh, she's all smiles and everything, but sometimes I see it out the corner of my eye. That look of pity. I never wanted that from her. Why do you think I kept my early life quiet all these years. She was the only person in the world I could relax with. I could park the Sally with all the baggage, which came from living where I did, and be the Sally that laughed and joked with her and her brothers and sisters. The Sally that drank tea and ate biscuits at the Bullens, as if she didn't have a care in the world. That has gone now, all smashed to pieces. Miriam knows for sure now, that I am damaged goods. Oh I'm sure she still loves me and will always look after me, but which Sally is she doing it for now? The Sally of old, or the one she just met. The broken one.

I can't stop the past invading my brain. I've tried to block it out, but the overwhelming shame I've carried since finding that little black book keeps pushing and goading me so much so, that the colours. Red for anger. Yellow for calm. Purple for indecision, are all merging together making brown and I can't think straight. I know that going back to Mulberry Crescent is what I need to do. It will make Megan think I can cope on my own, but then I'll only have myself for company and there will be no distraction from the flickery silent movie running on and on in my head. Even so, I have to give the illusion of normality. I have to show them that even someone as fractured as I am can manage without Miriam there to stop me self-destructing. Maybe things can get better. Maybe if I give Miriam a break from all the madness, things will go back to normal and she will realise it isn't the same without me. I know that I am the most important thing in her life. She has known me the longest out of anybody, and I know she will choose me when push comes to shove. It will soon, mark my words. I guess showing her that I am coping at Mulberry Crescent will make her proud of me. I've always been good at bluffing. I've made a career out of it.

Megan has moved our sessions away from Miriam's. I was worried when she first suggested it, but now I have had time to mull it over, I think it's for the best. I know I have to give her something more than I've touched on in my letters if she's going to deem me capable of living alone, but the thought of just me rattling around in the house where I killed my husband terrifies me. On the other hand, having people in my home watching my every move, coming shopping with me, invading my thoughts, is even worse. I can't put my plans into action when I have an audience. No. I have to do this. I have to make her think I'm ready to go it alone.

I don't even think about Audrey Brown anymore, I did that to death. I know I could never change the fact that Larry thought she was superior to me in every way, and by stealing her things and going through sex scenarios in my head I was only torturing myself. I am trying to separate the colours in my head, to find the yellow and hold on to it for all I'm worth, which isn't much to be fair. So what if she scored an eight, six whole points more than me. It didn't matter if she had a slim figure and a great bum, or if she left me in the dust in the shagging stakes. I'm over it, honestly. I mean it. I'm completely finished with all that. You don't believe me, do you? It's true, I haven't been there in days. I need to put all my energies into appearing normal and getting Megan off my back. What is normal anyway? I sure as hell don't know, I don't think I ever did, but let's face it, I didn't have the best role models. A drunk, a rapist and an absentee father. I didn't stand a chance, did I?

I've decided to be a bit more forthcoming with Megan. She will only keep on pressing on the sore bits until I do. She wants me to talk about the stuff I'm writing in the letters. I thought the whole point of putting it down on paper was so I wouldn't have to say the words out loud, but she says they were only ever a starting point. A kind of springboard to help me sort out my feelings going forward instead of always dwelling on the past. No need for that now. I'm coming to the end of what has been a life of pain, fear and lies because everybody lies. Everybody. Even me.

Miriam

I'll tell you something! I never thought I'd live to see this day after all we've been through. It's been bloody hard. The weight of all Sally's shenanigans looked set to bury me and Brian, but we've come through it, even if it's taken nearly every bit of strength we had. It's Monday and Sally has finally agreed to go back to Mulberry Crescent, after a bit of persuasion from Dr Megan I shouldn't wonder. The first part of last week, I truly thought they'd have to take her to the funny farm, and we all know how she feels about that place. She'd started to peer through her fringe again and doing that weird little two-step when she walked. She hardly spoke, acting all shifty with her shoulders right up to her earholes. On Thursday though, it changed as if by magic. When she came back from her session with Dr Megan, you'd have no clue that she'd been through anything like what she has over the last few months. Especially not stabbing her husband. It seemed as if the old Sal was back. She's still strange, you understand, she's always been like that, but at least she was talking normally again, and not muttering about lists and Lycra. She still stuck to me like glue, that didn't change, but right out of the blue she suggested we go shopping for a few new bits and pieces for her house. Sally ruddy hated shopping. The crowds, the noise. She reacted to it all. I said it was lovely that she wanted me to go with her, but I was a bit tired, and I was, bone tired. Our Garry came round to see us when Sally was out and he said I'd aged ten years, cheeky beggar. It's true though. I'm a shadow of me former self. And Brian? A stiff wind would blow him over. Garry wants to bloody kill Sally for bringing all this to our door, but it wasn't her fault really. I was the one that invited her to stay. One thing's for sure. If I'd known then what I know now, I never in a million years have done it.

Sally was packing. She didn't tell me what happened in the meeting with Dr Megan, but she said she knew now she had to go back. She said she wanted to build a new life. To try and put the past behind her. I was a bit sceptical to tell you the truth. What a turnaround! It was far too quick to my mind. Only last week, I thought she was on the last train to LaLa land and now this? I didn't know how she was going to manage. She can only just cope with making a cup of tea these days. I know it sounds horrible, but it was someone else's problem now, I'd done me bit. We all had. It was up to her now. I keep turning what she told me about her brother that day over and over in me mind. I don't remember what came out of my mouth on that freezing floor, but I do remember being scared to death of saying something that would set her off again. As it was she'd caught me on the cheek when she was flailing her arms about, trying to pull her hair out. She didn't notice and I didn't react. After what she'd just told me, I don't think she was even aware she was there with me in my little kitchen. Her brain was fried. She'd calmed down eventually though. I just kept whispering in her ear, just talking rubbish really but she seemed to be listening. Afterwards, Sally kept asking me if I thought she was somehow to blame for what Jim did to her. I told her not to talk daft, that it was out of her control. What she told me that day is probably the tip of the iceberg, but I'm glad she won't be here to tell me anymore of what happened to her. Which is a bit selfish of me, I know, but I wouldn't be able to change anything, poor love. That's why I'm taking a very large step back and leaving it to the professionals. In fact, I'm going as far as I can go without abandoning her altogether. As I said, I've done my bit. I miss Jill and Mandy, I miss my cuddles with Sarah. All I need now is a little bit of normal.

I told Dr Megan what happened that day. She probably already knows, she's just not allowed to tell me. On the one hand, I understand that, but on the other hand it would have been good to have a bit of a heads up, so I would know how damaged she really is. I don't mean that in a horrible way, of course I don't. Those terrible things had been done to an innocent child and it wasn't her fault. But I've been her crutch for the last thirty-five years, and if I keep going down this road, it'll be me what needs looking after in the funny farm. I'm chuckling to meself now, cos in me head, I see me in one room in The Chimes and Sal in the room next door. I don't know why I'm laughing. I can't think of anything worse. Thank God Brian was asleep when it all kicked off that day. I had me hands full with Sally in a heap under the table without him shouting and banging on the ceiling making that God awful lampshade shake. He hasn't been sleeping properly since the heart attacks bless him. Yesterday he told me that he'd actually been feeling ill for a good while before it happened. It'd coincided with Sally coming to stay. I think having her at our place, when they've never really got on, stressed him out. To make matters worse, Brian watching me run ragged, and not being well enough to help, dented his male pride a bit, and we all know what comes after pride, don't we?

Dr Megan is coming for Sally in a minute. I'm staying out of the way, I said my goodbyes to her last night. She wasn't really with it to tell you the truth. Her eyes were jiggling about in her head and her body was jerking all over the place, like she had Saint Vitus dance. I don't ruddy blame her, it was a lot to take in. Everything would change for Sal after today. She kept saying that she would see me tomorrow. I didn't want to lie to her, so I didn't say anything. I just changed the subject. Dr Megan thought it best I didn't go with them to Mulberry Crescent and I'd agreed straight away. Sally would have hidden behind me, used me as a shield. It's what she's been used to, I know that now. Protecting her all those years hadn't helped her really. I did my best, but I was hardly qualified and it made her dependent on me, and less able to sort her own problems out. Dr Megan said it was time for Sally to face her demons. I thought to meself Sal would have to be ruddy Mike Tyson to fight all she's got going on in her head, but I didn't say it out loud. She's got people that are going to work with her and get her settled so she won't be totally on her own. Sally was adamant she didn't want anyone staying in the house with her, but she accepted help with the shopping and a bit of cleaning. That tickled me, because you won't find a better cleaner than Sal. She's had years to perfect it. Larry was a sod for that. Everything had to be spotless or else. I didn't know if she would let someone take that over, or whether she would go behind them and do it all again out of habit. Time would tell. I wished her all the luck in the world, but I need to focus on my own family now. Did I tell you I am going to be a granny.

Megan

I'm going to ring Moira in a minute. I haven't spoken to her in a while but, when I'm in this frame of mind, I need her quiet reassurance and sense of reason. She is my oldest and dearest friend and I miss her terribly. She lives about three hundred miles away and I only see her once a year but, as she is so fond of telling me, that is what a telephone is for. Today Sally goes home and I, quite frankly, am dreading it. She seems too calm and resigned to her fate and that's what's worrying me. It feels too easy. I would at least have expected some reticence about leaving Miriam. This could go two ways. We could expect fireworks or she could put up the barrier I was so used to seeing and go quietly. Neither Miriam or I knew which one we were going to get. That's why I need to speak to Moira. I can't tell her the specifics of the case of course, but I won't need to, she can read me like a book. She will know the right words to say to bolster me, to give me the strength to deal with whatever arises.

Sally has given me another letter. There is a part of me that wants to tear it open now, but another part worries it will open up a whole new can of worms for me to make sense of. I'm supposed to know how to help the poor woman. After all, I have been in this job a very long time, but Sally's reluctance to engage when we meet makes it extremely difficult to discuss the revelations that keep on coming in each new missive. Honestly, I've thought about giving up and letting someone else who isn't approaching retirement and has dodgy knees take over. But I owe it to both Sally and Miriam to see it through. They have both been through so much recently. Miriam, nearly losing Brian like that, has shaken that wonderful lady to the core. I am extremely frustrated that I can't share the contents of the letters with her. I think, had she known about some of the things Sally had to endure in her early life, she wouldn't have been broadsided by her friend's increasingly erratic behaviour and would have felt better equipped to deal with it.

I've had a long chat with Moira and she has reminded me that, despite being old and decrepit, I am actually quite a strong person, one that very rarely gives up, so I've taken it on board and decided not to be so hard on myself. I would deal with whatever comes when we get to Mulberry Crescent and so would Sally...

...She was too calm. When we walked through the door to the house where so much had happened, there was just a slight hesitation, a small step back, but then she walked in as if she'd just been out to the shops for a bag of sugar. As she moved down the hallway, she walked over the place where Larry had lain without missing a beat. She put her bag down on the kitchen counter and slid her coat off her shoulders. Sally looked at me as if to say, you can go now, but I wasn't satisfied that she would be all right on her own just yet. The lady who was bringing

Sally's shopping wasn't due for half an hour, so I said, "Why don't I put the kettle on and we can have a cup of tea before we get you settled?" She gave me a tight smile and said "I'll do it," then turned her back on me. I took that as another dismissal, another 'I can manage on my own thanks', but I stayed right where I was. It was a test really, to see if me going against her wishes would result in a meltdown. It didn't. She was ice cold. I didn't like where this was going. I couldn't stay if she didn't want me to, but I felt it was important to be there when the home help came. I wanted to introduce Mrs Waters as someone Sally could trust.

It went as well as it could have done under the circumstances. Sally's slightly chilly demeanour toward Mrs Waters was a step up from the Arctic conditions she displayed earlier toward me. Her attitude though did nothing to dent the woman's warm sunny personality. "Please call me Debbie," she said brightly. "It's a pleasure to meet you, shall I put the kettle on?"

Sally nodded stiffly and we all had another cup of tea. Debbie put the shopping away, all the while chatting to, well, me mostly, because Sally hardly uttered a word. I could see she was looking a bit tired and overwhelmed, which was understandable, when you took into account what had happened here and that two hours ago she was still at Miriam's, her place of safety. From now on she would, for the most part, be alone. We both left soon after Debbie had confirmed the dates and times she would be coming. It was clear Sally needed to be on her own for a while. She needed to get used to being back in the house where her husband met his end. I hoped we were doing the right thing. Time would tell.

Sally

This letter has been difficult to write. Oh, not because I find it hard to spill my guts any more, on paper. I don't really. It's just that I'm getting bored with it. I know you say it's easier for me to write things down. Well. Get ready. Here goes…

I killed my mother. Oh, it's of no loss to the world, believe me, and it happened a long time ago, when I was a teenager. I had gone back to the house where I used to live a few weeks after I'd met Larry. I'd been staying round his place for a while because, quite frankly, I couldn't stand living with Mother a moment longer than I had to. Larry shared the flat with a mate, but he was always round his girlfriend's, so we had the place to ourselves mostly. The parents still had my birth certificate which I would need to get a passport. Larry was going to take me to Spain, another foreign country I didn't know anybody in. I didn't want to go, but if I hadn't agreed, he would have gone without me and I didn't want that either. I'd had enough of being alone.

I pushed open the rusty gate, It protested loudly, announcing my entry with a deep graunching sound. I wondered if Mother could hear it, but the curtains went un-twitched. As I moved down the garden path, the prison I never expected to see again loomed large. It felt exactly the same to me then, as it did when I was a child. It was never a home. It was a place to be feared, and I felt instantly as shackled to it as I did when I came in from school every day of my young life. The garden, rife with weeds and brambles that pricked and poked the untended soil with spiky fingers, spread themselves along the ground with menace. Big, grey flint rocks stuck out of the ground at all angles like the plates of a stegosaurus. I remember now. There was never any colour. Never any warmth. Never any happy there. I knocked on the back door and as usual no one came, so I tried the handle. It was unlocked. I could smell the alcohol as soon as I stepped foot into the kitchen. It made me gag and a slew of terrible memories assaulted my head. I shook it violently, so they would fly out my ears and be gone forever. No such luck. I was burning to get out of there but I was on a quest. Nothing would stop me getting that piece of paper. I didn't have much to show for seventeen years on this planet, but that document was the key to my shiny new life, and I wanted it so badly I could taste it. I thought I'd remembered where they kept the important papers so I went there first. They weren't there.

The acrid smell of piss and vinegar was getting stronger, so I followed it up the stairs to the front bedroom. Mother lay, prostrate on the filthy bed snoring her head off. Oh God, she disgusted me for so many reasons. I prodded her arm with the tip of my finger hard. She stirred slightly then went back to sleep. Drool ran out of her open mouth and down her cheek like a tiny river. She had been sick on her housecoat, which looked like it had been lived in every day since I left a few months before. I'll tell you the next bit in a minute, I just need to take the rubbish out. It's Friday and I don't want to miss the bin men. I'm trying to be useful, so that Miriam won't send me away. Since I told her I was raped, she's treated me with kid gloves, been extra nice. See. I told you people would treat me differently. I was right!

I'm back now, I just caught them. They don't wait for anybody these people. I saw old Steve Whichelow struggling down his drive with his wheelie bin last week and they drove right past him. Anyhow! Enough about that, back to the last time I ever saw that house, back to the first time I ever came out on top. I left her bedroom and went to where my father slept. They hadn't co-habited in years. There was never any emotional connection between them. Now you can see where I get it from! I don't really blame my father for not wanting sex with someone that pickled herself in alcohol and rarely showered, but I don't blame her either, for not wanting to lie with someone who had all the warmth of a polar icecap. It couldn't have worked between them anyway. All Mother's affections were directed towards my brother, so she was happy with separate rooms.

I reached down under the bed, careful not to pull all the years of detritus down onto the sticky carpet. I figured that this would be the only other place they would keep them and Bingo! My fingers brushed the old brown case that had always held the important papers. I opened it quick. The whiff of old libraries crept up my nose, a welcome respite from the stench of the house. My birth certificate was in amongst old, yellowing bills and receipts for unknown transactions. I took it out and glanced at it. My first name seemed to fade away and all I could see was Agatha. Oh I know it wasn't really there, but I just couldn't shake it. I didn't mind Ruth though. I wished it could have been my first name, but it was hastily added at the registry office, because they were asked for one. Ruth was the name of the manager of the off-licence Mother used. She was nice though and often gave me a packet of sweets, or a bag of ready salted crisps when I went in. Of course, you couldn't get away with sending children to buy booze these days. I folded the paper up tightly, sealing my name inside. I put it in my pocket, turned to leave and came face to face with Mother.

"What the hell are you doing here?" she slurred. "Get out of my house, you good for nothing piece of shit." I thought that was the pot calling the kettle black so, I didn't dignify the remark with a reply. Instead I went to push past her, to get as far away from her as possible. Was Spain far enough? Was Antarctica? I didn't think so. She stood firm in the doorway, arms and legs splayed, blocking the exit like a black widow spider and my anger went straight to red. I pushed her out of the doorway with a strength I didn't know I had. She stayed upright and pushed against me with all her twenty-stone frame. So there we were. A Mexican standoff, each pushing the other back and forth. I didn't realise she was so close to the top stair, so when she tumbled backwards down the whole flight, I was shocked. I called her name, but didn't get an answer. When I got to the bottom of the stairs, I soon saw the reason. She lay at such an angle she looked like the number seven. Her legs bent sideways at the knees, her head lolling to the left. There was nothing anyone could do, so I stepped over her and walked out of the door and out into the whisky-free air. That chapter of my life was done and dusted. I was just seventeen. I was numb. Feel free to judge me. It could have just as easily been me that was tipped headlong down the flight of filthy, uncarpeted stairs, she was pushing just as hard as I was. It was anyone's game.

Miriam hasn't relented like I thought she would. I'm definitely going back to Mulberry Crescent tomorrow. Oh, being alone doesn't bother me. I have been my whole life if you think about it. I just hoped that when I met Larry that would change, but he put the kibosh on that. I didn't fight back though, did I? Well until I did, with a knife with a stainless steel blade and a *rubber handle. We got them as a free gift when we bought the cooker. It said on the box that they were sharp and could be a hazard, bla bla bla, but I can see why the manufacturer didn't print 'could be used to kill someone' as part of the user manual. Oh, I'm not naive. I know he would have left me eventually, for Audrey Brown or Nina big tits. I prevented that at least. To tell you the truth, even when he was here, he wasn't really. I had more lonely times throughout my marriage than I ever had as a kid, because when I was young, I had Miriam and the Bullen family, and Barney, for a while. Of course Miriam was still in my life, but what with her being with Saint Brian and me with Larry, I saw her a lot less than I liked. I'm sure she felt the same. I've got to go now. Make of this letter what you will. I can smell the dinner cooking. We're having lasagne and chips for dinner and Miriam makes the best lasagne in the world.*

Miriam

I've just had a ruddy good cry. Brian thinks I should be doing the Macarena round the kitchen in me pinny. He's all set to hang out the flags now that Sally has gone, but I am worried about her still. Brian says she's a grown woman and she can take care of herself. I know he's right really, after all she has come this far on her own. She puts a lot on the fact that she had me and me family to help her out when she was a kid, and she did, but it was an hour or two each night after school. All the rest of the time she had to run the gauntlet of her bloody crazy family. She must have been so lonely, poor love. When I get me bearings, and I can move without me shadow, I know that I'll be happy to have me house back. I must admit it has been a bit like walking through a minefield some days, having Sally here. Brian and me were constantly weaving round her, trying not to say something that would send her skyward. It wasn't easy, I can tell you! Now, I can make a cuppa anytime I like without getting cold looks from the tea police. I will miss her in a way though. She's been here nigh on four months, or a quarter of a bloody year as Brian keeps saying, and that's a long time in anyone's book, especially with all the baggage she brought with her.

Dr Megan says the CPS are close to making a decision about what's to happen to Sal. I hope and pray they let her go, it isn't as if she did it deliberately. Larry was a bastard. There's no other way to describe him, except maybe a narcissist. In all the years she was with him, I never heard him say a nice word to Sally and it wore her down to a stub. I remember one time she was a bit late home. I had dropped her off round the corner. We didn't want him to twig we were still friends. If he'd looked out the window it wouldn't have been good at all for Sally. I didn't just drive away. I fiddled about with me seat belt for a minute or two, till she got to her gate, then I pootled down the road to turn in the cul-de-sac. As I got a couple of houses up from Sal's, she was still on the doorstep. The door opened with a crash and I saw him grab Sal by her hair. He yanked her inside, smacking her nose on the door frame as she went. What could I do? If I'd gone in there shouting the odds when I wasn't supposed to be there, Larry could have killed her for lying to him. I just had to leave her there and keep driving. I don't know how the ruddy hell I got home, I couldn't see the road for the tears. True to form, he'd scuttled off to the pub that night and I had to take Sally to the hospital. I'd have been long gone if he'd been my husband, but then I had a completely different upbringing to hers. I was always taught to stand up for meself and others. I wouldn't have taken the crap Larry dished out. Mind you, Sally's mam wasn't good to her, to say the least, but I always had encouragement from mine and she's the best anyone could wish for. She puts us kids first, and it's made us stronger, more confident somehow. Me dad were wonderful too. We counted. We were important. And we were loved. We always had a ruddy houseful an' all, but there was a lot of fun and laughter and people to confide in, at Sal's, there wasn't any at all.

Dr Megan is going to ring in a while and let me know how it all went. She said they found a nice Lady called Debbie, who would be there to do the shopping and that a few times a week. I feel a bit better knowing that Sal won't have to cope all on her own. It's going to be different, for both of us, but in a good way. I'll have less washing for starters and Just cooking for me and Brian from now on will be a lot cheaper too. If there's just us, I can get away with buying one pack of chops and whatnot, but when there's an extra person, then you are straying into two pack territory, because one would never be enough. They did give us a bit of extra money, you know, for having Sal, but it never goes far these days, does it? Brian is wobbling the ugly lampshade again. I can hear his dulcet tones. I'll have to go and see what he wants. I expect his book has slipped off the bed again. I told him. I said, if this keeps happening, I'm going to put him in a ruddy cot. Me legs have developed muscles I didn't know I had since Brian has been consigned to the bedroom. It hasn't done anything for me figure just yet though. I live in hope!

Megan

Today has been a really hard day. Not just because I have just had to leave Sally at Mulberry Crescent on her own, but because my joints are seizing up. I've been in pain all day and despite anti-inflammatories hastily taken at Miriam's, they are now getting to screaming point. One piece of good news is that the Crown Prosecution Service have decided not to charge Sally with anything. They took a long time examining all the evidence and decided that she acted in self-defence. They took into account the witness statement from Miriam about the abuse she had suffered at Larry's hand. It's the right result. Maybe now without that hanging over her head, she'll feel able to open up a little and let me in.

I can hear Gina calling everyone to dinner, Charlie's yelling yippee. I think chips are on the menu. The company round the table will be a welcome distraction from worrying about Sally, and with some food on board I can take stronger painkillers. Something's changed with me. I don't usually worry about my patients like this. I have a duty of care and I help them all I can, but I've never had sleepless nights worrying about them, like I have with

Sally Wilson or even Miriam come to that. I want to read the letter she gave me before I finish for the evening, but it's my turn to put Charlie to bed. He has decided that we have read *The Very Hungry Caterpillar* thirty times. He tells me the caterpillar has eaten lots and lots of food, not to mention a little boy's tummy every night, so it will turn into a very beautiful butterfly indeed. We are moving on to *The Gruffalo*.

Cuddled up together on Charlie's tiny bed, I read it for the first time. He didn't know what to make of it in the beginning, but when he realised the Gruffalo wasn't really scary, he enjoyed it very much. In fact, I had to read it twice before he would settle down to sleep. I have always had that rule. Only two stories a night. If I hadn't, Charlie would run rings around me and I would be there till all hours. He knows, and accepts the rule, but it doesn't stop him trying to push the envelope a few times. Tonight I held fast. I still had work to do and my eighty-year-old body began to push ninety. I needed to get my feet up to stop my knees complaining, so I kissed his downy head and turned on his nightlight. Immediately the room took on a feeling only an inky blue sky could provide. As I closed the door, a red and gold nebula floated past his little face draping him in a rainbow of soft colour. On the ceiling the planets and the stars kept watch over the most precious thing in my world.

This letter is the most complex to date. I've had to read it quite a few times to try and understand it properly. Sally has blatantly told me she killed her mother, but that it was an accident. What do I do with that? As I said before, I believe she is telling me the truth in her letters, but her perception of the events could be so very different to mine, especially as it is coloured by the neglectful, and quite honestly horrific upbringing she's had. I'd like to say I was shocked at the way Sally relayed events, but I wasn't. The matter-of-fact delivery was typical of her. Her mother was dead. Full stop. No need to phone an ambulance. Was there an element of psychopathy? Or was it learned behaviour from the ones who were supposed to protect her? To Sally, her mother became like Barney then, like the flies. Irrelevant. She had never experienced love or comfort from her mother so, in turn showed no emotion when she saw her broken body at the bottom of the stairs. The fact that Sally uses the words 'I killed my mother' didn't mean she had done it deliberately, but it didn't rule it out. Her curt explanation blamed the woman for starting things by using her size to overpower her much smaller daughter, trapping her in the room. Sally deals with trauma or violence like you or I would ponder over a shopping list. She puts the hurt, the pain and the terror in categories, just as we would with meat and fish. Crossing each one out as she stores it away in the filing system in her brain, where it can't overwhelm her. I'm sure she must have a whole library of beatings, rapes and unimaginable loneliness locked in that head of hers, and for that, I feel truly sorry. I could picture Sally pushing against her mother, pushing against the squalor and the smell of the place she grew up in. I hoped, that in telling me about that awful day, she was at last, putting her trust in me and I sincerely hoped I wouldn't let her down. I don't need to file Sally's letters with the police as she hasn't been charged with any crime, but they would be safely stowed in my locked cabinet where I could find them should anything change. Examining every word carefully, at times, I could feel her apprehension. When she spoke about Spain and Antarctica, places far away from Winston Green, where she knew no one, but might yet be forced to go. It linked back to her childhood, being pulled along by her father, to places she wasn't ready to visit, being made to do things she wasn't willing to do. The clipped sentences felt like armour to me, a way of giving her protection as she stepped back in time, into that house. I wondered what was going to happen when she was finally made to confront everything her life had thrown at her. Would her armour hold, or would it fail and push her right back to being that little girl and break her. I hoped and prayed Sally was stronger than that. That she would come through all the trauma, a lighter, stronger, happier person.

My knees were so sore that I felt like using my dad's rusty old chainsaw to alleviate the problem but, instead, I took some more painkillers in the hope I would get some sleep. You never know? Miracles happen every day. I woke in the early hours and had an epiphany. I knew in that moment, Sally would be my last ever client as a psychiatrist. If the pain was almost unbearable now, Lord knows what new heights it could reach in the next year or two. The specialists have been talking about knee replacements for a while now. I've held off, wanting to get to retirement under my own steam not with the aid of a whole series of nuts and bolts, but now, I just want the horrific pain to end. I'll call my consultant in the morning. I just hope I can hold out long enough to see Sally's case through. I can't rely on Miriam to help anymore. The poor thing is almost as burnt out as I am. She deserves to live a quiet life with Brian, especially now they are going to be grandparents. By taking her case I have a duty to Sally, to help her to move forward, but in order to do that I have to do something for me first. New knees it is.

Sally

So that's it! I'm alone again. I couldn't wait to see the back of Megan and Debbie but, once I'd slammed the front door behind them, part of me wished I hadn't been so hasty. Oh I don't mind being on my own, I have a degree in it. It's just that my eye keeps landing on the spot where Larry left this world. To be honest, I'm glad that he's dead, but my mind keeps seeing him still lying there, and if I can see him as clear as day what is to stop him rising up and hurting me all over again?

I think I made a good show of being their version of normal while they were here. I must have done, or Megan would never have left. When we came in, I'd walked through Larry, making sure not to do my one step back thing and went about filling the kettle. Making three cups of builders' tea grounded me. I was used to being tea lady at Miriam's and if I closed my eyes, I could have been in her bright kitchen with Radio Two in the background. She loved that I made the tea. Saint Brian was a big drain on her most of the time, so it was one less thing for her to do. I'm sure she would have preferred it just to be the two of us, but there is a bit in the marriage vows that says for better or for worse so I guess she felt she had to honour it. I did too, although mine was mostly for worse. I really can't remember much of the better, if there was any at all.

Larry is still lying there and I'm starting to worry. What if all I ever feel in this house is black? What if all the violence, anger and loneliness got sucked into the walls, only to bleed out and seek to engulf me? What if all I ever see is a dead body with scarlet staining his chest? If that's all there is to look forward to, I had better put my plan into action fast. I've tried phoning Miriam. I just wanted to hear her voice, which I suppose I did in a way because I got the answer machine. I'll try again in a minute but I need to get out of this hallway. It's too near the swing bin and Larry is starting to breathe.

I'm in the sitting room now, the furthest I could get from him and I've calmed down a bit. I'm trying to find my mobile. I think I might have left it at Miriam's. I'll have a look in my suitcases in a minute, but that means braving the hallway and passing the kitchen again to get upstairs. If I close my eyes and run, I could do it, and if the phone is there, it means I won't have to use the landline by the front door when I call her again. I don't know what to do now. It's lunch time now and I'm hungry. I need to get to the kitchen which means coming within inches of Larry. I'm peaking round the door frame in the lounge but it's too far away and I can't see if he is still there. So taking a deep breath, I close my eyes and go for it. I'm used to navigating this house with my eyes shut. It was something, if you remember me telling you, I used to do as a child, because of Barney going blind. I never got out of the habit. It meant I could go anywhere in the house in pitch darkness, which has been a bonus to tell you the truth. Many times I've managed to slip away from an angry Larry and hide. He tried following me once. Stupid fool could have just turned the lights on, but in his haste to get to me, he rammed his shin into the table on the landing when he took a wrong turn. I kind of wish I'd stayed in the bedroom and let him slap me about, because when I came out of my hiding place, hoping he had fallen asleep, he was lurking behind the bathroom door. He beat me almost senseless, then got into bed and went to sleep. I woke up five hours later on the floor on the landing. I couldn't really tell if it was day or night because my eyes were swollen shut. As I was lying there I thought of Barney and I felt something that wasn't exactly love, I think it was understanding.

Miriam must be out. I've tried her a few times now, and left messages on her answerphone. I'm sure she'll call me back the minute she gets home. I'll pop and see her tomorrow. Oh I won't go to the house. Megan thinks it would be good to give Miriam some time alone with Saint Brian. She doesn't call him that of course, I named him all on my own. I think I'll write her another letter and post it on my way to Miriam's. This will be the last one, and then she will know everything. Talk about bleeding a person dry. I'll hide across the road from Miriam's in the bushes. I won't be seen. I have become an expert at lurking, what with the whole Audrey Brown thing so I'll be fine. Mrs Bronstein's hydrangea is in flower and it's massive. I'll be able to watch over Miriam from there without being detected. I just want to see her face, check she is all right. I know what time she goes to the shops, so if I go at half past eleven I should catch her leaving the house. I want to go to bed but it means braving the hallway again, buy I decide to bite the bullet, do a Barney and get to the stairs. It's then I make a big mistake. I open my eyes and glance in the mirror. There, just over my shoulder, Larry raised his head.

Miriam

I've had to turn off the ringer. The ruddy phone went every couple of minutes for at least an hour. At first, I nearly answered it, then I heard her voice on the machine. Dr Megan said to let her settle into Mulberry Crescent without using me as a crutch, so it would be best not to speak to her for a while. Brian's going spare. He wanted to pull the ruddy cord out of the wall. He keeps saying we are never going to be free of 'that bloody woman', his words, not mine, but I must admit I'm feeling a little uneasy about how this is all going to pan out. I hope Sal is all right, but due to the amount of calls, I very much doubt it. Brian says I should put me energy into me own family and stop worrying about everybody else. By everybody else of course he means Sally, cheeky beggar. It's only been a day since she left, so I haven't had time to focus on anything, except three tons of ironing and changing the washer on the kitchen tap. I had to do it in secret mind, so as not to hurt Brian's feelings. He wasn't up to messing about with a drippy tap yet, but you try telling him that. If I'd told him about it, he would've been out of that bed like a shot, giving himself another heart attack I shouldn't wonder. No, best I do it. Quick and painless. Well I say painless, I cut me ruddy finger on the metal bit, didn't I? Silly mare.

It's in times like this I thank God I haven't got a mobile. I refuse to have one. When I'm out of the house, that is my time. I doubt anything major will come up in the half hour I'm in Tesco's. I say that, because the minute I plugged the landline in, it started ringing. It didn't take an O level in communications to know who it was. I didn't answer. For one, I was trying to get ready to go shopping, and two, I didn't really didn't want to drag everything up again. Dr Megan said if it became a problem I was to get in touch with her, so I did, quickly. She said that Sally was probably feeling a little bit out of her depth and needed reassurance, but that she should settle down soon. I hoped so, because to tell you the truth, I felt awful ignoring anyone, let alone me friend who was still very much to the left of centre.

When I got back from the shops, I unpacked me groceries and had a cheeky slice of devil's food cake as a treat. I got a BOGOF on toilet rolls, I'm pleased about that. I don't know how we get through so many, I really don't. I only bought a nine-pack last week. I suppose having an extra person in the house used it up quicker, and I reckon Brian stashes it somewhere in case there is a ruddy apocalypse or something. It's them ruddy books he's reading. They're putting all sorts in his silly head. Something felt a bit weird when I left the house this morning. I could have sworn someone was watching me. Of course, there was no one there, but it did give me the heebee geebees for a minute. Mercifully the phone didn't ring for the whole afternoon and I managed to get a bit of me knitting done. I'm making a layette or two for the baby, and a jumper with a cow on for little Sarah. Garry says she's obsessed with them. I got her an Ermintrude soft toy from the Magic Roundabout for her birthday and she carries it everywhere, even though she hasn't a clue who it is, or what the programme was about. I found a DVD of the series and gave it to Garry to put on for her when they want a bit of peace. That's what I used to do when he was young, and it worked a treat. Let's hope it works with Sarah because when the baby comes, they'll need all the peace they can get.

I'm doing fish and chips for tea, and I thought of Sally because that was one of her favourites, that and lasagne. She loved my lasagne. She was especially partial to me home-made garlic bread an' all. I haven't a clue where she put it. Sally's as thin as a rake, but she could eat for England. I wish I could eat a double helping of summat and look like that, but I'm more likely to look like Mister Blobby. I wondered what she would be having for her tea. I knew the lady called Debbie had got a week's worth of shopping, so she had food in. I just hoped Sal was of a mind to cook it. Dr Megan is popping round here tomorrow. It'll be nice to see her. I've made another devil's food cake so we can have some with our tea. Another one of Sally's favourites. Bless her.

Megan

I popped along to Mulberry Crescent before I went to see Miriam. I thought it would be nice to give her an update on how Sally is doing but she wasn't in. I thought she just might not have wanted to answer the door, but when I came back down the path I met her next door neighbour, who said she had gone out early, about nine, and had not yet come back. I chatted to her for a while, not letting on who I was and after ten minutes I knew all her children's names, how many times she had been married and a whole host of other snippets of information. I thought to myself, I'd better try and remember it all in case there was a test, she was that intense. When I got back to the car, I tried Sally's mobile. It was switched off. I waited for a while hoping she would come back, but I couldn't stay long as I'd got to pick Charlie up from his morning session at nursery after seeing Miriam. Gina normally went, but she had an appointment at the doctors and was afraid it would run over. That didn't matter. I loved picking him up. He'd chatter on about who he'd played with and what he'd been doing, but my favourite times were when he came out with paintings in his fist. They were usually brightly coloured scribbles that you had to guess at, but he'd be so proud of them. Most of the time you wouldn't need to see them to know what colours he'd used, they'd be all over his hands and face. When he came towards me today though, he had a face like thunder. "Hello Bear," I said, wrapping my arms around him. "What's happened today for you to make your frowny face?" What he said next was epic.

"My girlfriend doesn't want to go out with me anymore, because Daniel pulled her hair and said it was me, but I would never do that, Nanny, I love her."

"Don't worry, Charlie," I said with my jaw clamped tight, trying hard not to laugh. To him, it was the worst thing to ever happen, so I had to treat it with the solemnity it deserved. "Has Daniel said sorry?"

"Not to Eloise, but he said sorry to me, so he's my friend again. Eloise is going out with George now." His little face all scrunched up, trying not to cry nearly broke my heart. I wanted to hold him, just like this forever, to freeze us in time, I wanted to say don't grow up, don't get a girlfriend, a job, a family. Stay my wonderful three-year-old grandson for the next twenty years, but of course that couldn't happen.

I didn't start thinking about the opposite sex until I was in middle school, and that was only because my friends did. It was in secondary school that those feelings properly kicked in. I had said it to Leo and Gina many times, that Charlie was three and a half going on thirty, but it wasn't just him. Children seemed to grow up much faster these days. They leave behind their teddies and dolls at three or four nowadays, and glue themselves to the nearest console. I wish sometimes that we could turn the clock back to a time when kids weren't playing video games twenty-four-seven, or were allowed mobile phones and social media accounts at primary school age. What was wrong with writing a letter, or actually playing outside in the fresh air with your friends. I did. It never did me any harm. "I'm sure Eloise will stop being cross tomorrow Charlie," I said. "You'll see."

"Women!" Charlie said suddenly and I couldn't hold it any longer. I roared with laughter. Charlie joined in too and we skipped to the car. Well, he did and I limped but we got there. Together. When we got home, I got Charlie settled with a snack and a drink and put *Charlie and Lola* on for him. He likes it, because the little boy in the programme has the same name as him. It kept him quiet while I tried Sally's mobile again. Still it went to voicemail. If I couldn't get hold of her soon, I would have to do another visit. If she didn't answer then, because of her vulnerable state, I would have to phone the police to do a welfare check. I dreaded doing that. You were never sure what they were going to find. I had done a forced entry before when I couldn't get hold of a client. I had only seen him for the initial visit, but I knew he was depressed. I hoped to be able to work with him, help him to feel better, but when the police got there it was too late. He had taken his own life. It was so sad to think that a person gets so low, so desperate, that they think that suicide is the only option left to them. It never is. The trick is making them see that before it's too late. Seeing that poor man slumped in his chair with the television still blaring out has stayed with me and I don't want that to happen to Sally. At the moment I wouldn't rule it out. She has been so erratic and so incredibly unhappy. Even when she was living with Miriam we could all see it. Having Sally's sessions at my office isn't working either. She only came once. Of course, I can't make her come. She is free to do as she pleases now, but I still think she could benefit from them. I know my office is impersonal even though I try to make it homely. I think a person with heavy baggage like Sally would do better in familiar surroundings, although, I know in her case, it may be different because of what has happened there. Just then, a thought occurred to me and I gave Miriam a quick ring. I asked if Sally had been in touch with her at all today? She said, apart from the one this morning that Brian told her not to answer, she hadn't. I told her I was going back to Sally's this evening when Charlie was in bed to check on her. Miriam asked me to let her know if I managed to speak to her. I told her I would. I probably shouldn't have worried Miriam, but I knew that she would be the only person Sally would go to in a crisis. Miriam said the next time Sally phoned, she would be sure to answer. We said goodbye and I rang off.

When I got to Sally's that evening she was there. She took some time getting to the door and when she opened it, her face was pale and sweaty. "Hello Sally," I said calmly, "I haven't been able to reach you on the phone today, so I thought I would come and check if you needed anything."

"I'm fine," she snapped. "Why were you trying to call me? I didn't do anything wrong. You can see I'm fine, Goodnight." She shut the door in my face. I didn't want to distress her any further, so I spoke to her through the letter box. I told her I would see her at my office tomorrow for our usual session. She didn't answer. I went back to the car and wrote the exchange down in my notebook word for word. I didn't want to forget anything, because I would certainly be asking her about it when I saw her next. I had expected some teething problems. Being back there alone, after the hustle and bustle at Miriam's, could be throwing up thoughts and feelings she wanted to forget. I believed Sally to be stronger than she thought she was. She just needed to be given time to come to that conclusion on her own. However her reaction to my presence, just then, was a little extreme.

When I got home, Leo and Gina invited me to movie night. Normally, I would love spending time with them. Watching some psychological thriller or a rom-com whilst stuffing my face with popcorn. But to tell you the truth. I just wanted my bed. My hips and knees were doing the tango and I needed pills to turn it into a waltz at the very least. It was a cup of herbal tea, a bath and a good night's sleep that this doctor ordered. Tomorrow was another day and could take care of itself. I had had enough.

Miriam

Brian came down and sat in the chair for a while this afternoon. It was Wednesday and there was a programme on animals with David Attenborough on the telly. We both liked him. I'd bought us a little treat from the bakery in town while I was catching up with Jill and Mandy. We have to have something with our cuppa of an afternoon. As usual, Brian had a doughnut but I fancied a custard tart, I hadn't had one of them for ages. Jill couldn't get over how well I was looking. She said I'd been looking like death warmed up for weeks, but she didn't like to tell me. Mandy agreed. We had a lovely chat. It was nice just to be meself, and not have to watch what I said all the time like I had to with Sally. It was exhausting. As I was queuing up for the cakes though, I could have sworn I saw Sal go past. She couldn't have seen me or she would have said hello. She was gone when I got outside, but I was glad she was out and about and not stuck in that ruddy house on her own. Maybe she was picking up a few things before she went to see Megan. Wednesday was one of her days.

Brian's doing a bit better lately. He still isn't sleeping

properly though bless him. He's been having a few nightmares. After, when they've gone, he can't nod off again, and when he's awake, I'm awake! Dr Kelly gave him some pills, but I was only to give them out when he really needed them because they were strong enough to knock an elephant off its feet. I could have made a joke about elephants and Brian being a bit big round the middle, but I kept quiet. These days Brian seemed to have had a sense of humour bypass as well as his heart. I'm sure he'll come right when he gets back to doing a bit round the house, and can see his mates again. He hasn't seen Alan and Colin for a long time, in case he should catch a cold or something from them. They were champing at the bit to have a game of gin rummy and half a lager together. Well, Brian tells me it's gin rummy but I know they play poker for money. I don't care as long as he's having a good time and doesn't bankrupt us.

The phone hasn't rung all day, apart from Grace letting me know when she's picking me up to go for the scan. I'm going with her because Garry has to work and can't get out of it. I was so happy when she asked me. I get to see my little nugget of a grandchild on a TV screen, fancy that. I did have a couple of them when I was pregnant with our Garry but you don't take it in, do you, when it's you on the table? I was always so scared that something might be wrong, I never looked at the screen in case the baby had two heads. I was happy just to hear his heart beat. It sounded like hundreds of horses going full pelt, I've always loved that sound. When you're young and pregnant, you get overwhelmed with it all. Your head is full of all sorts especially, when it's your first, but I'll be able to enjoy this one while Grace lies there, bump in the air, keeping the baby safe and warm for another couple of months yet.

Brian's gone back up to bed. He can only stay down for a little while before he starts yawning and whatnot. It's a bit odd, because when he gets up there he can't sleep, so he reads everything he can get his hands on. It's costing us a fortune in Stephen Kings' and whatnot. Still, it gives me time to work on me knitting. Little Sarah's cow jumper is proving a ruddy nightmare. I've had to make the pattern smaller and I'm having a hard time getting me head around it. I hope it turns out nice in the end. I'm giving it to her as a present from the new baby when it comes. Garry and Grace thought it'd be nice for her to get something from her brother, yes! It's a boy, folks and they're calling him Brody. I don't know? I just got through telling you the phone hardly rang all day, when it has burped three times in ten minutes. Every time, I get up to get it, I have to put a stitch marker in me knitting and haul meself up, but when I say hello, there's nobody there.

.

Sally

I shouldn't have reacted like that. Megan isn't stupid. She'd have picked up on the fact that I'm stressed in a heartbeat. I should have been nicer, but then she would have seen through that as well because I never am. I just panicked, I guess. I couldn't let her in though, could I? I couldn't let her see Larry. I could feel his eyes boring into the back of my head, willing me to slam the door in her face. He always got what he wanted. Well, until I stabbed him to death with a kitchen knife, I'm sure he wouldn't have wanted that. I would probably have to answer for my behaviour tomorrow with Megan, if I was to go, which I don't think I will. I can't see the point. I can't tell her I'm seeing my dead husband lying in the place where I took his life, and not only that! I'm doing his bidding. She'd have booked me a bed in The Chimes straight away. I don't think anyone can help me now. That's OK though. I know what I have to do. I have to keep an eye on Miriam. She's bound to be missing me. I know it's only Tuesday but I have to check she's all right and not seeing anyone else. I was only going to wait until she came out of her house, see she was fine and go home, but something made me follow her to Tesco's. It's only a ten minute walk and I know how to keep hidden, so she didn't know I was there. I left her when she was safely in the bakery on her own, and I caught the bus back to Mulberry Crescent. As soon as I'd got in the door I could see him. He appeared to be dead, or playing possum, I didn't know which, so I stepped over him quickly in case he reached out and grabbed my ankle. I made it into the kitchen, made a cup of tea and stepped back over him to get to the sitting room. I was safe in there for the moment. I didn't think he could actually get up off the floor, but I was sure I kept hearing rustling in the hallway. It was only a matter of time. He was gaining strength. I shut the door and turned the TV on to drown out the noise. It was nearly time for *Coronation Street* anyway. The powers that be at ITV had switched it to a Tuesday this week because of some football match or other. It makes me angry because they never move *Emmerdale*.

On Wednesday morning when I should have been on my way to Megan's office, I was going in the opposite direction. I got to Miriam's a bit before ten and thought I would watch the house, just for an hour. I didn't expect to see Miriam coming out and turning left towards town. Just like yesterday, I followed her and what I saw cut me to the quick. She looked like she had forgotten all about me. I could see her plain as day as I stood in the window of the shop opposite, until I started getting funny looks from the shop assistant and had to move. Miriam was chatting with the two people who were always on the sidelines, threatening to take her away from me, as if she hadn't a care in the world. They were as bad as Saint Brian, taking all her time, leaving none for me. She had her head thrown back and she was laughing hard. Were they laughing about me? I had seen enough to know that if I didn't act quickly, Miriam may forget me, replace me with others that could never mean as much to her as I do. If all that's left for me is my deceased husband for company, I may as well just end it now.

Megan

Sally didn't show on the Wednesday, or the Friday. I have been to her house every day since, but she either was not in, or was not in to me! Technically, she didn't have to come anymore. The police had cleared her of any wrongdoing, so she was under no obligation to finish the sessions at all. That didn't stop me worrying. Especially now I know she carried the burden not only of Larry's death, but that of her mother's too. I think she feels angry with me and abandoned by Miriam because, in Sally's eyes, she wasn't welcome there anymore. We made her leave. Maybe she feels that she has no one now, even though I've made it clear I'm still happy to see her in our sessions, but it was Monday now and I still hadn't seen or heard from her. I rang Miriam when I got home and she hadn't heard from her either, although she did say she might have seen Sally in the precinct on Wednesday, but wasn't sure, because Miriam knew she was supposed to be with me. I asked her to ring me immediately should Sally get in touch and she said she would.

I must admit I forgot all about Sally when I got home. I'd been in for less than half an hour when Gina came running into the sitting room in a bit of a panic. "Mum! Daniel's dad has just rang and asked if I knew it was World Book Day tomorrow. I told him I hadn't a clue and asked why it was important? He told me that because the primary school is dressing up. The teachers thought it would be fun if the nursery kids dressed up too. I didn't get the memo. I have twelve hours, that's if I don't sleep, to come up with not only a character from a children's book, but to make a whole costume. Daniel's dad said we are not allowed to buy one because that would put the families that couldn't afford one at a disadvantage. There's a prize for the best one. Help!"

We called Charlie into the room, and asked him who his favourite character from his night time reading books was. I thought he would say *The Gruffalo* or *The Very Hungry Caterpillar*, but no! *"The Tiger who came to Tea,* Nanny, that's my really really favourite," he said, jumping up and down. Gina and I looked at each other in a panic. How the devil were we going to make Charlie into a tiger in twelve hours. It looked like I wasn't going to get much sleep either. "Are you sure, Charlie Bear? Is there another one you really love?" I coaxed him gently.

"I like George, not George at school, but the George who is Peppa Pig's little brother. He has whiskers and his daddy goes oink oink." That was it. Charlie was off, running round the living room oinking. He oinked in my ear, he oinked as he hugged his mummy and he was still oinking, although not quite so enthusiastically, ten minutes later. "That's it, the tiger it is. I don't think I can make the nursery suffer with all that oinking," Gina said in exasperation, although I still don't have a clue how we we're going to do it?"

"When in doubt," I told her, "visit the Internet. There must be some suggestions in there somewhere." There turned out to be hundreds and we were spoilt for choice. Suddenly Gina stopped scrolling and shouted, "That's it, that's the one! It can't be all that hard. Can it?" She pointed to a small child in a onesie that had been painted to resemble a tiger. The maker had added ears and a tail to complete the ensemble. She looked very sweet. "He has a beige onesie that's nearly too small for him," said Gina excitedly, "I'll go and get it." She raced off, leaving me to decide what the hell we were going to make ears and a tail out of. It was going to be a long night.

Sally

Larry was dead when I left the house today. He didn't even flicker an eyelid in my direction. He'd been dead yesterday too which I was grateful for. I did keep peeping into the hallway to see if he was lulling me into a false sense of security, but so far so good. I had been back here for three weeks now, and all the old feelings of dread and uncertainty were creeping back, as was my fixation with walls. I felt cheated though because I couldn't even sit on my stair to think. Oh, Larry had got that sussed hadn't he? He could see me from his vantage point by the swing bin. I knew that one day he would take my stair from me, I just didn't think he would do it as a corpse.

As the days went by I was getting more and more lonely. I suppose I had Larry, such as he was, but he wasn't a great conversationalist. In fact he never spoke a word. He would just leer at me or stare me down, but the worst was when he smiled. It was a cold, mirthless grin that made him look like one of those ventriloquist's dummies they had in the old days. It terrified me, and that made the pink begin to fizz once again. It turned to orange when it dawned on me that he still ruled the roost. He was still made me scared to live in my own house. I wanted to stab him all over again, but there was no fun in that because he couldn't feel it, could he? It would be pointless, and it wouldn't get rid of him. No. Larry was here to stay. So far, this week, he hadn't left his position by the bin, but I read somewhere that when dead people return to the place they died, it means they have unfinished business, and that it takes time for them to gain strength, to be able to walk through walls, or kill their wives.

I was frightened, I wanted Miriam. I had spoken to her a couple of times on the phone and she sounded like her old self, asking me how I was doing, had I seen Megan? I said I had, which was true. I saw her going into the chemist in the precinct. She didn't see me, but as Megan had said, I was under no obligation to see her if I didn't want to. I didn't really, but I had realised that if I pulled away completely, it would look to her like I was hiding away, unable to face things, so I told Miriam I would go on Wednesday. She said that was wonderful, but although she was friendly, she didn't invite me to her place or anything. That was Saint Brian's doing of course. I still worried that she had replaced me with Jill and Mandy, and they now were the benefactors of Miriam's devil's food cake. I bet they weren't always having problems that Miriam had to fix, or seeing dead husbands lying in their hallway.

I can't bear to think Miriam had stopped caring about me, and I can't think of anything else so I have to find out. I'm keeping watch outside her house every day now. I'm trying to pluck up the courage to ask her face to face. Somehow it didn't seem to be the right time, when she was leaving to go and laugh with her friends at the coffee shop. At least she didn't take them to The Cakehole, that would have been the ultimate betrayal. That was our place, just mine and hers, but so far she hadn't. Another reason I hadn't asked her was because I was afraid of the answer. I went there every day too, because I needed to see her face, it had always calmed me and I needed that right now. She had been my safety through everything with my mother, and father and Jim and Larry. Even though she never knew what they were doing to me, she knew I needed love and reassurance and had always given that in abundance. I had found lots of new vantage points to watch the house. I thought it may look a bit odd to the neighbours if they saw me in the bush all the time and they might have said something to Miriam. I found I could get round the back of the building, where a large privet hedge in the lane hid me completely. It was even better than Mrs Bronstein's hydrangea, because hers was on a corner, and there was always a chance that Garry would see me from his van when he came to see his mother. He did that quite a bit, now I had left.

One particular morning when I saw Miriam leave to go shopping, I didn't follow her. Instead, I waited until she was out of sight and crept up to the sitting room window. I cupped my hands around my eyes and peered through the sparkling white nets, which were Miriam's pride and joy, to check whether Saint Brian had deemed to rise from his bed. He had lorded it over Miriam since his heart attacks, pretending to be bedridden so she would wait on him hand, foot and finger. I couldn't see him, so I quickly ducked up the side of the house to the back door. It was open. I pushed the door into the room a few inches, just enough to squeeze myself through. I knew that it squeaked if you opened it fully and I didn't want to attract attention. I had no idea what I had come in for, so I just sat at the table and looked around. Everything was familiar, reassuring, and a big plus! It didn't have a dead body lying half in, and half out of the kitchen door. The smells of baking and last night's dinner sent me back to when Miriam cared, when I'd sat at this very spot and told her about Jim. As I got up to look around, my elbow knocked the bread bin into the tea caddy, which in turn, fell on the floor. All of a sudden, the lampshade wobbled and I heard Brian shout, "Is that you, love?" I picked up the spilled teabags and hastily shoved them into the tin, replaced the chair and hurried away, shutting the door quietly behind me. I wondered how long it would be before I went back into the warm, bright kitchen with its safe and familiar smells. Not long now if things went according to plan. Not long at all.

Miriam

Brian was in a right old tizzy when I came home from the shops. I went straight up to our bedroom when I saw the lampshade doing the hula hula. He kept saying there was someone downstairs, and asked if I'd come back for me purse or anything? Which I didn't. I told him to settle down, or his blood pressure was going to go into orbit and I didn't fancy a trip to A and E. He did calm down a bit, but was still adamant that there'd been someone moving about in the kitchen, about an hour since. I went downstairs to see if anything was disturbed, and on the way, I realised the stairs had started to squeak like a trapped mouse. I reminded meself to talk to Garry about fixing them along with the loose floorboard in the loo. I don't know if it's just me, but the house seems to be getting as old as I feel lately. All creaky joints and rusty hinges. I don't know whether it's all the stress of everything and whatnot, but I'm wound tighter than me grandad's old Timex. That's a bugger to get going an' all.

When I got to the kitchen I knew Brian was right. One of the chairs at the table had definitely been moved and there was a teabag lying on the lino next to the ironing board. I know I think I'm going as doolally as Sally sometimes, but I'm damn sure I didn't drop it. I hadn't gone that far yet. Although, if things didn't get back to normal soon it wouldn't be long. Garry and his family come regularly now and I'm loving being a granny. Little Sarah is a joy. She never stops nattering. She already calls me gran gran and that is near enough for me. I can't wait till little Brody is born, then I shall have two to spoil, shan't I? It's great to see them, they're a right tonic and Brian's getting better slowly. We have to keep his blood pressure under control still, but things are looking up. The only fly in the ointment is Sally. I think she is following me. I've seen her a couple of times now in the same shop, hiding behind the baked beans, or walking down the main drag of the precinct a little bit behind me. I don't know if she realises, but you can see people coming in the reflections of the windows opposite. I used it the other day to avoid Mr Ahmed. I saw him as he locked the door of the dry cleaners and turned in my direction, so I ducked into a vaping shop hoping he wouldn't see me. I felt a right fool when the man behind the counter asked me what flavour I wanted? I hadn't got a clue what he was on about so I said "Sorry, wrong shop," and left sharpish. Thank goodness Mr Ahmed didn't see me. I like the man, don't get me wrong, but gawd can he gossip. He always asks questions about Sally too, which can be really difficult. I'll use the window thingy from now on. I don't want to meet her yet. I just don't want to go back to how we were. It was becoming a bit toxic, I could see that and it was upsetting Brian no end. Things change, don't they? I have me other friends now, and Sally will meet people I'm sure, when she stops being weird. Come to think of it, she has always been that. It's no wonder when you've led the life she has. Please don't think I don't care about her, I do, but our lives are different now and it's time to let go, for both our sakes. Following me has got to stop 'an all. I know she's free to go where she wants, but stalkers are creepy. They peer into people's windows and watch your house. I didn't think Sally wouldn't do that to me, but I don't seem to know what she's thinking these days. I'm going to ask her about it when I phone her next. Dr Megan said to keep it to just once a week for a while. She said that Sal needed to make new friends and take charge of her life, and she wouldn't learn to do that, if she felt she could hide behind me all the time. I understood, and I agreed with her to a point, but it still felt a bit like I was casting her adrift. I said if only talking to her on a Wednesday made her follow me all the time, then wouldn't it be best to ring her a bit more often and maybe she would ease off a bit. On second thoughts, this is Sally we're talking about, who knows what's in her head at the minute? We have to take into consideration that she's gone from living here with all the hustle and bustle of family life, to being completely alone in a place that was never really home, cos of Larry and his shenanigans. I know he isn't there anymore, but it must feel strange to walk over the place he died to get to the kitchen every day if you get my drift. I do feel sorry for her, you know? Poor mare, but I have to think of my family now.

I made up my mind to talk properly to Dr Megan to see what she thought about me ringing Sal more often. I know she hasn't been going to the clinic much. Dr Megan told me that last week when she popped by. Which is the opposite to what Sally had told me last Wednesday, but the police have finished with her now, and she doesn't have to go to therapy if she doesn't want to. Personally, I think she should go every day. I know she's me friend and we have a lot of history, but that doesn't give her the right to come in me house uninvited. I'm sure it was her the other day? The chair she always sat in was the one that had been moved. She had attempted to put it back in the right place but there was a stain on the lino, and I always put the leg of the chair over it to hide the mark. The browny green blob was the shape of the Eiffel Tower, and, as much as I liked France, I didn't want it on me floor. I'd tried everything to get it out but nothing would shift it. I got a faint whiff of the softener she uses 'an all. Clean linen. Brian says I should call the police, but I can't do that to Sal. I'll tell you one thing though. It won't happen again, you can be sure of that.

Sally

Surprise!! You won't be expecting this letter from me will you? I know we don't have to see each other anymore, but I want you to know I am getting the voicemails. Sorry, I've been too busy to reply, you know how it is. Since we've stopped seeing each other I've been spending all my time with Miriam. I'm looking to the future now. I think I have a solid plan. I have also been thinking about the past a lot too, most of it unbidden. It has spurred me on to end these feelings of never being good enough, never being wanted by anybody, except Miriam of course. Oh, I see images of so called happy families in magazines and on the television, but are they just that? Images. Do they really exist? Take Miriam for instance, she thinks she's happy with Saint Brian but all she does is wait on him, fulfils his every need. When is she going to be free to choose what she really wants. I know she would choose to see me more, to get back to when it was just me and her. Only me and her.

My life has been unusual by some people's standards. Tragic, by most, and absolutely pointless in my eyes. Having been dragged up the way I was though, has made me see things in black and white. Well! With a little hint of grey and other colours here and there, just to keep things interesting. The way

I understand life is, you either have, or have not. You eat, or starve. Kill, or be killed. As you know, Larry wasn't the only person that died at my hand. There are more. My mother, as I have said, is of no loss to me. In fact, I'd felt lighter than I had in a very long time. I feel I must confess to you, she was no accident. Oh, it happened the way I said it did, except for the almighty shove I gave her at the end. Watching her do a triple somersault down the stairs was exhilarating. I scored her six point five for artistic interpretation, but she was a bit shaky on the dismount. I should imagine it was quite a feat for her. One moment she was a sad, obese sack of whisky. The next, she was just like me, a fly, an ink blot on the table, inconsequential. Come to think of it, it's the only time I felt any kinship with her. I remember looking at her when she landed, and being disgusted to discover she had nothing on under her robe. The thick rolls of fat, separated by lines of sores and filth looked like ruts on a muddy road, a putrid smell so thick I could chew on it. It took me back to the stink of Audrey Brown's perfume, you could cut slices out of that let me tell you. I was so angry with Mother, and myself if I'm honest. I had allowed that person to make my life hell, but she can't hurt me anymore. It was a fitting end for an incestuous paedophile who made my brother become a monster. I'm glad Jim got out. Oh, don't get me wrong, I hated him for what he did to me, but equally, I hated her for what she did to him. Like follows like.

This brings me to the other killings. I was not entirely to blame for the foetuses. Jim had to take some responsibility too. The first was killed when it was twelve weeks old and the second at sixteen weeks. I have touched on that earlier on in my letters, said I miscarried them. What I failed to mention is that I would have dug them both out of my belly with a spoon, rather than keep them in my body a second longer. Believe me, they were better off going where all the unborns go, than having a mother like me. I wonder what kind of monsters, incestuous products of a shadow and a demon would make. I'd told the doctor I had been raped, which I had, but I didn't go into detail. I expect she thought I was on the game. I lied about my age and probably, because I'm tall, I got away with it. In hindsight, if I had told the truth, they would have taken me away. I would have had a different life from the one I was forced to live, and we would not be where we are now. I suppose when you're fourteen, you haven't got the wisdom, or the inclination to help yourself, and I truly believe that if I had said something, Jim would have killed me. He, like me, had no empathy. We could feel, I guess, in our own way, I think what I feel for Miriam is akin to love, and I sort of cared about Barney. The babies were just blobs, an assortment of cells which were probably twisted and deformed, unimportant. I just thought I'd better tell you everything. You know? For clarity. Get my affairs in order so to speak. Don't cry for me, don't give me a second thought. I'll be better off where I'm going. Some people believe in heaven and hell, I'm on the fence but we shall soon find out. When Miriam dies, I won't have time to mourn because I'll be right behind her. Oh, I just remembered, for the sake of full disclosure, I strangled the cat as well. She ate my rat, what was I supposed to do? As I said before, she didn't mean it. It's instinct after all, but I was angry and the orange very quickly turned to red. Before I knew, it the cat was limp in my hands. I put it in a black bag, slung it in the wheelie bin and forgot all about it. Much like I did when I killed Larry.

I have another confession, but I'll wait a bit before I tell you about that. Incidentally, I've been thinking about my father a lot lately. Don't get me wrong, I couldn't care less whether he's alive or dead. I've been turning over and over in my mind what I found, when I was searching under his bed on the day my mother went to Hell. Whilst I was looking for my birth certificate, I came across my father's private papers. All at once, I knew why he was never in the house, I knew where he had been going all that time. The reason he didn't care about us was no longer a mystery. He had another family. He was a bigamist. Well, I don't know that for sure, because he may not have married her, but, it turns out I have three other siblings. I saw a photo, they all looked normal. Like one of those images in a magazine. I hated my father at that moment, more than I had ever hated him. Not because he did the dirty on my mother, I can't blame him for that, but what I can blame him for is throwing me to the lions, then playing happy families with Mrs Bun the Baker's wife, and their three little doughnuts. It wasn't that I wanted to be with them. Nothing could be further from the truth, but anything would be better than the hell he chose to leave me in. And another thing. If my father could love his other family, why couldn't he love me?

When I met Miriam, a bit more normal began to creep into my life. Knowing her, and being wanted by her and her family gave me more confidence and self-belief, although that got knocked out of me when I married Larry, but I'm grateful to Miriam for giving me that brief time of almost happiness. They included me. They made me feel like one of the family, even though I had a trunk and three suitcases full of baggage. I'm going to have to wrap this up soon. Larry is stirring. He's always here. Sometimes dead. Sometimes standing behind me, but always here. Needless to say, I won't be sorry to see the back of the shit show that has been my life. I can't take any more shame and hurt and rejection, I'm too tired. I can't even put it to rest for a few hours each night, because I can't sleep without Larry pawing me. Oh, he's up and about, wants me now. Well *he can't have Audrey Brown, can he? He can't leave the house. That has been a godsend to tell you the truth, because I can shut the front door behind me, go and find Miriam and have a few hours when he's not leering at me with that supercilious grin on his face, and I don't have to see the big red stain on his pristine white shirt. I suppose at least he is company but it's hard to miss the hole in his chest. It shows his black heart. Oh, I know he can't hurt me, can he? I guess I've learned to live with him in death, as I had in life. Cautiously! When I go downstairs in the morning he's always dead again, which of course is how I like him, but I know that soon he will begin to breathe, to taunt me, to get my pink fizzing. It's all getting a bit much to tell you the truth. That's why I've decided that Wednesday is the day. That's the day Miriam doesn't go out. This will be the day we get to spend together. The last day. It will also be the last day I have to spend with Larry in Mulberry Crescent, the last time I have to see his shit-eating grin. I am ending this now. I am sick and tired of people trying to keep Miriam and I apart. It isn't what either of us want, and if we can't be together in this world, then we'll be together in the next. I don't want to hurt Miriam. She has always looked out for me, has gone into bat for me and I thank her for that from the bottom of my heart, but I have no choice but to do this. If there is a heaven then she and I will get to be together for ever. If not, it will stop anyone else having her love, her time. Time that should be mine. It will be all over when you get this. That's why I put a second-class stamp on it. You should get it on Thursday or very soon after. Stamps are pricey, aren't they? They've doubled since I last bought some. I don't understand that. You would think that with the invention of text messages, that they would lower the price to make people buy them. Not many people write letters anymore, they should.*

Now to my other confession. I tried to kill Saint Brian. Oh, I didn't think it would happen that fast, and certainly not on a day when we had a doctor in the house. I cocked that up good and proper. He did die for a minute or two I suppose, so in a way I was successful, but of course, it didn't last. I wanted Miriam to be free. She didn't need him running her ragged all the time. I was trying to do her a favour. I can't tell you how many times he banged on the ceiling. She would roll her eyes and heave her not inconsiderable body out of the chair, to struggle up the stairs to do his bidding. The 'eye roll' was her way of telling me her life was becoming too much of a burden. Finally now, I can repay her for her kindness to me. I can save her. Going back to Saint Brian. I had found an expired box of his blood pressure medication when I was looking for the jam. It was a sign. I decided there and then to do it slowly, so no one would suspect anything. I put it in his tea. Why do you think I wanted to be tea lady? Oh I don't hate him, not really. Hang on, that's a lie and I promised myself I would tell it like it is as this is our last missive. It was quite simply done to help my friend. He needed to be gone. As that never happened, I had to change plans at the last minute but this one feels right. I want what I had before. Just me and Miriam against the world. I don't profess to believe in God, but I want to believe that people who should be together in life will be so in death. I'll feel safer knowing that wherever we go, she will be there to look after me, to keep me safe. I have no idea how it's going to go on Wednesday. I'll have to think on my feet like I always do. I'm sure it will be OK.

Thank you for trying to ease my burdens but, quite frankly, I don't think there is a psychiatrist in the world who could do that. By the time we met, I was too far gone. They say some people shouldn't have kids. That was certainly true for my mother and father, but also for me. The unborns dodged a big

Sally-shaped bullet there, I can tell you. As I said thank you for trying. I won't say thanks for caring too, because you are paid to do that and it doesn't count. Nevertheless if you see us in the next life. You are welcome to come in for a cup of tea. I promise not to put anything in it as long as you leave again. Miriam and me. Friends forever. That's the way it has always been and that is the way it has to be. You can see that can't you?

Goodbye

PS. I've left you Wendy, my spider plant in my will. Well, it's not a proper will. It's on a piece of paper on the kitchen table at Mulberry Crescent. My will, not Wendy. She's in the bathroom. She likes the steam. I didn't think Brian would appreciate her somehow, and Larry hates plants.

Sally Wilson

Megan

Charlie looked adorable. Gina and I stayed up until stupid o'clock painting his onesie orange. When that was dry, we painted the tiger stripes in black. For two people who both failed GCSE art, I think we did a good job. The ears and tail were made out of a sheet stuffed with the innards of an old pillow, also painted. I don't want to blow my own trumpet, but I was amazed at how well they turned out. I had to hunt for the sewing machine which hadn't been seen since 2012, I hadn't a clue where I'd put it. Leo thought he may have put it in the loft, so spent half an hour looking in bags and boxes with a torch in his teeth. When he came down he had a sneezing fit because of the dust that had accumulated over decades. Needless to say the poor thing couldn't find it. I eventually located it in the cupboard at the bottom of the stairs under the Christmas tree. I hoped it would still work. We were in luck.

As Charlie lined up with all the Matildas and the Harry Potters and most amazingly, a giant peach, he had a smile a mile wide. I took a picture, so I could embarrass him when he got his first girlfriend, Eloise not-withstanding. I remember my mum showing my ex -husband a picture

242

of me in the bath when I was about eighteen months old. We had only just started courting at the time, and I thought to myself, that's it. He won't want to go out with a girl that has a mad woman for a mother showing all in sundry my baby photos, but that turned out OK. Until it went wrong. I wouldn't really do it to Charlie, bless him, but I might tease him with it.

My marriage on the whole had been happy. Michael was my toy boy, and gorgeous to boot. He was almost fifteen years my junior. It didn't matter to us. We were happy, potless, but happy. We had Leo quite early on and we both fell in love with the slippery purple little person straight away. Leo had let out this huge wail and had pooed at the same time, all over the bed, and me. We couldn't care less. He was here, he was safe and he was ours. We weren't blessed with any more children although we would have loved them. Michael has always been a great dad, and he was a wonderful husband, until the womanly wiles of the buxom blonde, in the coffee shop opposite his office, turned his head. She was younger and way more attractive than me. For a start she didn't have frizzy hair and a size sixteen bottom. They fell in love, gazing at each other over cream cakes and sandwiches. Then, he left me after twenty-seven years. We divorced. He married her and had three more children. Laura was now six, Melissa, four, and Thomas two. Leo gets on well with Linda, and he loves his siblings. He has taken Charlie over to play with them many times, and he loves going. Michael and I remain friends and his wife is very nice. I was bitter for a very long time, but now, I can see he is much happier and I am content with my lot in life. I'm too old to go looking for love now, besides who would want a clapped out psychologist with a big bum and dodgy knees.

When we got home from dropping Charlie off at nursery, I went straight to the office. It was Tuesday. I was beyond tired having stayed up half the night making the tiger costume, but I had an important meeting at the Social Services office, about a young man who used to be a client of mine. He had been discharged from a psychiatric hospital, and was doing well, but now needed housing. His social worker asked me to be there for the meeting, as I had built up a good rapport with him and he trusted me. She thought it would be continuity for him and I was happy to do it. It was nice to see the positive side of our work and was a welcome distraction from worrying about Sally and Miriam. I was retrieving his file and answering a few e-mails, when I became aware of a fragrant figure in the room with me. I looked up, and Isobel, our wonderful secretary, stood at my desk with a beaming smile and a waft of CK1. I knew that smile, it was loaded. All of a sudden she whipped a huge pile of mail from behind her back and plonked it on my desk. "Happy reading," she said, winked, then turned on her heel and left the room as I tried to stop a landslide.

I quickly scanned the mountain of post, separating the wheat from the chaff. A few looked important, a few invited me to this lecture and that meeting. I filed the really unimportant stuff, such as a flyer for the latest candidate for the upcoming election in the bin. The mildly important ones went into my in tray, and I stuffed the really urgent ones in my bag to deal with at home. One of the letters caught my eye, because I recognised the handwriting. It was from Sally. I was surprised because we hadn't seen each other for weeks, and all my attempts to phone her went to voicemail. I shoved it in my bag along with the others, to read whenever I got a chance, and left to meet my client. The discussion had gone well. My client had agreed to go into YMCA accommodation until something more permanent could be arranged. He looked so well now. I was proud of him for overcoming his quite severe problems, and having the guts to ask for help, instead of just drifting. I couldn't help but compare him with Sally, who, in my opinion was not trying at all, She has blocked all attempts both by me and the social services to have any input, and seems to have disappeared off the face of the earth, well except for the couple of times Miriam thought she glimpsed her out the corner of her eye in the precinct. She couldn't be sure, because surely Sally would have gone over to speak to her, wouldn't she? Leaving the office, I shoved my weary body in the car and drove on autopilot towards home. I was on call again later, but I wanted a hot shower and a nap before then. As it turned out, I needed it. I had the night from hell.

I got called to Winston Green late in the evening, to assess a young man who had put his hand through a plate glass window, whilst trying to outrun a pack of zombies. I quickly worked out that far from being mentally ill, he had drunk a bottle of vodka on top of snorting a nose full of cocaine. That will do it every time. I wasn't there long, thank goodness. I yearned for sleep, but then Charlie had other ideas. The poor little mite had a temperature of thirty-nine and had been sick twice. I suspected the start of an ear infection, he was prone to them. The giveaway was that his ear was as red as the tomato I had in my sandwich for lunch. I couldn't go to bed and leave Gina to cope alone. She was as sleep deprived as me, and Leo had a six o'clock start in the morning so he needed his rest. It was after three when Charlie finally tired himself out from all the crying, bless him. I crawled into my bed and must have fallen asleep as soon as my head hit the pillow. When I woke at eight-thirty the next morning, I felt surprisingly spritely. My knees and hips were on the downlow for a change, and my age slid from ninety to around forty-five. I don't think it would ever go as low as sixteen again, but never say never. I finally have an appointment to see a consultant, so who knows. New knees, new me!

I was ready for a coffee and some of Gina's soda bread toast before I sat down to read Sally's letter. She makes it herself. I don't know where she finds the time, but I'm mightily glad she does, it's delicious. Charlie made a miraculous recovery and wanted to go to nursery, so whilst Gina took him, I opened the light blue Basildon Bond envelope, which, I noticed was too big for the paper inside it. I bit into heaven on a plate.

I scanned the letter, meaning to go over it with a fine tooth-comb when I got home from work this evening, but I catch sight of a sentence that makes my blood run cold. "Oh my God!" I shout out loud. "What day is it? What day is it?" I swallow quickly to clear the last of the soda bread and whip round to look at the calendar. It's Wednesday. D day for Sally Wilson. The day she has chosen to end her life and take Miriam with her. Sally hadn't meant for me to see the letter until it was all after the event, but it came to the office earlier than Sally had anticipated. She had banked on it all being over before I even knew about what she was planning. Thank God for Isabel and the fact that I came into the office at all that day.

I pick up the phone and ring Miriam. No answer. I try Sally. The same. I leave a note for Gina saying that I've had to go out on an emergency, grab my keys and almost fly to the car. I put my foot down, ignoring the sudden crescendo of pain assaulting my joints, all the while wrestling with calling the police. I need to check on Miriam first, to see if she has seen Sally today, before I turn up with the boys in blue, and scare her and Brian to death. My heart is in my throat. Miriam has no idea of the danger she is in. If Sally follows through on her threat before I get there. I will never forgive myself. I hope and pray she has a change of heart, or if not I get there first.

I'm stuck in a traffic jam on the Edgerly Road. A lorry carrying barrels has shunted the number fifteen bus to Waverly Cross under a viaduct and the massive kegs are rolling all over the road. Finally I see a space. I'm flooring the poor car, please God, don't let me run out of petrol, I had been meaning to top up for a while now, but I was waiting for the beeper. I've been calling Miriam's house constantly from my phone on the dashboard. Still no answer. It's going to take at least twenty minutes to get to them at this rate. Shit! Shit! Shit! I can't believe I didn't see this coming. Sally is unwell, but I never had her down as a cold-blooded killer. I know in her mind, she thinks she is saving them both, that they will be together forever but poor Miriam is the innocent in all of this. If Sally killed her mother and it wasn't an accident, I have to question the death of her husband too. The attempt on Brian's life alone is enough to see her go to prison for years, or, more likely, see her shut away in The Chimes, if she's

247

still alive when I get there. As psychiatrists, we are taught to read between the lines. People leave clues when they talk to us. The things they don't say are as important, and often times more crucial than the things they do. I missed something with Sally. I know I haven't been on the boil lately. Pain does that to you. It wears you down, keeps you tired. That is why I had decided to retire. It's no excuse and I hold myself accountable for anything that has, or is likely to happen. I have failed both Miriam, and Sally but I'll play the blame game later. There is something I can do now, and I hope with all my heart I'm not too late. I call the police.

Sally

I'm here, at Miriam's. She, however, is not. I've checked. All I found was Saint Brian snoring his head off. His mouth was so wide open, I could see the crown that cost Miriam a bomb. I bet he's had one of his pills. One less thing to worry about. It isn't a very auspicious start though I'll grant you, but I should be used to it by now, it's the story of my life. I guess I was a bit naive to think this would be any different. It's Wednesday. Miriam never goes out on a Wednesday. I just hope she's not with Jill and Mandy, they are scary. They have the power to take her away from me, I'm under no illusions about that. She seems so happy when she's with them, I've seen it every time she meets them in the café. I can't seem to do that for her anymore. I'm not sure now, that I ever did. That's another reason why it's got to be today. I can't take the chance that she'll forget me. I think though, that when all's said and done it will be me she chooses over everybody. I'll wait it out. She shouldn't be long. She never leaves Saint Brian more than an hour or two. I check my pocket for the bag containing the crushed diazepam the GP gave me. It was supposed to calm me down. It didn't. I hope they have more of an effect than that today. I am using all of them so it should do the trick. I'll dissolve it in the tea. Miriam has hers so strong she won't even notice, especially if I put an extra sugar in it. I wish I'd had some of this when I tried to do Brian in, but I only found blood pressure medication, and it was out of date. Mine isn't.

The incessant ringing of the phone is giving me a headache. I don't know how Saint Brian is sleeping through it. I've a good mind to answer it next time and give the caller a piece of my mind. They are welcome to it. There's far too much going on in my head for one person to handle. Miriam had better be back soon, I'm starting to get twitchy and I need the company. I keep thinking about Larry, if he's awake? I hope, now I'm not there anymore, he will die again and stay dead. I don't think he'll follow me. He can't leave the house, can he? I have enough to deal with without him leering at me from Miriam's hallway. I don't want anyone barging in on us either, so I've bolted Miriam's back door just in case. I'm always telling her not to leave it unlocked. You never know what type of people are going to invite themselves in.

I can smell last night's lasagne. If I was on death row, I would like that to be my last meal, but only Miriam's would do. In prison, you get anything you want to eat before you walk the green mile, well, within reason. I had toast and gooseberry jam for mine and all the time I was eating it, I could feel Larry's eyes staring at me from behind the sofa watching every mouthful, it was a waste of his time, he couldn't eat any. Oh well. Hey ho. Hang on! Do I hear the door? Yes! She's home. She's going to be so pleased to see me.

Miriam

I feel it as soon as I open the door. Something's out of whack. My immediate thought is Brian. I go towards the stairs, but catch sight of something moving in the kitchen. "Hello!" I call out, trying to sound brave, but just so you know, I can be a bit of a coward at times. I take Brian's brolly out of the massive vase me Aunty Sandra got us one Christmas. It's far too big to put a plant in, unless you've got a ruddy aspidistra, but it works great for an umbrella stand. "I'm armed," I shout. "Show yourself!"

I rush to the kitchen, brolly raised and… "Bloody hell Sal, you nearly gave me one of our Brian's heart attacks. What are you doing here, lovey? Is something wrong? Don't tell me I left the bloody back door unlocked again?" Sally doesn't answer. She's sitting, bolt upright in the chair she always sat in when she was living here. She's calm, but her face looks different. Wrong. I start to worry. What the hell does she want? Her eyes look as if she's travelled far away and having a struggle getting back. What the bloody hell do I do now? The phone is ringing off the hook in the passage. It seems to be getting louder every second. Me brain is racing and I can't take anything in.

There's a stranger sitting at me kitchen table, the phone is doing me head in and I can't seem to string two thoughts together. I turn to leave the kitchen to answer the phone and I've never seen Sally move so fast. She bars the door to the passage, and me mind goes straight to the picture of a praying mantis I saw in a *National Geographic* at the doctors. "Hello Miriam," she says, so quietly I can hardly hear. "Since you haven't come to see me and Larry at all at Mulberry Crescent, I thought I'd visit for a while as I know you miss me. Sit down there," she says pointing to the chair dead opposite the one she got out of. I do it because I don't want to rile her up, but all the while me brain is whirring, trying to find a way to keep the storm in the teacup. She sits down again and stares at me across me table. There's something in her eyes I haven't seen before, something final. I can't keep me hands still. I try to look normal. Did she say Larry?

Me knees are shaking as bad as one of them jellies little Sarah likes. She loves the raspberry ones best. I want to fill the silence with questions, but if I start, I'll find it hard to stop. I ramble when I get scared and Sally knows it. So I take a deep breath and swallow the verbal diarrhoea. "It's nice to see you, Sal," I say as cheerily as I can muster. "Want a cuppa?" Sally nods and her face begins to relax. As I'm filling the kettle I've got all sorts buzzing round in me head. I don't know what to do for the best. What if I say the wrong thing and set her off? I'm not so sure I could talk her down this time. Something's definitely changed. Her eyes are too bright, her body's too stiff. The phone burps yet again, but rings off before the answer machine kicks in. I reckon it's one of them scams our Garry keeps going on about. Probably someone wanting to rob us of our life savings. They'd be welcome to it we only have £204.50 in there at the moment, that'd get them a nice lunch. I tell you, I'd rather give them all we've got, than be here with Sally at the minute.

Me mind's still going like the clappers. I'm worried about Brian. I hope to God he's all right. What does she want? I need to fill the silence as usual, so I say, "Hey Sal, while the kettle's on to boil, I need to nip to the little girls' room. Can you warm the pot if it clicks off before I get back?" She nods again, but doesn't speak. Instead, she looks up from the table straight into my eyes. Suddenly it is as if all the air has been sucked out of the room. The hairs on the back of my neck are standing to attention and I'm waiting for something to kick off! I turn and leave the kitchen on rubber legs. As I go up the stairs towards me hubby. I'm praying to all that is Holy that he's OK. I don't want to think Sally would hurt him, but the woman sitting in me kitchen is not the Sally I know. The phone keeps burping. Instinct tells me to answer it. Fear lets it ring. I Can't help it, but I start to cry when I see him there, curled into a ball snoring his head off. I give him a kiss on the cheek and breathe in the familiar smell of the man I love more than anything in this world. It's time to put me big girls pants on. I tell meself I would do anything to get me and my Brian out of here and away from danger. Away from Sally.

Megan

I have a thought and try Brian's mobile but it's switched off. So is Sally's. I'm still a little way away from Miriam's but at least I've cleared the worst of the traffic. I'm going over all the letters in my head, looking for clues, or something I missed. I had Sally pegged as the victim, and she is, in lots of ways. She is, no doubt, the product of a severely dysfunctional family. She'd been ignored, used and abused in the worst ways possible, but I saw her as someone with no confidence who was trying to make sense of the hand she'd been dealt. What I see now, is someone who is protecting herself by lashing out first. She harbours resentment against everybody she believes has slighted her, and uses it against them when she feels backed into a corner. In this letter she's telling me loud and clear, she has nothing to lose now. By ending things on her own terms she's finally in control of what happens next, the feeling that's eluded her for the whole of her life. I feel responsible, I am responsible. I encouraged Miriam to take Sally into her home, to give her a real sense of family, of safety then I wrenched it away and sent her back to the place where she only knew pain. She needs Miriam now, just as she did when she was a child. She still wants to feel loved by someone. Who doesn't? In Sally's mind, Miriam was the one that led her to that joyful, messy house after school. Miriam is the one who was always there to make everything better, everything safe and Sally needs that like we all need air. Sally is thinking only of that now and it's become an obsession. She sees Miriam as her saviour. I didn't see it and if anything bad happens to either of them, I will never forgive myself.

Sally

Miriam's been a long time in the 'bathroom'. Oh I know what she's doing. I'm not stupid. Saint Brian, once again is her main focus, her darling hubby and what do I get? A pig of a husband who rated me a two, and is still watching everything I do. He's just as bad as the people I was forced to live with as a child. Why am I always something to be stepped on, then scraped up like dog shit on a shoe? She's taking too long. I need to find her, but first I need to stop that phone ringing, so I pick it up and slam it down just to relieve the pressure in my head. Find Miriam, the voice in my head is saying, she'll make you safe. I start up the stairs and meet her at the top. She looks scared. I don't like it, so I say, "Don't worry, Miriam, I haven't hurt him this time. He isn't a problem. Let's go down. I've made the tea."

Miriam

What does she mean this time? Has she hurt him before? Oh my God! She didn't make my husband ill surely?! She might be bonkers, but she's not a bloody murderer! I can't get me head round it. I want to ask her what she did to him, make her understand how close she was to taking him away from me, but I know that will make her mad, well, madder than she already is.

Sally is talking to me, but I can't catch anything she's saying. She's muttering something over and over, but I can't quite catch the words. Me head feels like it's in a washing machine, me thoughts on a fast wash and getting ready to spin. I'm trying to calm down, to listen to her, but me whites are getting mixed with me coloureds. She's asking me something? Focus Miriam, focus!

"Why don't you want me anymore?" she's asking. "Why are you replacing me with Jill and Mandy? Why did you send me back to Larry? Oh I get it now! It was all so you could laugh at me behind my back. I saw you in the coffee shop, having a joke at my expense the three of you."

That's it! She has finally lost what was left of her marbles. "I would never laugh at you and I didn't send you away neither, Sal," I told her gently. "It was just time for you to go home. Being here was only meant to be temporary, while they sorted things out at the house, you knew that. Dr Megan thought it would do you good to have a bit of time to yourself away from this madhouse. Larry's dead, lovey, has been for six months. He can't hurt you anymore." She stands up straight as a stair rod, then sends the chair right across me lino. "If that's what you think, you haven't a clue! He's with me every minute I'm in that house. He touches me. Makes me do things. I don't like it! I want things back to the way they were before, when we had each other. When there was no Larry, no Brian. Just us. That's all we need, Miriam. Just us." Sally's eyes are wild. She can't seem to focus. She's swaying all over the place and I'm glued to the spot. I could make a run for it down the passage. Try and get help, but that would mean having to leave my Brian. I can't do that. There is no telling what she'll do to him in this state.

"Why don't we sit down, lovey?" I say softly. "We can have our tea. There's some devil's food cake in the tin, you know it's your favourite. Come on, Sal, pull up the chair and get it down you." I sit down and thankfully, Sally picks the chair off the floor and does the same.

"Right Sal, You cut the cake, I'll pour the tea and we can have a chat, just like we always do, eh? Now, what's wrong? What makes you think I don't care about you anymore, lovey?" What Sally says next, knocks me bandy.

"I'm sick of everyone trying to make you hate me. All of a sudden I'm not worthy of your time. Jill, Mandy Megan, Garry and his family, and worst of all bloody Saint Brian, they take everything you have and there's nothing left for me. I want to leave this life, but I can't be alone. I don't know where I'm going and I won't know anyone. No one will see me all over again and they won't have walls to keep me safe. I don't count, you see, I never have. Not to the people I lived with when I was a child and not to Larry. You have to come with me, then I won't be scared."

I'm struck dumb and my Brian will tell you that never happens. I open me mouth to speak, to ask her to explain what she's on about. Then it's like Sally flips a switch. She looks at me with stone cold eyes and she says, "Drink up, Miriam, our tea's getting cold. Everything will be all right. I promise."

Megan

I'm pulling into Miriam's road now, but I can't find a parking space so I double park outside her house. Grabbing the phone from the dash I get out of the car and dial Miriam's number. It goes to voicemail again. This time I leave a message. "Miriam. This is Dr Megan. I've had a worrying letter from Sally. I hope to God I'm reading it wrong, but I think she's planning something and it's not good. Lock all your doors. I'm on my way. Ring me if you get this first." I hang up. I'm a few steps away from Miriam's door, but as I'm about to knock I hear a bloodcurdling screech. I need to get to her now! I'm looking for a way in as I call 999 again. I tell them that things are escalating and to get here as quickly as possible. I am starting to panic and that won't help anyone, so taking a few deep breaths, I calm down enough to think clearly. All the windows are shut tight, I'll have to smash one to get in. I'm looking around for a rock to break the glass, when I suddenly remember something Miriam said, about a key on a string behind the front door. God I hope it's still there! I put my hand through the letterbox and fumble for it, find it and drag it through the flap. Opening the door as quietly as I can, I take a few steps down the hall. I can see into the kitchen from where I'm standing. Miriam is visible but she doesn't see me. She's rooted to the spot at the kitchen table, terrified, but alive! Sally's already here. I can hear her pitch rising. I can't quite understand what she's saying, but by the sound of it, she's spiralling.

Miriam

Sally hears the voice message and she looks shocked for a minute, then she opens her mouth and makes a noise that doesn't sound human. I look at her face and all trace of the Sally I knew has gone. I've got to get out. Get help for Brian. I look towards the passage, and lock eyes with Dr Megan. For a minute me heart lifts, but me head says, now it's another person in the mix. How did she get in? Of course, I think to meself, the ruddy key on the string. I don't know whether to be happy or sad that she's here. I don't want anyone getting hurt, least of all the woman who has come to save us. I don't know what to do? I can usually calm Sally down when she gets het up, but I think that ship has sailed. Sally doesn't know Dr Megan's here and I have to keep it that way for now, make her think it's just me and her.

"It's all right, Sal," I say. "Calm down, eh? I'll help you, lovey. Haven't I always done that? What was Dr Megan on about on the phone? You wouldn't want to do anything to hurt me, and I know you didn't mean to give Brian a heart attack. You know he means everything to me, don't you, Sal?" As soon as the words came out of my mouth, I knew it was the worst thing I could have said. Sally went nuts! The chairs went flying. She tried to tip the table up an' all. I'm ruddy glad she changed her mind cos the boiling hot tea pot would have landed in me lap.

Sally

"Now I know you would put Saint Brian before me? I don't believe it! I've known you since we were eleven. He came much later. We meant everything to each other didn't we? I'm obviously a burden to you. You've just been pretending all this time. You are just like all the others. You used me to feel good about yourself. Let's help the charity case. Poor little Sally. Never mind what I'm feeling, what I want! Everything's going wrong! This isn't what I planned! Why do you keep looking into the hallway? Is someone here?"

Miriam

Now I know she's potty. We have history yes, but things change, people move on. They get married, have families and they, in turn, become the most important thing. I know I have to find all the right words now. Our lives may depend on it. Before I can speak though, she goes from raging to dead calm. I'm frozen to the spot when she smiles at me, her eyes like obsidian. "I didn't mean that, it's just that I don't want anyone to ever come between us again, that includes Megan who I believe is here with us. Show yourself, Doctor. You're just in time for a cup of tea."

Megan

Sally is too calm now. It tells me she is on the edge and about to fall into the abyss. The police aren't going to get here in time. Think, Megan! Think! Do I do what Sally wants and step into the kitchen, or do I check on Brian? Miriam's eyes drift towards me seeking solace and it hurts my heart. A shake of her head tells me no don't come in, stay put.

Miriam

I tell Dr Megan to stay put in the passage with my eyes, so Sally picks up me teapot and throws it into the sink. It was me favourite. She bought it for me for Christmas. I jump to me feet, sharpish, to avoid the hot liquid flying everywhere and back away. Me bum finds a wall and I press into it, as if it will keep me safe.

"I know you're there. It's all your fault!" she screams at Dr Megan. "Go. Leave us alone! We don't need you! We don't need anybody, do you hear?" She sweeps her hand across the worktop sending me china-ducks salt and pepper set flying as she comes around the table. Hang on, what's she got in her hand? Oh bloody hell! She's got a knife!

Suddenly Sally turns sharply to the right and is staring at the bin. She's muttering something but I can't make it out? Is she talking to someone? I wouldn't be surprised, I don't think this can get anymore barmy. I hear the cars outside, I hear Sally getting louder but what I don't hear is the front door slamming. I was praying Dr Megan would go for help, I should've known she wouldn't leave me. She's only ever tried to make things better for Sally, for me and she saved my Brian. She doesn't deserve any of this. I can feel the wee running down my leg, but I stay put and squeeze me thighs together to stem the flow. I daren't move, cos all I can see is the table's reflection in the blade in Sally's hand.

Megan

I speak for the first time. Now Sally is in no doubt I am here. "I'm here. I'm not leaving you," I tell Miriam in a strong voice that belies my fear. The police are coming. Hold on."

"It's all your fault!" Sally is screaming. "Get out! Get away from us. You've ruined everything!"

Sally still has the knife and starts toward Miriam, then, she stops dead, turns her head and looks towards the bin. Her whole body is rigid with terror. I can see her shaking from my vantage point in the hall. It's as if she can see something Miriam and I can't.

"Why are you here? Why are you following me?" Sally whispers to a spot on the floor. "You weren't supposed to come here, never to Miriam's. Please Larry, I need you gone. I tried to make you go that night. Miriam! I'm frightened! Send him away! Go! Go!" Sally is screaming now and waving her arms about like she's swatting flies. I gesture to Miriam to stay put, but she's still pressed up against the wall, her face white, so I don't think she could if she wanted to. A dark stain is spreading down the leg of her trousers and my heart goes out to her. Then her courage astounds me when she says, "It's all right, lovey. I'm here. Larry's gone now. He can't hurt you anymore. I'm here. I've always been here haven't I? Put the knife down, darlin', and have a seat, you still haven't had your cake." Sally starts to relax as she listens to her friend's voice. She puts the knife down on the counter. Miriam nods at me to come in and I take a step over the threshold. My mind is racing a mile a minute. I am the professional. I should have this under control, but the pain in my body is ramped to the max and I can't hold a thought in my head. Sally looks straight at me with a hatred I have never encountered and screams at the top of her lungs. "Get out! You did this! You ruined it all! It wasn't supposed to end like this!"

I try to reason with her, but it's not my voice she wants to hear. All of a sudden, she picks up the knife and rushes at me. I turn back towards the hall to put some distance between us, to try to summon help, but my knees give out and I stumble. Sally keeps on coming!

Miriam

"Sally! No! Stop! What the bloody hell are you doing?" She's finally snapped! Like that girl in the film I told you about. It's all happening too fast. I can't help but turn me thoughts to Brian upstairs and I pray he stays asleep. She lunges, brings her arm back and rams the knife home. Dr Megan falls forward onto the floor and lies too still. So much blood is spreading across the blue jacket she always wears, turning the world purple.

"You killed her, Sal! You've bloody killed her! All she ever tried to do was help us." Sally is standing there like a bloody statue and time freezes. All is quiet. I can't even hear meself breathe. I need to give me brain a rest, just for a minute. I come to me senses and rush towards Dr Megan who lets out a whimper. Thank God! Then Sally lifts her arm for the second time. I don't have time to think. I grab the nearest thing to hand and I swing it. Sally collapses on top of Dr Megan. The blood from the jacket staining her face. Sally isn't moving. The knife falls from her hand and clatters to me laminate. Oh God! What have I done?! Dr Megan groans again. I whisper to her. I tell her things will be OK, although I don't believe me own words. Things won't ever be right again! I have no way of knowing if she can hear me, but I keep on talking to her till I hear the cavalry coming. I can't whisper to Sal. She won't hear me. She'll never hear anyone ever again.

Megan

Something is crushing me. I think I see blood out the corner of my eye, but everything is in soft focus. I hear Miriam saying something, but she sounds as if she's underwater. I can't understand her. Am I dying? I won't get the chance to say goodbye to Leo, to Gina, and I didn't get to hold my Charlie Bear one last time. I'm sorry. I love you all. The weight is lifting. I'm aware of Miriam's tears on my face. She's stroking my hair, and muttering gently. I hear sirens, and the last thing I see is blue, fading to black.

Epilogue

Miriam

I'm listening to the radio in the new house, and Brian is making me a cuppa. The garden is lovely and it's a nice place to live, though I liked my old street where I knew everybody. We couldn't stay there, not after Sally. We haven't gone far really. I still see Jill and Mandy once a week for coffee and a cream cake. We still put the world to rights, but my world has changed and I'll never get the old one back. Sally was ill. I have to remember that. She didn't mean to do what she did, I'm sure of it. It makes it hard to think about what I had to do. I'm knitting some cardis for the grandchildren. They go through them like a dose of salts, you know.

I didn't tell you, did I? It turns out Grace and Garry had twins. You could have knocked us all down with a feather. Little Maya was hiding right behind Brody and even the scans didn't pick it up. Brian and me, we're over the moon. He's fully recovered from his heart attacks and we are grandparents to three lovely kids. We couldn't love them more. Sarah is a brilliant big sister and helps Grace out no end. The twins are nearly a year old now. You should see Brian rolling around on the floor with them,

I think he's having a second childhood. I don't blame him. He says we've got to make memories while we can. None of us know what's around the corner, I know that better than anyone. Time flies so fast, doesn't it? Blink and the twins will be twenty-five with kids of their own, and Sarah, with her brains, will probably be a doctor or something, but I don't want to wish their lives away Life is precious. You have to take it minute by minute and make the most of every good thing that happens. Having Sally in me life for all them years has taught me the true value of family. You have to praise them, guide them, love them and, God willing, they never have to feel like she did, like they are nothing.

That day stays with me, and never leaves. Brian refuses to mention her name, or talk about her at all. I think he can't get over the fact that he nearly lost me that day, and I know he feels guilty for sleeping through the whole nightmare. I tell him it wasn't his fault. He'd taken two tablets instead of one cos he hadn't been sleeping at all, and they knocked him for six. I'm ruddy glad they did, cos if he'd come down, I could have lost him too. Time has helped us both though, so did moving house, but I go over and over it in me mind, trying to work out if I could have done or said anything different. I don't think I could.

When Sally drew that knife and did what she did, I had to try and help Dr Megan. She was only there because of me. Because she read something in that last letter that scared her to death. I would never have forgiven meself if I hadn't tried. I just reacted. I only wanted to stop Sally, but the only thing to hand was the knife block. I didn't have time to realise that I was doing to her exactly what she was doing to Dr Megan. When I swung the block, one of the knives came loose and hit Sally in the neck. It severed an artery. It was instant.

I have killed someone. I have to live with that forever, but I did it to try and save someone else. No one knows what they would do if they were faced with a situation like that, do they? I hope you don't judge me too harshly, though nothing you could say would be worse than the blame I put on meself. I speak to a psychologist sometimes, being as Brian can't talk about it. It helps me to remember that I'm a good person that a bad thing happened to. The police said I couldn't have done anything else in the circumstances, but I wish with all me heart that it had ended differently. Me family's brilliant, and I've got everyone around me, but I haven't got Sal. I miss her, no matter what she did, and I hope the next life she wanted so badly, sees her loved and wanted by somebody. I think of her a lot and I'll always know in me heart that I loved her and I didn't set out to kill her.

Megan

It's evening here, and the most glorious sunset is making our little bit of beach soft and fuzzy round the edges, like a photograph out of focus. The waves are crashing onto the rocks loud. Unrelenting. The wind whipping them into a frenzy. I can see Charlie running up the sand carrying a bucket of water for his moat, which is fast disappearing as the tide tries to claim it. My mum is laughing as Leo sweeps him up in his arms and blows a raspberry on his tummy. Gina is in hospital at the moment. She has been diagnosed with breast cancer but it is treatable and she will be one hundred percent cured when she's had the op, and life at the beach will be the best thing for her recovery.

I'm witnessing life outside my window. Raw. Vital, but I can't be out there with them. Not yet. I haven't left the house since we moved. It's too hard. Mum and I pooled resources and bought our little beachside haven as soon as we could. I needed to take myself right away, to heal. What happened in Miriam's house that day changed my life, but more importantly, it changed me. I'm to blame for it all. I read everything wrong and, because of that, someone died. I will carry that with me until the day I meet my maker. I know it may sound selfish, when Sally isn't here anymore, but I thank God that Miriam saved me. I will always be grateful to her and the fact remains, if I hadn't gone in, we would be looking at two, possibly three deaths. My sensible side says I should have waited outside for the police, let them handle it, but the side of me that rushes in like a fool where angels fear to tread won out, I'm glad it did because Miriam, a beautiful soul, is alive and well, at least physically. Now she can enjoy her husband and family in peace.

Right from the start with Sally I went down the wrong path. I misread some of the signs she was trying to convey through her letters. I saw her only as a victim. A bruised individual who had been used to the fullest extent, then cast off like a leaky boat. She was all that, of course, but she was also so much more. I should have known that you can't live the way she did without carrying a lifetime of anger, resentment and fear. It all had to go somewhere and she chose to direct it at anyone she felt had hurt her in some way. The only person who showed her any kindness was Miriam. I could see that Sally was dependent on her and sought to correct this by sending her back to Mulberry Crescent. I realise now, by doing that, she got to the point where she couldn't cope, making her need Miriam even more. Because of what happened, and the fact that I nearly died too, I have a form of PTSD and agoraphobia.

It's strange how things can change. At one time I would be treating these conditions, now I'm a walking advert for them. I'm getting better every day though. Cornwall is weaving its magic and I hope that soon I'll be whole again. I'm longing to be able to build sandcastles with my amazing Charlie Bear, Leo and Gina, feel the sun on my face and warm my knackered old joints. I wish I hadn't answered the phone that day. Someone else would have taken the case. Someone with excellent joints, who was definitely more on the ball than me. It wasn't fair to Sally, or anyone else involved. I will never forgive myself for what transpired in the eight minutes it took the police to come. Life can turn on a sixpence. One minute you are someone you know and the next, a stranger looks at you in the mirror. With time, I'll learn to accept the new me, but In my heart I know I will never lose who I am completely, because the constant love of a small boy will show me the way. He is my light, my reason to get dressed every day. I still, however, have to be careful on the stairs, because Charlie's car collection has grown exponentially. Life is being lived to the full here in this house every day and I'm so thankful for that, but on the flip side it makes the guilt harder to bear. To Sally, wherever you are…I'm sorry.

At Miriam's

"That was 'Don't let the sun go down on me' by Elton John. I am Amy Roberts at WGFM. More music in a moment folks, but now we head over to our newsroom and Raun Nixon for a breaking news story."

"Thanks, Amy. Emergency services entered a house in Nightingale Terrace in the early hours of this morning after a fire broke out in the rear of the property. Whilst securing the premises, the skeletal remains of a female was found in an upstairs bedroom. Early indications are she had been stabbed. A knife was located at the scene and was taken away for forensic testing. A police spokesperson said they believe it to be the owner of the house Audrey Brown. They say the condition of the body could mean she has lain undiscovered for over a year. Neighbours say the woman had been talking about going to stay with her sister in Australia, so no alarm was raised. An investigation has now been opened. More information as we get it. Amy. It's back to you in the studio."

The End